Trapped!

I cut my cape in two and my new friend and I each wrapped a half around our left arms for protection. We had just finished when they came in sight. They halted in a cluster, the men in front and the dogs behind.

"We're going to take you, Conan," their leader announced.

"You may," the man with me said, "but first we'll take some of you!"

Ace Fantasy Books by John Myers Myers

THE HARP AND THE BLADE
THE MOON'S FIRE-EATING DAUGHTER
SILVERLOCK

THE HARP AND THE BLADE

JOHN MYERS MYERS

ACE FANTASY BOOKS
NEW YORK

THE HARP AND THE BLADE

An Ace Fantasy Book / published by arrangement with
Starblaze Editions of the Donning Company / Publishers

PRINTING HISTORY
Originally published by E. P. Dutton in 1941
The Donning Company / Publishers edition 1982
Ace edition / February 1985

ISBN: 0-441-31750-2

Ace Fantasy Books are published by The Berkley Publishing Group,
200 Madison Avenue, New York, New York 10016.
PRINTED IN THE UNITED STATES OF AMERICA

TO MY FATHER
JOHN CALDWELL MYERS
Who gave me the best to read and drink.

THE HARP AND THE BLADE

Chapter
  One

"If Charlemagne was alive," the big Frank shouted, "your lousy princeling would be lucky to get a job as swineherd!" He roared at his own jest, but it turned and bit him.

"He's already a swineherd," the slim, young Saxon was sticking up for Otho, the capable emperor of his own people, "and the pigs he's chivvying are Franks!"

That was fighting talk, too near truth to be said or accepted good-humoredly. I had been bored by their bellowing, but then I looked up from the Ovid manuscript on which I had been reading proof. The stinking little inn had but one window, and we three as the only patrons had commandeered the two tables it lighted. The others were practically shouting in my ear, but the rest of the room was too dark for my work.

I finished my wine and looked enviously at the large flagon they were too drunk to appreciate. Then I looked more closely at the men. The Frank's face was not too dissipated, nor was it weak or stupid; but it showed that curious arrogance that is not in itself ruthlessness as to other men's rights. It springs instead from a bald incredulity that such rights exist. The Saxon's countenance was less definite, not marked enough to show how he would be, but he looked like a decent enough lad.

Just then, however, he was talking out of turn in view of the fact that he was on Frankish territory. I shook my head. In times like ours it isn't safe to discuss politics with a man who

1

has more than one arm unless he is known to concur. But that isn't likely, what with so many factions there are hardly enough men to go around. And the big fellow was not, I was sure, going to let the matter drop. He was very angry, and I judged him the kind to take his anger seriously.

"Just because you German lice have beat up on some Huns and Wends," he began ominously.

"And Franks," the younger man taunted. "You may have had an empire once, but what good does that do you, now you've lost your guts? Otho's kicked you all around the place; and you know the only reason he hasn't taken you over?"

"No, but I'd like to." The Frank was almost sober through sheer force of rage, and I shifted uneasily. He was then a dangerous-looking man if I ever saw one. The boy, on the other hand, though he was being very noisy, was just talking, hugely enjoying having the upper hand in the argument. He wasn't going to stop talking, either.

"No, Otho can't be bothered ruling you," he rubbed it in.

"You haven't said why." His companion spoke with alert quietness, and the tensing of his body told me he was ready to act.

I almost intervened. First I thought of warning the youth, but that would no doubt have resulted in having them united to avenge my impudence. There was something reasonable I could do, however. From where I sat it would be a simple matter to conk the young fellow with the empty flask on my table, explaining to his companion that I, too, could not bear to have Franks insulted. My hand closed on the decanter, then drew away. I shrugged. It was none of my business if a man didn't know whom to get drunk with.

"Well, it's this way," the Saxon laughed, and I gripped the table, waiting. "Otho doesn't want any washed-up has-beens in this empire. He likes to rule *men*." He threw back his head, the better to enjoy his mirth; and as he did so the Frank drove a knife in his throat.

That was that. It had happened, and I had known it would. There was nothing to do or say now. I watched the killer draw out his knife and the blood follow as the corpse collapsed.

The Frank took a long pull at his glass, then looked around for something on which to wipe his dripping blade. My manuscript caught his eye. Probably he didn't think, and just as probably he wouldn't have cared if he had; but before I could stop him he had caught up a carefully written page and cleaned his dirk on it.

During the murder the life in me had been stilled, but now it awoke in a rush of fury, due only in part to the killing. That page not only represented hard work, but it was vellum, expensive and not easily come by. I caught up my stool from under me as I rose. Though not as big as the Frank was, I'm big enough for most purposes.

"You'll have to pay me for that," I said, giving him a chance.

He hadn't really seen me before; but my face told him the anger my words withheld, and he reacted in kind. Grinning, with the murderer's fire still in his eyes, he crumpled the vellum and reached for another sheet. In case he never knew what hit him, it was the stool I swung from behind me. He went down with a gashed forehead and lay still.

It seemed probable that he would be out for some while. I rifled his wallet for indemnity, then as compensation for injured feelings helped myself to some badly needed wine. As I put my cup down the Saxon stiffened with the first onset of *rigor mortis,* and the uncanny twitching drew my attention. With the drunken flush sucked from his face he looked younger than ever, and there was a clean, winsome cast to his features that made me wish again I had obeyed my impulse to save him. I cursed the Frank, but I was no friends with myself, either.

There had been no scuffling to speak of. Doubtless it was rather the sudden silence that caused the landlord, a dark, shrewd-faced little fellow to emerge from the kitchen. He stopped in the doorway and crossed himself, but he didn't cry out. He, like all of us today, had seen too much of violence and death to be shocked or even especially surprised.

"Both dead?" he asked me.

The quiet impersonality of his voice relieved me of any fear that he might shout for help. "The big one's just knocked out. He killed the other."

He nodded. "I heard 'em quarreling."

"I had to hit him. He was going for me, too," I explained, but he was thinking about something else and not interested.

"You robbed 'em yet?"

"The Frank destroyed something of mine, and I saw to it that he paid me back; but that's all."

He started to make up for my negligence, pleased and mildly amused. "Finicky, eh?"

"Maybe." I was in no mood for jibes. "Does it bother you?"

"No, of course not. I ain't got anything against you. Look, I'll even give you some good advice. Get as far away from here as soon as you can."

I thought he was probably right, but it was getting late, and I didn't want to leave if it was avoidable. "Why?" I asked.

He touched the prostrate Frank with his foot. "A gang of this guy's men will be back here pretty soon. They're just down the road rounding up some cattle and sheep that don't belong to them."

I started rolling up my manuscript. "Who is he?"

"His name's Chilbert, and he runs things around here." The landlord pursed his lips. "He says he's a count, and maybe he is. He came to these parts with a gang a few years back and built a fort. You know how things go now. Anything belongs to anybody that can take it, and nobody but the guy who's being robbed cares. So I guess he's a count, at that. He can make it stick."

He filled the dead man's cup and drank moodily. "I suppose you think I'm a thief."

"And a corpse robber," I pointed out.

"It'd be no use to the lad now," he shrugged. "As for Chilbert, he and his men never pay me for my wine. He burned my first place because I cussed a bit when he wouldn't pay the score."

This recalled my own obligation, but he refused my money. "You won't take your cut, but the wine's on the house. Besides, it was worth it to have the bastard knocked out. He hung my brother because my brother didn't like his pigs stolen."

I thought that over while belting on my sword. "Why don't you finish him, now you've got the chance?" I inquired.

"Aw, his men would just go on a murdering spree, then one of them or somebody just as mean would move in and claim as how he was count. So what's the good?"

My harp twanged deeply as I picked it up. "Won't Chilbert get nasty when he finds his money gone?"

He smiled cunningly. "After I've hidden the loot I'll make a bump on my head and lie down. They'll find me unconscious, then I'll tell the count how you frisked him."

I started to get angry, then laughed instead. "Get me a skin of wine," I said, putting down a coin. "I may need something to keep the chill out tonight."

He was back in a minute. "Too bad about the lad."

"Yes," I said, my conscience itching again. "Who was he?"

"Oh, one of Otho's men sent down to look the situation over, I guess. Boys shouldn't be used for such work. They can't help strutting as if they'd made an empire themselves."

As I passed Chilbert I dropped my Ovid by his unconscious head. "What did you do that for?" the innkeeper asked.

"He paid for it," I said. "Didn't he ever tell you he was fond of poetry?"

The landlord's all but emotionless acceptance of things was in its way as oppressive a part of the inn's atmosphere as its normal stench, the smell of blood, and the presence of death. Outside there was the freshness of early summer in a green land. And in spite of the fact that I didn't know where I would sleep that night it seemed well to be traveling again.

From force of habit I started toward the amiable nag I had purchased after landing at Nantes a few days before. But there were two other horses hitched near it, both of much greater beauty and far fewer years. Moreover, one, at least, was short a master. There was a trim, little mare, undoubtedly the Saxon's, and a tall, powerful bay with lines promising speed as well as endurance. I gasped at my good fortune. The landlord might not have understood the difference between stealing money and taking the legitimate spoils of war, but it was clear enough in my mind.

The horse jibbed a bit while I was arranging my gear, and I saw from his hide that Chilbert wore spurs and used them roughly. I didn't try to be too friendly, but let him get the smell of me before I mounted. "This is your lucky day," I assured him, adding as a courteous afterthought: "And mine, too."

Down below us to the right, visible in small, shiny patches through the trees, the Loire ran. To the left there were a few fields, one or two small ones under cultivation. Beyond was unbroken forest banked on low hills. Our road ran east and west, parallel with the river. It was mucked over from recent rains, but it was firmer and broader than most roads, at that.

Some say Charlemagne had it made, some even that the Romans built it. It was very old.

While I was making sure my harp wouldn't chafe my mount I saw a group of horsemen ride into view a few hundred yards to eastward. East was my own direction, but after one look at them I resignedly headed the bay back whence I had come. Meeting Chilbert's men while straddling his horse was no part of my plan.

My mount set off at a canter, and I did not try to hurry him. It would be some minutes before they could find out what had happened, and in any case I wasn't worried about being caught. My own judgment of horse-flesh aside, it was reasonable to suppose that the count's steed was better than that of any of his followers.

As I had seen to it that the Frank had paid handsomely for the Ovid—worth it, though, if he could read, which was unlikely—I was no longer short of funds. That was a good thing, for with that part of the valley closed to me I was forced to take a circuitous route that would not lead past the valley monasteries where I had counted on exchanging poetry and scholarship for hospitality. That is if I happened to strike abbeys where the *monks* could read. With many of the abbots, themselves fighting landholders who had not even bothered to take orders, literacy was playing an increasingly minor role in religious houses.

The tree closed over the road to make the air fine and cool. I looked back to make sure there was no pursuit, then as I rode on I pondered the changed state of things. They say that in other days there were kings strong enough to order their realms, laws that guarded and controlled men, and a priesthood that as a body strove earnestly for learning and a reasonable amount of godliness. I had traveled much in my thirty years and was yet to see any of those things.

They say even that there was once peace in my own land of Ireland, but that I found hard to credit. Some scholarship was still left there, but most of the great schools were wrecked by the Danes. Not that the Danes were worse than anybody else, if they could only get over the idea that a book was something to burn. They didn't fight more than other people, though they generally fought better and in more places. They were in England, too, where in concert with the Welsh, Scots, Picts, and the English themselves they were making certain that everything that Alfred had built up was falling apart.

Dissolution was the story the world over, but in France, where Rome was and after that Charlemagne, things were worst of all. There were Danes again, of course—what part of the earth didn't have them, except perhaps Denmark and Norway—but their depredations were for once matched by those of Moorish pirates in the south. Then Otho and his Saxons were grabbing off chunks of territory to northwards, a great push of the Huns was driving lesser savage tribes west against the Franks, and there was much doubt that the Spanish Goths could keep the Moslems from flooding across the mountains again.

As for the Empire itself, all that was really left of it was the Isle de France, a territory a good man could spit across with a favoring wind. The rest of the domain was picked to pieces and fought over with disorganized viciousness. Anybody who could claim even a one-eyed dwarf as a follower tried to set himself up as a baron. Most of the cities were no longer inhabited, and the monasteries were filled with merchants whose only religious fervor sprang from a hope of thus saving their remaining wealth. As for the generality, the passive hopelessly let the waves roll over them, the less resigned ran in the woods like rabbits. They dropped their young as indiscriminately, also, and not too many knew or cared who their father was.

I was glad Charlemagne didn't have to know what had become of his people, and I was saddened to think how rogues like Chilbert were taking the place of Roland and the other great peers as counts of France. Many claimed that the ill state of the Empire was a sign of fulfillment of the old prophecy that the world would come to an end in the year of Our Lord one thousand. That was a good fifty years off, so I didn't worry too much.

Although I had continued to take things easily, there was still no sign of pursuit. Chilbert, whom I had not sized up as a forgiving man, was either too sick for vengeance or despaired of matching his own horse. I had been looking for a road running north, but when I found one at last I gazed at it uncertainly. It was little more than a set of wheel ruts and might not go very far. A little ways up it, however, the forest was broken by a clearing in which a squat, frowsy man was grubbing over a small grain field. A stranger was an enemy in those parts, so he started to run lumberingly as I approached to question him.

Having expected something of the sort, I got the jump on him, and herded him up against a haystack where he hunched, panting, hating and frightened. He probably connected all men on horseback with Chilbert and his ilk.

"I'm not going to hurt you," I said. "I just wanted to know where this road goes."

He relaxed. "I don't know."

"But you live here!" I protested. "Does it peter out soon or does it go on?"

His eyes were vacant with ignorance and a horrible want of curiosity. "I don't know. I've been up it a ways. It goes farther than that."

I tried another tack. "Any strangers ever come down the road?"

"Sometimes. Not often. I don't know where they come from." He didn't care, either, and it was obvious that names, directions and distances, even if he had heard them, would mean nothing to him. It was likely enough that he had never been two miles from the spot where he stood.

He had, however, told me that the road was not just a dead end, and I didn't want to retrace my way west any further than I had to. I decided to chance it.

My planned itinerary had called for following the Loire up to Tours, then cutting north to Louis' capital at Paris. After that I had thought of trying my luck at Otho's court, where it was said a good poet was always welcome. I didn't shine to a devious detour that might include risky cross-country traveling, but that I would be killed if the count got his hands on me was a far more unpleasant certainty.

For the first time I hurried my horse. Dark wouldn't fall until about ten at that season, and I had hopes that in the dozen or more miles I could cover before then I might unearth some sanctuary. During the next hour, indeed, I did pass a couple of peasant hovels, but the damp and mild chill of a summer night were small terrors compared with me behind such doors. Then, save for the road itself, I saw no sign of men. Meanwhile the sun went down, and twilight could do little to alleviate the gloom of that deep forest.

When I finally did come out into the open even the final phase of dusk seemed almost dazzling. It was no man-made clearing, or if it had been so started it bore no traces then. It stretched into the woods and out of sight behind a hillock which in turn slanted down to a stream running at right angles to the road. I dismounted and drank, noting how my long face and long, fair hair were caricatured in the slightly rippled water, then rose to look the situation over.

I had to rest sometime, and the meadow's thick heather offered the best bedding I was apt to find. But the place had a feeling about it that made me somewhat uneasy. I was half minded to go on, but the foolishness of riding in weary aimlessness through the dark was apparent. Oh well, I thought, it wouldn't be so bad with wine for company. I had a pull at the skin, felt immediately better, and started following the stream in search of a likely place to camp.

I skirted the base of the first hill, and it was then that I saw it. A dolmen stood on the second hill, two tall upright stones capped by a large slab, within a ring of smaller standing stones. I had known there was something queer about that meadow. Not that it was the first one I'd seen. I had run across them in Ireland, among the Scots, in Pictland and England as well as in France itself on previous trips; but the sight of one never failed to get under my skin and crawl.

Some say it was giants that built them, and some that it was done by magic. The Church claims there is no magic, but I notice it believes in it right enough if a saint is the performer. Of course, all those things—dolmens, cromlechs and standing stones—are very old, and maybe there's not much power connected with them any more. But I wouldn't want to bet on it, especially as they invariably instill the feeling that unseen eyes are all about, watching without friendliness.

Then, too, though some forests look peaceful at night that one didn't. The trees, dim, and merging one with the other, seemed to be waiting for something to happen. And the heather stirred restlessly before little gusts of wind.

It wasn't good there at all, but though I myself could bed down anywhere, the chances were against soon finding a place where there was as good forage for the horse. So letting him amble where he would, I set about making a fire. Then with my back turned carefully to the thing up on the hill, I proceeded to encourage my drowsiness with long draughts of wine. It didn't take very long in my weary condition. I soon wrapped my cloak around me and hunkered down in the heather.

Chapter
Two

My fire had gone out when I was awakened by the howling of wolves—not just moon-baying but the cry of the pack on the trail of something. A wolf's call is fine to hear when a man's safe in a house, just as the sound of wind-driven rain increases the coziness of lounging sheltered and warm; but it carried no cheer then. I felt as chill and naked as a worm with a hen's eye fixed on it. Not that they might be even after me, but if I waited to make sure it would be too late.

There were stars but no moon as yet to help me locate the horse, so I gave that up. The cry came again, seeming surely to come from the road I'd been on, and I peered around wildly. The trees by the stream were small, easy to shin up but offering no perch on which to wait out a siege; and among the great trees of the forest I might look in vain on a dark night for one I could climb. There was the dolmen, however, a dark bulk against the sky. I caught up my sword and wine and sprinted for it.

All along I'd had the fatalistic feeling that I couldn't avoid that thing. I hoped that any powers that still watched over it wouldn't mind. I thought of crossing myself but decided it was too risky. Well, they had no particular reason for picking on me. I wasn't much of a Christian and had respect for old things.

Tossing my weapon and the skin up to the cross rock, I got a toe-hold where a stone was weathered, reached up and pulled myself on top. I was just about in time, too. I had hardly stopped panting enough to have a drink when the lead wolf ran out of the night. About fifteen others followed.

Switching from the horse's scent to my fresher tracks was something I had been afraid they would do, but it was all to the good once I was in haven. I put the wine down and laughed. "No wolves served," I told them.

The pack leader looked up, growled, and jumped. But that was just swank, of course. He was three feet short. They all yapped a bit and nosed vainly around, then sat whining expectantly, as if they thought the next move was mine. "I'm not coming down," I remarked.

After a while they saw that I meant it and went off, sniffing for signs of other game. Had it been in the winter they doubtless would have been uncomfortably persistent, but food wasn't all that scarce then. Nevertheless, I stayed where I was. They had given me a nasty minute, and I was taking no more chances in that vicinity. For a while I was fearful that they would pick up the bay's scent, but when I again heard them give the hunting call they were deep in the forest. If, therefore, they hadn't frightened the horse away by their howling, all should be well. It was chilly on that stone without my cloak, so I didn't try to sleep. Instead I worked on the wine, speculating as to how far out of my way the road I'd chosen would take me and into what sort of community it would first lead. All places were upset and lawless and all roads perilous, but not for me as a rule. Except when, as in the case of Chilbert, I had offered special grounds for enmity, my harp and my poems gave me a general passport of good will. That was natural enough, too. With everything from empires to ethics being fed to the hogs, poetry was the one sound thing left. Even the Danes, who systematically destroyed most things, made and liked good poetry, though their taste was limited.

I could make poems with varying degress of skill in four languages and recite them in seven, so I could go almost anywhere and find an audience. Irish I was born to, and Danish I had learned nearly as early from Norse who'd settled on the Irish coast. Latin had been the only language permitted at the monastery school, and French I had worked at enough to be handy with in the course of two previous sojourns among the Franks. The others, English, Welsh, and Pictish I had acquired for recitative purposes as needed.

My only good work was in Gaelic, and most of that wasn't for the casual commercial market. The traveling bard, if he is fond of eating, cannot waste time trying to improve the taste of his hearers. He must give them something they're in the mood for at the moment, and only the simple, old things like bawdiness washed down with a sip of moral justice are sure fire.

But every man must pay his tax to Hell in some manner; and he can still do good work if it is within his power. I wasn't certain of the reach of my capabilities; but I had hopes, and I loved the work.

Then, as at many other times, I turned to my craft for life when nothing else was vouchsafed. Starting with the thought of the languages I had mastered, I began considering how interesting was the relation between the habits of a people and the nature of their prosody. But before I'd got very far with that thesis my hair stood on end. I heard voices, although it seemed absurd to think that any group of people would be abroad in that waste at such an hour—or it would have seemed absurd had I not been on a dolmen.

Staring anxiously at the part of the forest the sounds appeared to come from, I saw flickering lights moving toward me. Fiends making a night raid was the first and only explanation that occurred to my startled mind. I wanted to run, but if they really were fiends they could catch me anyhow; if not I was as safe where I was as anywhere. Stretching out on the rock, in hopes I might not be observed, I watched them in fearful wonder.

In a moment or two the lights emerged into the meadow and began weaving more or less directly toward the dolmen. I groaned and sneaked my sword out of its sheath. I might accomplish nothing, but at least I would make the effort. There were, I could by that time count, a dozen torches, and the bearers were chanting to a rhythm that was not quite music. It had something of the quality of plain song, though it was divided into shorter phrases.

Straining my eyes to see what kind of thing was doing all that, I saw that the leading figure, their chief or priest, had no torch. He carried a wand and nothing more; but the rest, little, hairy varmints dressed in skins, all had either a spear or a club. They could have been gnomes, but if they weren't that I was damned if I knew. I held my breath, expecting to be discovered, but a torch, though it gives good light, also casts black shadows; and none of the creatures came very near the dolmen.

Instead they started to weave in and out among the circle of standing stones. I had just been flattering myself that I knew all languages spoken thereabouts, but, whether gnome-speech or not, I could make nothing of their words. They continued repeating their chant, and as nothing ill was happening to me I got interested and started to analyze the verse form.

It didn't have much form in the strictest sense. The lines, which apparently could be of any length, were tied together merely by a recurrent phrase. It reminded me of certain Pictish poems, and at the thought I almost snapped my fingers. Trim one of those ratty elves up a little and put a trifle more clothes on him and you'd have a Pict, if you wanted one.

I began going over the poem, which I then knew by heart, and found that though some of the words were strange quite a few closely resembled Pictish words. If I was right the gist of the chant was that it was dark and they wanted light, although why they didn't go to sleep and wait for dawn was more than I could figure.

Suddenly the leader left the circle, marching up to the dolmen to stand right beneath me, and as he did so the others ground out their torches. In the abrupt want of light after the glare I could see little, but I could hear him intoning urgently in a high, sweet voice. He hadn't spoken ten words, either, before his feet glowed like phosphorus.

For an instant I was stunned, then I turned to look behind me. The moon had just peaked above the horizon and was striking directly between the upright stones that supported the rock I was on to light up the little man before anything else in the world that we could see.

It rose swiftly then, a full moon, picking his body more and more strongly out of the dark and making his shaggy white head wondrously bright and shining. How he had timed it I didn't know, but the effect was as if he had called the moon up over the edge of the world. It was the most impressive single thing I had ever seen, and I had once been present when a murdering, usurious louse of a king was withered to a sniveling suppliant by a bishop who turned him over to Hell with no hope of pardon, knelling him to everlasting punishment with bell, book, and candle. That was very good, too, except that it made my stomach crawl. This was clean, heartening beauty.

Just as I anticipated being discovered, however, and was trying to calculate how they would react, the ceremony was over. They turned away and made silently for the forest through the now coldly smoldering heather. But relief had had scarcely time to set in before I heard a slight scratching sound. The next moment the old man's head popped up over the rim of the slab.

Seeing me, he almost fell backward in his fright and amazement, but I collared him, held a hand over his mouth and dragged him up. If I let him yell I'd probably have Picts throwing spears at me for the rest of the night. "It's all right," I told him, hoping he knew enough of the words I was using to get the general sense. "I was chased up here by wolves, and I'm going away in the morning." I repeated the assurance for luck, then as his friends had disappeared I let him go.

He had recovered his poise and sat up, giving me a slow and careful examination. "You're not one of us," he finally observed, "but the speech you used was ours, though there were a couple of words you said twistedly."

Notwithstanding the dialectical differences he had observed, we weren't going to have trouble in conversing. "I learned it from a people," I looked at the moon to make sure of my direction and pointed northwest, "who live on an island off there." Now that the excitement was over I felt cold again. "Have some wine?"

He was more than willing, and when he finally took his mouth from the nozzle things were on an amiable social plane. "These men who talk like you," I said when I had drunk in turn, "fashion a brew out of heather which tastes milder and can make a man drunker than anything I've ever had."

He smiled and then grew thoughtful. "They must be of our people. Though I didn't know there were any left except ourselves. But we used to own the world."

"Yes?" I said politely.

"Oh yes. I remember."

I was startled. Rome had been a long time ago, before Christ even. "How old are you?" I asked cautiously.

He put the hand on the rock. "As old as this."

I understood then and nodded. Among the Picts the man who conserves the old knowledge and wisdom of the tribe is believed to have lived always. Well, it would be some while before day returned, and maybe I'd learn something interesting from the fellow. I passed the wine again. "You must have had quite a life."

This remark seemed to please him. "I have. I've seen everything in the world come and go. First my people were here, and I had them put up the stones because there are powers that should be honored. Then, as I say, we ruled everything until men came who looked like you and talked like this—" Here he astonished me by speaking words that sounded something like Gaelic.

"Well," he went on, "they were here a long time, and those of us they didn't kill lived as best we could. We thought nobody could defeat them, but a new people finally did. They spoke like this—" and though the words were slurred they were in Latin—"and were great builders. But they made it harder for us than the others because they cut down the forests." He stopped and chuckled.

"What's so funny?" I asked.

"Well, I'm still here, and they're gone; or if there are any of them left they don't know it. The language they spoke and the things they made and knew are no longer theirs."

"Meanwhile," I pointed out, "the Franks have come."

"Yes, and Bretons," he nodded. "We have been crushed as never before because of their wars on our land, but maybe they'll kill each other off."

"They tried hard," I admitted. "Still you're getting weaker all the time." I was not drunk but had yet taken enough to push discussion solely on its merits without too delicate a regard for feelings.

He didn't take offense but smiled pensively, fingering his great, moon-glowing beard. He looked as though he might actually have been as old as he said he was. "Perhaps I'll die," he spoke again finally, "but if I do everything really good will die with me. After my people are gone nobody will ever really know how dawn holds life in check when the mist rises white above the heather or how the trees move and change shapes at night. They won't know how a friend's eyes can look, warm over the ale, or how the beauty of one of our girls—for there are no others of any worth—can stir a man. They won't know how fine a thing it is to be of the land or be honored in the tribe."

I shrugged. "I suppose all peoples feel that way."

"Do they?" he challenged. "Then why do they all come here, leaving their own lands, often leaving their tribes or, yes, even their women behind? You, for instance, who are you?"

"Finnian. An Irishman."

That meant nothing to him, but he wasn't interested in details. "You're from somewheres else, too. What are you doing here?"

"I'm a bard," I explained. "I travel around singing wherever men will pay to listen."

"Won't they listen in your own land?" he inquired with a suggestion of a sneer.

"Of course." In spite of myself the thrust injured my professional pride. "I am welcome anywhere."

"Why not stay home in that case? Isn't the land good?"

"It's all right," I said, "but so are a lot of other places."

That seemed to annoy the old fellow, and he snorted. He was getting into the spirit of the thing and drank without invitation. "Do you like it where your own gods aren't worshiped?"

"Why, as for that, they make it easy for us these days. Word's got around that there's only one god for all people everywhere."

"Drivel!" he snapped, reminding me of an Irish priest commenting on the claims to supremacy of the pope at Rome. "Do you believe that?"

"I don't care much one way or the other. I was trying to be disarming but achieved no such results.

"You don't care about your land or your gods. Why don't you at least stay and stand with your tribe?"

"Oh, the clan's getting along all right." I shook the skin and felt relieved as it gurgled encouragingly. "They don't need me."

"They're probably better off without you," he said bitingly.

His obvious spleen about something that was so little his concern amused me. He was all priest in his worrying about who had which gods and what other people did about life. "Maybe," I said placidly.

"A man who lives away from his own country and people," he stated, "doesn't live in reality. He knows nothing that is really happening, nor is he truly a part of life. He is merely suspended in it."

That caught my attention, for in a purely general sense I had found it so. "Possibly that's why I like it."

For a little old man he certainly could hold a lot. "You like nothing that's worth anything to a man!" he scolded when he had wiped his mouth. "You travel alone, don't you? I suppose nobody wants to be seen with you!"

"You seem to like to drink with me," I pointed out.

"I do not like to drink with you! I just don't hold it against the wine if the company's bad." He released the skin grudgingly. "What's your woman doing while you're running all over places you don't belong?"

"I haven't got one and don't want one."

I expected another outburst, but the statement seemed to leave him speechless. Hunched forward, staring at me, he was an eerie and angry figure swaying a little in the moonlight.

The moon was by then well up, and the rim of the forest looked no longer ominous but as soothed and relaxed as my mood. If the night had been as cool as I had thought, it was so no more. I was beginning to feel that it wouldn't be difficult to sleep, but his next words changed that.

"Always after the others leave when the moon ceremony is over I sit up here to wait for signs. I had thought that you might be a good omen, but you are bad." He was leaning forward, peering fixedly at my face, and though I met his eyes I was not happy. All my uneasiness about the stones and their makers came back with a rush. This was the servant of those wild, old powers, and he had become malevolent toward me. "You care for nothing," he accused again.

There was no use mentioning poetry. A priest can't get over the notion that a good poem is a hymn. Of course, sometimes it is, but not often.

His words were coming a little thickly, but he knew just what he wanted to say. "You serve nothing and help nobody!"

As he said that my mind went inevitably back to the Saxon youngster, and I felt shame again that I had not so much as stretched out a hand, no, not even spoken a warning. My efforts might not have been effective, but I had foreknown and hadn't tried.

The old Pict was leaning so close by then that I could smell the wine on his breath; and he got it! Whether it is done by magic or not, there are some men who can reach into another's mind and pull his thoughts out whole. That man was a priest of an ancient, strange race, probably versed in wizardry, too, and he read me out. "You let a man die today because you couldn't be bothered!"

"It wasn't my business," I muttered.

He saw he had me on the run and that increased his sense of power. "You think nothing in life is your business!" he howled. "But I'll make it so things will be!"

"For an instant I merely shivered, then pure, scared rage made me pull myself together. I shoved his face so hard he fell over backwards, then I caught up my sword. "You try to curse me, you damned hobgoblin, and I'll chop you up for dog meat!"

Far from being taken aback, he defied me in a voice crackling with vindictive glee. "If you don't believe in any gods, what are you worried about?"

"I'm not worried," I blustered lamely. "I just don't like to be cursed."

"You're not worth a good curse," he informed me, sitting up as I took the point of my sword away from his throat, "but I'll put my will on you."

"Go ahead," I said sullenly. "Not that anything will come of it."

"Oh yes it will!" I waited alertly, ready to kill him if he voiced anything that sounded as if it might be a spell, but he only looked at me hard and said: "From now on, as long as you stay in my land," here he swept an arm to include all directions, "you will aid any man or woman in need of help."

That didn't seem so bad, and my relief was mixed with mortification at having been so afraid. In the past couple of minutes, however, I had become nearly sober and thus conscious of the chill and the stiffness in my weary muscles. Rising, I stood with my back to the Pict, stretching and looking hopefully for some sign of dawn. There are limits even to the elastic hospitality of inebriety, and after having threatened to kill another, a man could not—or I could not—go on drinking with him. I hoped he'd take the hint and go away.

When I heard a slithering noise, therefore, I didn't turn immediately. I waited awhile and then looked around to find the slab empty—completely empty. He had taken the last of the wine with him. I spotted him then, a blur just merging with the apron shadow of the trees. My first impulse was to leap down after him; but I'd never find him, and the Lord alone knew how many other raffish demons he could conjure out of ratholes or in whatever other appropriate places they lived.

Impotent to take it out in any other way, I stood and howled my fury like a child. "You thieving night crawler! You bat's louse!"

All I got in return was laughter and the valedictory retort, which undoubtedly gave him a great deal of satisfaction: "I didn't think you'd care."

It was an hour before I ceased mouthing oaths, as different aspects of the enormity that had been perpetrated upon me kept cropping up in my mind for wrathful consideration. Nobody but a priest could share a man's hospitality, butt into his personal affairs, exact a penance that was to his own advantage, and leave with the additional pleasure of feeling self-righteous.

Thus I fretted out the nub of the night, growing more miserable as it waxed progressively cooler and the wine ebbed in me. Then with the first light I plodded through the cold, dew-soaked heather to find another unpleasant surprise. Some rodent had gnawed its way into my scrip and eaten my small stock of provisions. I looked at the dolmen and shook my fist. All that would be needed to make disaster complete would be the loss of my horse. Thoroughly disgusted with an ill-run world, I started to search for him.

Chapter
   Three

A LITTLE scouting around showed me that the bay, whether or not he had been stampeded by wolves, had strayed north up the road. By that time I was so accustomed to bad chance that I would have suspected trickery if anything pleasant had happened. That wine-stealing Judas of a Pictish wizard was doubtless responsible for everything, and my only recourse was to get out of his domain. Feeling much put upon, I wrapped my saddle and smaller belongings in my cloak and slung the whole over my shoulder. My harp, which I usually so carried when afoot, I tucked under my arm.

Walking thus loaded didn't help my hunger or my disposition, but it warmed me up in short order. My burdens were not too heavy, but they were awkward; and a long sword wasn't designed for a pedestrian. In consequence, though the new sun was soon lighting a very fair day I wasn't favorably impressed. I don't suppose I'd gone more than three miles before I caught sight of the horse, but it seemed as if I'd been walking for a week.

When I called wheedingly the animal looked up from some young shoots it had been nibbling and trotted a ways further. Restraining the impulse to run in pursuit, I put down my things and commenced stalking. It teased me for more than a mile, but, finally perceiving that it was not going to be allowed to eat in peace, it yielded. It was laughing at me, having enjoyed the fun thoroughly, but I was so pleased I condoned its misplaced humor. The bay's recapture marked the first good thing that had happened since finding the dolmen, and I hoped that my ill luck was ended.

After retrieving my gear, which had not, as I had half anticipated, been somehow stolen I pushed on at a stiff pace. With a horse under me my appetite no longer seemed likely to prove mortal, and I regained much of my lost good humor. Till well past noon I passed nothing of man's save a couple of burned-down shacks, but that didn't much matter. I was traveling in fine, new country on a fine, new day, and the road could be counted on to take me somewhere. Even the food problem wasn't insoluble. As I told the bay with a cheerfulness he might have thought in bad taste, I could always eat horse meat.

The road had been dipping into and out of a series of small, shallow valleys, and from the top of one of the dividing hills I at last saw what looked to be an abbey. My surmise was correct. In another half hour or so I rode into a wide sweep of field under cultivation, with a monastery, possessing on closer inspection many of the aspects of a fortress, as its hub.

Whether the force came from piety or arms, strength was present. There was an air of settled prosperity rarely found; and the peasants didn't run at the sight of me or even appear concerned beyond a natural curiosity.

As I approached the abbey gates I examined the place with interest. It was a genuine stronghold all right, and no doubt needed to be. There was a huge, iron knocker, but just as I was about to dismount and use it a long, raw-boned monk appeared on the top of the wall and looked me over leisurely. "Good afternoon," he finally said. I liked the looks of his rugged, weather-beaten face, but his tone was not encouraging. "Have you business at St. Charles?"

He spoke in Latin, which proved that I had found a monastery where some tradition of learning was remembered. After turning my horse so that he could see my harp, I answered in kind, asking courteously for entertainment.

"Another minstrel," he said without inflection.

"No," I corrected him with a touch of pride, "a maker." Then, as that did not appear to impress him sufficiently, I added: "And a scholar."

"You don't look like a priest," he pointed out.

Several comments occurred to me, but I refrained from giving voice to them. "All cannot be fathers of the Church," I answered instead. "Some of us have to content ourselves with being merely sons."

He grinned at that, and I began to hope that we might get on. "That's a remarkably long sword for a poet." He hesitated just long enough. "And a scholar."

I understood his attitude. Every petty faction had its spies and secret agents, so every stranger was automatically suspect. "Alas!" I droned, "a peaceful man and a Christian meets many who are not either these days and must protect the life God gave him as best he may."

"H-m-m. Where are you from, Christian?"

"I'm an Irishman and don't care what wolves eat what part of the Empire. Now speaking of eating, that's something I haven't done all day." While making this remark, I took the precaution of shifting my wallet so that the coins in it clinked musically.

His face became broodingly solemn. "You will be welcome to the hospice, my son," he said after a fitting pause for consideration.

Once I was inside he pointed out the guest house to me, then led me across the court to the stables. But things were not to my mind yet. The meager food of the hospice would serve in a pinch, but the monks were a hearty, well-fed crew. Their table, I judged, would be worthy of an appetite such as mine.

"What's your name, Father?" I asked my guide, who was appraising the bay with an expert's eye.

"Clovis."

"I'm Finnian and, as I've told you, a bard. When the fathers gather at the refectory couldn't I show my gratitude for the abbey's hospitality—in addition, of course, to my contribution for the poor—by reciting for them?"

He gave the horse a final, approving pat. "Have you poems worthy of these holy premises?"

"Oh no, not worthy," I said cautiously, "but possibly acceptable."

He rubbed his chin, and the sleeve of his gown fell back to show a big scar, not long healed. If that hadn't been made by a sword there would have been no use in his telling me so, for I wouldn't have believed him. "I haven't the authority to give you permission, even though I think gratitude is a very fine thing." That man and I understood each other perfectly. "But if you should come to the refectory when the bell rings," he suggested, "you could make your request to the Prior. Father Walter, our abbot, is not expected until somewhat later."

I caught a little sleep but made sure to be ready when the fathers filed in to dine. Father Clovis was friendly enough not only to present me but to state my purpose to the Prior, a small, alert, old man, who looked at me with some dubiety.

"What had you in mind to offer us, my son?" he inquired.

The monks were a noisy, cheerful lot; and they had reason to be. My mouth watered at sight of what was being set before them. "I know poems of all sorts, the works of others as well as my own poor efforts." I hesitated, then threw out a feeler. "The tale of a holy martyr might be too discouraging to weaker servants of God."

"That's sometimes true, my son."

The brothers, I observed, were not confining their talk to religious matters. "But good counsel," I pursued, "can be contained in other things as well as in sermons."

"An interesting observation," the Prior commented, looking more cheerful.

I knew them then, "I will give you," I said boldly, "a shocking song about the fate of a monk at St. Sulpice."

Poking libelous fun at the inmates of another abbey is one of the oldest and most reliable tricks in the book, provided one is certain of one's audience. All that's necessary is to pick out a rival monastery, preferably one in the vicinity, and make the necessary trifling alterations in the rhyme scheme. The Prior's eyes gleamed, but his face did not otherwise change. "We are willing to profit by the mistakes of those at St. Sulpice. Proceed, my son."

He rapped for silence, and I saw that the monks quieted instantly. There was discipline here for all the general air of rough and ready casualness. While I announced my intention I was fitting the name "St. Sulpice" into the poem. Then I struck a couple of jaunty chords on my harp and began:

> *A sacristan at St. Sulpice*
> *Admired his virtue without surcease,*
> *And, being mentally undersized,*
> *He shortly was self-canonized;*
> *But he did not come*
> *To Halidome,*
> *A fact at which he is still surprised.*

* * *

I played a little running tune before the next strophe while I looked around. They were encouragingly attentive.

> *He lived on weeds and cockroach soup*
> *And roomed with a he-goat with the croup,*
> *Then celebrated these foolish facts*
> *With vilely worded, mile-long tracts*
> *Whose vomitous cant*
> *Showed just how scant*
> *Piety is in a show-off's acts.*

> *At St. Sulpice, though, wits are dim:*
> *They loved this prig and boasted of him.*
> *No one could equal him, they agreed,*
> *At saving sinners by word and deed—*
> *The Devil, they claimed*
> *Could be so tamed*
> *By that old ass that he'd say the Creed!*

> *When Satan heard these words he laughed*
> *And came to challenge the mad monk's craft;*
> *But he, too witless to be afraid,*
> *Produced the latest tract he'd made,*
> *And the Devil winced*
> *At grammar minced*
> *And words strung out in a fool's parade.*

> *Satan whistled and shook his head.*
> *"Well, St. Sulpice is the first," he said,*
> *"Abbey in which I've ever been—"*

I had counted on that line for a laugh, and I got it.

> *"The rest have never asked me in—*
> *But I've never yet,*
> *Wherever met,*
> *Failed to detect a cardinal sin.*

> *"Pride," said Satan, "is what you've got,*
> *An excellent sin: it tops the lot.*
> *And I'll take all your tracts, what's more*

For though I've tortures by the score
I never had known,
Till just now shown
By you, the agony of a bore."
That sacristan of St. Sulpice
Is frying now in his own thin grease,
While Hell's most stubbornly hardened souls,
Who'd scorned to notice white-hot coals,
All writhe and sigh
And, unmanned, cry
At having read his monstrous scrolls!

Their applause was generous but not in itself nourishing or thirst-quenching. I managed to catch Father Clovis' eye and raised my brows pointedly. He winked and rose to the occasion. "Perhaps, Father," he addressed the Prior, "the learned poet would consent to share our small meal and entertain us again after dinner."

"If he so wishes, he is welcome," the other answered, and after thanking them I made dignified haste to occupy one of a number of vacant places. It was grand food in unlimited quantities, and I had just the appetite to cope with it. Having completed a manful job, I filled my glass with their white wine, which I had found especially good, and sat back to hold up my end of the conversation.

It promised to be a pleasant evening, for if, to judge from their discourse, the fathers did not run to profundity of scholarship, they were good fellows of reasonable education. The complexion of affairs changed in a minute, however. A priest followed by six other monks entered, and we all rose in greeting.

It was then that I saw what gave the place its air of having a backbone. The first monk was the Abbot, a broad-shouldered man with a strong, calm face. He himself said little, falling heartily to eating, but the turn of the talk was more businesslike after his arrival. It was evident from the words of the other newcomers that they had been on a scouting and skirmishing expedition. I had been right in appraising the place as one-part fort to one-part house of God.

A local faction, meaningless to me, was the chief subject of discussion so I kept silent and drank contentedly enough. The longer they sat and talked the more wine I'd have time to get under my skin. I was eventually conscious, though, that the Abbot had finished and was looking at me with his keen, wide-set eyes. "Who are you, my son?" he asked bluntly when I met his gaze.

"Finnian, Father. An Irish bard."

They were all looking at me now, Father Clovis sardonically, the rest with curiosity or suspicion. The monastery was off the main ways, although most likely it could be reached by more traveled roads than the one which had led me there. Still it was a time when all strangers must account for their presence plausibly. "I landed at Nantes a few days ago. My plan was to go to Tours," I told him.

His sonorous voice grew deeper. "You are sadly off your path then."

I held his eyes steadily. "I had to change my plans, Father."

"Why?"

It was chancy, for I couldn't know what alliances anybody around there had, but I decided there'd be a larger percentage of risk in evasion. "There's a man south of here called Chilbert who doesn't like me. I'm trying to skirt around his territory."

I had said something then, for the monks stared at me or whispered asides to each other. The Abbot thought it over and rose abruptly. "Come with me, my son. I'd like to talk to you."

With a regretful look at the wine I followed him out and along the cloister till he entered a room which proved to be his study. There was still sufficient daylight to illuminate it, complete with desk, shelves for parchment items, and a pair of chairs. He chose the one by the desk, and at his gesture I took the other.

"How well do you know Count Chilbert?" he wanted to know.

"Not at all and yet too well," I replied, the wine impelling me toward breeziness. "He wants to kill me, a familiarity I try to discourage from strangers."

He didn't laugh, and under the pressure of his waiting eyes I told him exactly what had happened, omitting only the exchange of my old nag for the bay. A priestly garrison might well commandeer such a fine horse for the good of my soul.

He nodded when I had finished. "The count's a cruel scoundrel, but he's a powerful figure hereabouts."

I shrugged. "I was given to understand he had plenty of followers. Otherwise I wouldn't have given his domain such clearance."

"I thought possibly," he hinted, "that you might have heard something about his general activities while you were in the vicinity."

"I might have, had I been interested. As it was I heard nothing beyond the usual story these days: everything's falling to pieces, and thieves are plundering the ruins."

He brooded, seeing a long way. "If some of the thieves are strong enough to protect what they take," he said at last and more to himself than to me, "it will mean some sort of stability. If the process of chaos could be stopped for just a moment something could jell to form a basis for rebuilding."

"Your thieves," I remarked, interested enough to provoke further discussion, "will merely try to take from each other when they've got everything else. Then where's your stability?"

As he answered I could feel the depth and passion of the man. "Chaos gathers speed from its own momentum and never ceases of itself. It must be stopped by force of will."

He paused, but I knew he would go on. He was in the mood to talk, and I was obviously an attentive listener. "I'm a father of the Church," he took a new tack, "and I hope not too unworthy a one. Originally, however, I did not take orders because I had an imperative call to holiness. But as a young man my crops were harvested by wandering outlaw bands three times running. Twice, also, my house was looted and burnt, and I had no recourse—no law or power to which I could appeal. It was too commonplace even to excite comment.

"Only the Church, even though much of its strength has been latterly worn away and dissipated, seemed to have the will to hold anything together. My wife was killed in the last raid, so I joined the fatherhood here. There are many in the Church these days for similar reasons."

I kept silent. He wasn't asking me for sympathy; he was telling me, and probably for a purpose.

"Because we are a united body and care enough," he went on, "we've been able to keep the wolves away. I'm abbot now, and I try to encourage learning and other proper functions of the monastery, but the bulk of my energies are of necessity used to see that on our lands men can work and live in a normal manner."

"You've got some very capable-looking assistants," I remarked, thinking principally of Father Clovis.

"I've needed them," he grimly declared. "Now as, as I started out to say, some of the robber chiefs are finally discovering that the pickings are getting poorer each year. As a result they're seizing what lands they think they can hold for their own. They're savagely rapacious, of course, but it means a settling of some sort; and to protect the revenue of their realms they will eventually have to establish some kind of order within them."

"I think I'd rather have no order," I said drily, "than one of Chilbert's devising."

"That's where you're wrong," he told me. "There must be a modicum of law, even if it's from a bad source, before anything can develop."

I hit nearer home. "Wouldn't an up-and-coming count like Chilbert think highly of rich, well-cultivated lands like yours so conveniently near his own?"

"Yes," the Abbot nodded, "but we're too strong to be conquered with ease. What he really wants of us is that we should hold our lands from him and pay him for protection—protection from himself as well as from others, naturally. He aspires to hold everything up to Normandy, and he may achieve it. He's a man of considerable ability."

The vision of Chilbert's ruthless face came before me unpleasantly. "I know the general state of the country and all that, but isn't there anyone who isn't a murderous brigand to stand against him? Or why don't you yourself try for the hegemoney?"

He shook his head. "That isn't my function. I admit I've been tempted; but I have given myself to the Church, and, as I said before, I have little enough time to be a priest as it is. If I went in for conquest I'd have none."

He was not a man to be friends with easily, but I liked him. "Isn't there anybody else?"

"There's a young fellow called Conan—a Breton, for we border on the march country. Though I'm not quite sure what he wants yet he comes of good stock and is, I think, all right. Nevertheless, he has returned comparatively recently after having been away since boyhood, and I don't yet know how capable he is or what a following he can eventually get."

"If you even think he's all right," I commented, "that puts him way ahead of Chilbert. Why don't you throw in with him?"

"I'm not throwing in with anybody yet," he said flatly. "I'm waiting to see who is strong."

"You mean to say you'll let a swipe like Chilbert seize more power when you might be able to check him by joining with a better man?"

He flushed, but his glance remained steady. "I'd like to see a good man rise to the top, but my first job is to look after the abbey."

"I suppose so." To my surprise I felt partisan about the matter and a little disappointed in this man, who had made quite an impression on me. Though God knows it wasn't my habit to pass judgment on moral issues.

He guessed what I was thinking and took me up on it. "There are two ways of looking at such a matter. Perhaps if I were a saint I'd fight blindly for universal good, even if I were convinced that nothing would be gained by my efforts. Being a lesser thing, I prefer to struggle for only the limited good that I believe is within my power to bring to fruition." He drew into himself a moment before he concluded. "There is a chance that even a saint might think something is better than nothing."

"Very likely," I conceded. He was doing his best in difficult times, and I was sorry I had been critical. "Just the same, I'm glad I won't be here when Chilbert's kingdom comes."

"You know from what I have told you," he said after another pause, "that I'm not anxious for him to succeed. Nor is it inevitable that he shall do so." He was looking at me earnestly, and I knew by his next remark that he had taken due note of the sword scar on my left cheek. "You're used to weapons, and you seem to nourish a strong feeling against the count yourself. Conan can use and will, I believe, reward experienced men."

So that was what he had been driving at! "And if he gets enough of them," once again I couldn't repress the slight taunt, "you might feel justified in being his ally."

"Exactly. Well?"

"No, Father. It isn't my affair."

Chapter
Four

AFTER a farewell salute to Father Clovis I headed north again early the next morning, having learned I had still some ways to go before I could make easting. Once I had ridden through the abbey's fields the forest closed in again, and I saw no more signs of habitation. The sky, mostly clear when I started, was overcast before noon with steadily thickening clouds. Smelling the air, though, I decided that it wouldn't rain for some hours, possibly not until night. That was considerate of the weather, because there was supposed to be a town of sorts up the line which I should have no difficulty in reaching by mid-afternoon.

I had dismounted to drink at a spring when I first heard them coming. All morning I had met nobody except a lone woodcutter, but these were riding men—several, to judge by the sounds and voices. Having no reason to anticipate trouble with anyone coming from the north, I wasn't especially concerned. None the less, I climbed on the bay and got off the road west, where there chanced to be less undergrowth. Thus I was still in sight but had comfortable room for maneuvering in case of need.

There were five of them, all well armed. The leader was somewhere in his thirties, a medium-sized man with black hair above a jolly, bearded face. Talking busily, he didn't see me until he was all but abreast of me. Then at his command they all halted and put their eyes over me. I had nothing to say.

"You're a stranger in these parts," the leader announced.

"Yes," I said pleasantly, "and one whose only interest in these parts is to get out of them."

His face was no longer jovial. "You're a liar!"

That was rude, but I wasn't going to do anything about it when he had four men with him. I waited.

"You're one of Chilbert's men," was his next accusation.

I thought the attempt would be futile, but I made one more effort to arbitrate. "I'm not his or anybody's man." I touched my harp and deepened my Irish accent as I went on. "I'm just an itinerant bard, and your lousy, local quarrels don't mean a damned thing to me."

Paying no heed to my statement, he edged his mount toward me, and I pointedly backed away. "That's Chilbert's horse," he said harshly.

I had been wondering what had sicked him on me. "It was," I acknowledged.

"He might lend it to a friend scouting for him," the fellow jerked his head and his followers deployed on either side of him, "but he'd never give that horse to anybody."

I swung the animal in question around. "We traded. Moreover," I pointed out, seeing that he had made up his mind to credit nothing I said, "I made an excellent bargain. I doubt if you can catch me."

But he was for trying. They all surged toward me at his word, and the bay swept away from them through the forest. We made fine speed, for the great trees were wide apart and the brush trifling. Dodging occasional low branches was the only real excitement in the business as they never had a chance of catching us. Nevertheless, they were hard to convince and didn't give up until, without especially pushing himself, the bay ran completely out of their sight at the end of a couple of miles.

Soon afterwards I breathed him, listening to make sure they weren't catching up. At the end of some minutes there was still no sign of them. "Nice work!" I told the horse appreciatively.

It was only then that I realized my new predicament. With a sunless sky and in a country where landmarks meant nothing to me the only possible way of retrieving the road was the laborious one of retracing my own tracks. And did I really want the road under the circumstances? Suppose that man who was so opposed to presumptive friends of Chilbert also reasoned that I would have to retrail myself and arranged to cut me off north and south. The more I considered, the more answerless my problem seemed as far as immediate action was concerned.

The best of all the undesirable courses that offered called for waiting over in the woods in the hope that the next day would bring a sun to guide me. But my mount and I would need water, and I had passed neither stream nor spring on the way in. Resignedly I started to wander in search of one or the other. If the road was still directly back of me, which it probably wasn't, north would be off to my right. I had to set some course, so, facing that way, I rode.

I fared slowly, for when going nowhere a man feels foolish to hurry. I was feeling sulky now. It was bad enough to be forced from my original route for being Chilbert's enemy. To be hounded from my alternate itinerary for being his friend was an irony too annoying to amuse me. And just how I was going to win free was more than I could guess.

My gloom was not so deep, however, that I didn't pause often to make sure that I wasn't coming near the road again. I didn't though, and so had one negative direction. Wherever I was heading, it wasn't east.

In about an hour I found a spring but didn't abide by my original and sensible plan of staying beside it. It was then only early afternoon, and I was far too restless to face waiting out the day in philosophic inaction. After letting the horse forage, I therefore went on. There was always the long chance of running across somebody or something which might be of help.

It wasn't for several hours that I encountered the first real break in the trees, but when I did it was a big one. A long while ago it had been a huge farm, and though stretches of it were badly overgrown with brush other sections had patches of tall grass scattered through the weeds. The horse could do well there.

I rode toward a likely looking portion, but stopped as I heard dogs bay in the woods downhill to my right. They were heading my way, the next few yelps told me, and I felt much cheered. The hunters would almost unquestionably be glad to share with me after the kill, and I could learn from them all I so much wanted to know about the lay of the land.

Following the course of the chase by the baying, I nodded

contentedly to myself. The quarry should break into the clear shortly.

Sooner than I expected the quarry did. It was a manhunt. Emotionless with surprise, I watched him wade through the brush and up the hill on a line that would pass me closely. He wasn't really running any more, though he was still trying. Twice he fell.

He had a bare sword he was using as a staff, leaning on it heavily as he plodded forward, head down. He was quite near when he first saw me and halted, swaying. He was too tired to have much of a face, but I knew what he was thinking. If I was an enemy the game was up.

Except that he was big, brown-haired and fairly young I couldn't tell anything about him. Maybe he was the kind of man who should be chased by dogs, but I gave him the benefit of the doubt. "No enemy," I called.

He still didn't move. Needing both mouth and nose for breath, he couldn't talk, but he pointed at my horse with his empty hand.

I cursed to myself. A fine animal like the bay could bear double for a while, but unless there was some refuge fairly near the pursuers would catch us, which included me. And if they killed him, as they presumably meant to do, it would be strange if they boggled at killing any ally they found with him.

A moment passed, and, though with a terrible finality, his arm dropped, he remained where he was. Once he had stopped he couldn't force himself to go on again. I saw him turn toward his pursuers, waiting.

Miserable with indecision, I shook my head. Meanwhile the baying of the hounds had taken on a horrible quality, now that I knew what they were after. They would soon be out of the woods, too; and I had better get away from there if I didn't want to watch the fellow torn down before my eyes. "Oh, well, Hell!" I swore bitterly.

"Look," I said after I'd boosted him into the saddle and scrambled up behind, "if you know any good places to go take us to the nearest!"

I was glad that I had traveled leisurely all afternoon. The bay retained strength enough to carry us, big men both, at a good pace. I looked behind as we started and saw the first dog break out of the trees, nosing the trail. Very likely the hounds would have a difficult time figuring out what had happened to their quarry at the point where he'd mounted. They might have to wait for the men to straighten them out, which would give us a little extra time.

My unwanted companion appeared to know where he was taking us. I would have liked to know myself, but he had no breath to spare for speech. We cut across fields toward the forest at a long tangent, and my physical discomfort as I bumped along astern of the saddle was only equaled by my uneasiness and disgruntlement. For a man who tried conscientiously to stick to his own concerns I seemed to be getting into an awful lot of trouble.

The pack cry of the hounds had dissolved into puzzled yelps, but as I looked back for about the fifth time, riders came over the rise. They shouted at the sight of us, the dogs started whooping over the new scent, and the sight hounds rushed to the fore. The bay was doing wonderfully considering the load he was bearing, but they were perceptibly gaining. "Have you any friends close by?" I asked the man in front of me; but he shook his head.

Reaching the forest, we skirted it while he searched for something. This turned out to be the hardly noticeable remains of a road, and we swung into it, threading through trees whose branches slapped and scraped us. The horse stumbled once and slowed to a canter. We goaded him on, but he never regained his full stride. He wouldn't be much use to us soon.

No doubt it wasn't actually so very long before we emerged into another spacious clearing. I only know we eventually did, and that I looked hopefully for a fortress. Instead there were only the ruins of a great stone building and that air of desolation peculiar to abandoned manholdings. As we passed the old house to go down the slope beyond I saw that the dogs had us in sight again.

I was about to tell my companion that we might as well turn, find a corner of the ruin, and die as best we could when he halted our mount in front of an arched stone vault in the hillside. The front wall had fallen, but it was otherwise sound, with a narrow front two men might defend—for a while, at least.

He slid from my saddle and lunged toward the vault, motioning for me to go on; but once having thrown in with him I could not leave him to it. Unloading my belongings I hit the

bay so that, lightened of us both, it hastened out of the way of
the imminent dogs to disappear in the nearby fringe of woods.
I watched him vanish, then reached the vault in time to be
ready for the first hound. In his excitement he leaped right on
the point of my sword, and I threw him off to watch him kick
out his life. I was then tired of being chased by dogs and killed
two more with savage pleasure. After that the rest decided to
wait for the men and stood around barking and snarling.

Seeing the situation was temporarily in hand, my companion had disappeared in the gloomy rear of the vault and so was
not apparent when the first rider arrived. He looked at me and
at the dead hounds; but the bay was not in sight, the swath in
the weeds showed he had gone on, and I was no one he knew.

I jumped him before he could come to any conclusions.
"Are those dogs yours?" I roared.

He was a bulky, hard-faced, red-haired man who didn't like
to be roared at, but he was still uncertain. "Yes," he said
surlily.

"Well, if you want any of 'em left," I snarled, "teach 'em
to tree what they're after."

A group of three more joined him as I said that. "He's
probably the fellow who picked Conan up," one suggested.

"If he is we can run him down later," the red man said,
"but Conan's the one we're after, and if he's riding the horse
alone now he has a chance of getting away. Get the dogs
going."

More horsemen had joined them during their brief counsel
and still more appeared as the hunt streamed away. "We may
be back for you," one of the first called to me.

I knew they'd be back. It wouldn't take them long to find
that the bay was riderless, but I could use the short reprieve.
Unbuckling my sword, I commenced stacking the loose blocks
of stone to form a rampart.

A loud splashing told me that there was water in our refuge,
which was good news. In another minute my ally reappeared
with dripping hair. He started to help me, but I waved him
aside. "Rest up," I ordered. "You'll get plenty of exercise
pretty soon."

He sat down and for the first time since I had met him he
spoke. "I've had some exercise already."

He was a fine-looking chap now that he wasn't gasping like
a fish on a sun-hot rock. He had a long, powerful body topped

by a long, exceedingly keen face, weathered but clear-skinned under his mop of light brown hair. His age, I judged, was about the same as mine, and he looked no more like a Frank than I did, either. Both from his name and appearance I picked him for a Breton.

Putting another block in place, I straightened and pointed to my scrip. "There's food in there. You'd better eat something if your stomach's stopped jumping."

"Thanks—and for the other thing, too. I'm sorry you didn't go on."

"There wasn't much sense in going on," I answered truthfully. "The horse was spent, and they would have had to follow me to make sure I didn't go for help."

"Yes." He moved his sword out of the way and reached into my scrip. "I shouldn't have got you into this, but I wanted something to put my back against."

I knew how he must have felt with those dogs getting steadily nearer. "Don't blame you," I said.

He took a huge bite of bread and meat, swallowed and took another, thinking hard. "Maybe," he said after he'd gulped down a third, "they'll let you go if I explain that you're a stranger who doesn't so much as know who I am."

"They won't listen," I told him. Besides, I'd begun to remember how the Abbot had spoken to me of a man named Conan. There couldn't, I reasoned, be many men so-called thereabouts who were important enough to be hunted by a small army. And I knew who was chiefly against him. "Are those lads Chilbert's by any chance?"

He nodded. "Oliver, the red-haired stench, is one of his chief lieutenants."

"Then they'll soon know," I snickered drily, "that I not only tried to save your neck but took you up on Chilbert's own pet horse."

He stared at me. "Why of course it was! How the devil did you get hold of it?"

"I liked it better than my own." I might have known, I thought, that Chilbert would continue to haunt me. That man had been fatal to me from the first.

My little wall was now nearly waist high, and I stopped there. "You're Conan the Breton with power in these parts," I said. "Is there any chance of friends finding you?"

He shrugged, not bothering to ask how I knew about him.

"They'll start looking, soon, I suppose. I was on a wolf hunt, lost the others, my horse broke a leg, and I got lost myself, what with no sun to go by. Then I ran foul of Oliver. I managed to hide from him first, but he got the dogs. My men won't know where to begin looking."

I went to get a drink then returned to listen. "They're coming back now," I informed him.

He rose to stand beside me. "What's your name?" He put his hand on my shoulder when I had told him. "Now we'll show them that it's one thing to corner and another to kill." He had recovered his wind, and the respite had given him time to call on the reserve strength of a mighty frame. In spite of the weariness he must have felt he looked very capable indeed.

I cut my cape in two and we each wrapped a half around our left arms to give them some measure of protection. We had just finished when they all came in sight, one of them, I saw with regret, leading the recaptured bay. Oh well, I conceded with wry philosophy, I would soon have no use for horses.

I felt very quiet. Nothing seemed quite real, and things happened with preternatural slowness. I was not bitter at being irretrievably trapped in a quarrel whose interests were not mine. Causes were no longer important in face of the actuality that was soon to be.

They halted in a cluster, the men in front and the dogs behind this time. "We're going to take you, Conan," Oliver announced.

"You may," the man with me said, "but first we'll take some of you."

The riders were looking the situation over and were not as cheerful as they might have been. Their horses would be useless, and not more than four or five could come at us without getting in each other's way. The red man looked at me. "We'll let you go free," he offered.

I spat. "Naturally. And you'll give me back Chilbert's horse, too." Conan laughed, and Oliver cursed me as grace before getting down to business.

At his order they all dismounted. Then five put their shields together and came at us. They had steel caps but no mail and muttered to each other, working themselves up to it. And suddenly anger rushed through me. My hour was near, but if it had to be I would kill meanwhile and like it.

"What's the matter with the red dog?" I jeered. "He's got

his tail between his legs before he's even been hit.''

Oliver ran forward at that and shouldered into the line just as it reached us. "That's better!" Conan approved and sliced off part of his shield.

The wall protected our legs, but they had bucklers for the upper half of their bodies. I caught two swords with mine, dodged under an axe, and swept my counterstroke at their shanks to make them step back. One of the others had his foot on the wall, and Conan took it off at the ankle. They all withdrew a minute to carry the maimed man away.

"Good work!" I applauded.

Conan picked up the foot and hit Oliver in the back of the neck. "You left something," he reminded them.

They were angry men when they came again, more swiftly. Holding shields together is sound defense; but it limits sword play, and they could only hack at me with overhead strokes which signaled themselves. The axe-man, however, was bothering me, for he kept trying to hit my blade and break it. But as axe work requires both hands he lifted his shield with every full stroke. With my left hand I drew my heavy-bladed knife and threw it underhand just as he was getting set for a blow. It stuck in his stomach, and he folded up, out of fighting for some days to come.

I had a couple of cuts but nothing worse, I saw, when they withdrew to get him out of the way; and Conan was only scratched. We had worked that time, though, and we were both panting a little. "That's what I call giving a man his stomach full," Conan cheered me.

"Did you nick any of them?"

He grinned. "Oliver hasn't as much of one ear as he used to have. The only trouble with whittling away that man is you improve his appearance."

He was enjoying himself, and I, too, was in a fine mood. We were no longer impersonal but good friends, and spontaneously we shook hands and laughed. They would wear us down, but meanwhile it was good to be giving them a rough time.

But they were in no hurry to come back, and it was easy to see why. The cloudy sky was bringing an early night, and the fact that we were in the vault looking out gave us a marked advantage of light that they naturally begrudged. They'd wait for morning, and I heard Oliver giving instructions anent preparations for the night. But they had scarcely unsaddled their horses when rain started falling.

"That means my own dogs will be of no help in locating me now," Conan said. "Still they probably wouldn't have found me in time anyhow." He raised his voice. "Hey, Oliver! Why don't you come in here out of the rain?"

Save myself no one present liked that joke. They had to stay right before us in the open or lose us. So they huddled wretchedly in the rain, which soon became hard and steady. Their sorry plight was a constant source of joy to us in the shelter of the vault, and we commented frequently.

Chapter
Five

OUR last sign of them as a black night fell showed that they and the dogs had formed a close ring around us. We were fairly satisfied, however, that none of them would risk attacking us when he could not see to strike. "Sleep if you can," I told Conan. "You've had a hard day."

Rainy nights are warmer than clear ones, so it was not too cool. I could see nothing shortly, and the teeming blotted out other sounds; but I kept some sort of watch. In the end, though, the myriad splashings worked on my drowsiness, and I, too, slept until a mighty yawn of Conan's reached through to me. It was still raining hard, and I could not perceive the hand I passed before my eyes to test the darkness. But the marked chill indicated it was well past midnight; and as it was, in fact, too cold for me to go back to sleep I sat up stiffly, shaking my head a little.

For the first time since having become involved in that disastrous affair I was neither too busy nor too tired to consider more than its factual aspects. Musing over the sequence of events responsible for leading me to where I then was, I couldn't help but seriously ponder the extent of the Pict's complicity. Well, if his had been the motivating influence he had certainly done a thorough job of fixing me up.

It was queer to sit blending with the night, conscious of savage reality that was yet rendered improbable by its silent invisibility. Out in the vague but proximate somewhere men were enduring the punishment of a ceaseless drenching in order to be sure of killing me come morning. They would be real enough then, but now, although they were hardly further off than I could toss a mountain, I couldn't so much as feel their vindictive presence, let alone picture them in their malice, fortitude and misery.

Conan, on the other hand, though equally concealed from me, had a credible existence. It was pleasant to know that he was stretched out a few feet away, a man I already thought of with a degree of warmth that surprised me. As long as I had allowed myself to be trapped I was glad to know that I had done so for no ordinary man.

He yawned again. "Giving up sleep?" I asked, hoping that he might feel in the mood to talk.

He grunted, and when he finally replied I could tell that he, too, was sitting up. "It gave me up. Next time you rescue me bring along a couple of blankets."

"Well, we're warm and cozy compared to the fresh-air fiends out there. Who do you think built this place?"

"It's Roman work. They had great farms hereabouts. I guess this was a cooler."

"It's a good thing you knew about it."

"I used to come here as a boy. This is my land, though I've been much away. I'm glad I'm dying on it."

"I never had any place," I said after considering his remark. "I made the mistake of being born to a third son of a chief, so all that they could think to do with me was to farm me out to the Church. But the only thing that caught hold was the poetry I found in the monastery library. So I left when I was ready and have been footloosing it ever since."

"I was in school in Ireland myself," he said. "My mother sent me there when my father was killed, so that his local rivals wouldn't have me done away with also. Yet this land always called to me, and I was determined to have it back. Danes captured me before I was ready, but I didn't stay a thrall; and I was glad enough to spend some years at Viking work to round out my education at points where it had been neglected. I returned about a year and a half ago."

"What did the family enemies do about that?"

"Oh, they were all dead or elsewhere, and this immediate district was in such a disorganized state that nobody had any power worth mentioning. The absence of any purposeful active force, not enemies to break, was the first problem with which I found myself confronted. Anyhow, I didn't really care about vengeance. All I wanted was my land and my people. After my father there was no one capable of looking after them.''

"A man who can look after himself is doing well these days,'' I said.

"Yes, but because I saw what had to be done, and knew how it could be done, and because men will follow me I could accomplish things for my people which they couldn't for themselves.'' He was citing a fact, not boasting, and I noted that he, as I had also caught myself doing, was thinking of himself in the past tense. "I didn't,'' he went on, "want my people to be forced either to rot as outlaws or slink through life like starved whores.''

"Chilbert was no help to you,'' I suggested.

"No. He used to pillage this locality and now in accordance with his new ambition to be a count he wants to own it. I've beat off his raiding parties, but this fall, I hear, he's going to start a concerted drive for conquest. Originally my scheme called only for retrieving my own, but because Chilbert would not be content with bullying his own domain I have tried to gather strength to break him. Well, I've lost out to him—lost other things, too.''

I took it that he referred to a wife and possible children—a man who had such definite knowledge of what he wanted to do with his time as Conan manifested would probably have an ordered domestic scheme as well—but I forbore to ask. There was no woman to mourn for me, I was grateful to think, and the few men who might care would never hear where and in what manner I ended.

I rose to see my last day, looking through the rain at the dim figures of water-logged enemies. "Did you have a nice night, Oliver?'' I called solicitously.

"A pretty seedy bunch, if you ask me,'' Conan said, clicking his tongue. "What do you figure they're doing out there, anyhow?''

"They claim as how they're going to fight us.''

"What? With just those few, scroungy, little warts?'' Conan raised his voice in protest. "Look here, Oliver; you'd better get Chilbert to send you some help.''

"They'd probably do better,'' I opined, "if they kept out of it altogether and let the dogs do the fighting."

Conan seemed astonished. "Why, hell, I thought they *were* dogs! All their parents were."

Some of them started for us at that, but Oliver snarled at them. "Wait till the light's better!" he ordered.

We ostentatiously ate our breakfast before those hungry men, then we stretched and flexed to work the kinks out of us. Shortly the rain slacked off, stopped soon after; and the sky began clearing. "The sun won't bother us till late," Conan remarked, "but then it'll shine right in our eyes and be the death of us—if we last that long."

Oliver had the patience of a good leader. He waited until his sodden men had some of the stiffness and dankness worked out of them, while we watched blue spread over a shiny green corner of the earth. "They're going to rush us this time," I said, watching them line up three deep.

In a minute they charged at us, four abreast. "Up on the wall!" Conan roared, and we leaped on it to strike down.

The men in front promptly became more interested in warding off our blows than in going forward, but the rear ranks had no such deterrent. They knocked the slowing leaders off balance, and we swooped on the confusion. My blade bit almost through a man's neck, and I heard another death cry as Conan struck.

The falling men in turn compounded the troubles of our attackers by tumbling back against the on-surging men behind. The force of the rush was broken, and while they jostled each other in an effort to close ranks we hewed at them to wreak havoc. I was wounded in the calf, but once they were no longer charging there were too many of them for their own good, a condition aggravated by the anxiety of all of them to do their share. I drew blood three times in return, and as the last of my victims stumbled I sliced him to his death.

Oliver, who had taken no part in the charge, was quick to see the futility of their broken attack. "Back out of there!" he howled. And then a moment later: "The shields, you fools, the shields!"

It was too late. They had drawn off without the corpses, not risking to stoop for them, and Conan was over the wall. Before they could do anything about it he had chopped the shield arms from two and tossed them into the vault. I have never seen a readier man.

Oliver was shrieking enraged commands, but I had worked the grips from the stiffening fingers by the time he had achieved any reorganization. It was certainly good to have a shield snuggling at my shoulder. I'd felt pretty naked before.

"This is more like it," Conan grinned. "Now we'll let them know they're in a fight."

"I don't think they'll rush us again anyhow," I said cheerfully.

As a matter of fact they left us entirely alone for a short time while Oliver took stock of the new situation. I tied up my wound, while my friend looked after a gash in his thigh. "Oliver's a sub-louse, but not an especially stupid sub-louse," he said in a low voice. "It won't take him long to see that the way to finish us is to keep hammering at us, never give us a chance to rest. Do you think you could give them a song while he's making up his mind?"

Pleased at the idea, I took up my harp. It would perhaps be the last time a song of mine was ever heard, for who can know that his work will live after him? I strummed, trying to decide which verses would be most fitting, then determined to improvise. My mind was quick with excitement, and line after line fell in place. The Frankish tirade, excellent for the purpose, was the form I chose. I didn't have enough time to polish it, of course, but it served well enough.

> *"The king of the rats once set his seal*
> *Pompously under this decree:*
> *Whereas cats use rats for a meal*
> *And whereas rats don't like it, we*
> *Order our subjects mercilessly*
> *To hunt down cats, vile each by each,*
> *Leaving none to prolong the breed;*
> *When the last one yowls its final screech*
> *Rats can—but will no more be—feed.*
> *Chilbert, Rex, his cross. All heed!"*

Some of the foe were trying to shout me down, but Oliver made them shut up. Not that he enjoyed my song, but he wanted all the quiet he could get while he thought things out. The fact that we now had shields as well as a wall to protect us was diconcerting him. I therefore directed the next strophe at him.

"*A rat whose hide was a dirty red*
Squeaked that the king had ordered well.
'A cat's most winsome when most dead,
Nine times dead and deep in Hell!
Come on,' he bragged, 'my wrath is fell!'
But when they'd tracked down two of the pests
He and his army stopped, perplexed.
'The king's decree,' he coughed, 'suggests
That we corner cats, but now what next?
There were no directions in the text.' "

Conan furnished my only applause. Oliver had turned his back and was beginning to give orders, so I raised my voice above his while I rubbed things in.

"*There were forty rats and only a brace*
Of cats, but these with great disdain
Yawned in the flea-scarred red rat's face
And entered a cave to dodge the rain;
While all the rats endured the pain
Of being washed, which is not their way
And they were foodless—the cats both ate,
Then snugly slept till a drier day
Making the bold avengers wait
Shivering under a sky in spate."

I didn't blame them—there wasn't anything else they could have done—but I knew that none of the survivors would ever think of that night of drenched discomfort without painful twinges of shame.

Oliver had found that more than four at our wall crowded each other. He was telling them off into groups of that number, and I gave them all a final boastful warning.

"*I will not say that the rats went mad*
(One needs a mind for a brain attack),
But they lost what minor sense they had
And rushed the cats, who cuffed them back—
But kept a few for the morning snack.
And so it went till the day was past,
When one they couldn't stomach—that's
The rank red rat—limped home at last.

*'Where are the rest?' asked the king of the rats.
'All traitors, sire. They've changed to cats!' "*

I had no more than time to put my harp down when they were on us, but we were not worried yet. We hunched behind our shields and took things as easily as possible, wounding two whose excitement allowed us good openings. After ten minutes Oliver called them back, and four others immediately faced us.

Defensive fighting is not so tiring, but by the time we had engaged all of the squads we were working hard. We'd been nicked in several more places, too, and sweat made the cuts sting. "We won't last another full round," Conan muttered. "Let's get rough."

They had become so used to having us conserve our strength that we took them grandly by surprise. "Over!" Conan yelled; and we cleared the wall before they were set and hacked at their legs. The two we slashed went down, and we turned on the others before help could race to them. Comfortably hedged but a second before by an additional comrade on each side, they were not steeled to meet us on even terms. They were more anxious to leave than to fight, and so did neither. We were doomed men for whom there was no such thing as risk, and they had no chance against our smashing charge as they tried to edge away. One we killed when his shield was riven by Conan's blow; the other we slew as he turned to bolt.

Then they were around us in numbers and all but cut us off from the wall. It was several desperate minutes before we saw an opportunity to jump back into our haven, and by that time we were bleeding from more places. It had been fine, swift work, but we were thoroughly tired for the first time. I thought longingly of the sweet spring in the rear of the vault, and I could hear Conan's breath coming heavily.

Still we stood them off, and eventually—I was losing even approximate track of time—Oliver ordered them to make way for replacements. He had taken no part in the fighting since the night before, but he included himself in this new squad. Doubtless he calculated that the kill was at hand, and he didn't want to miss it.

"Take this," Conan whispered, thrusting the hilt of his sword toward me. Then he tore a block from the barricade, brought it over his head, and heaved it. Oliver threw up his shield; but it was beaten in, and he went down. For the moment then his men were more interested in their leader than in us. They crowded to bend over him, and we had our first respite in perhaps two hours.

I sat down, glancing at my wounds with detached curiosity. It seemed not worth while to do anything about them. "You never can tell what you're liable to find under a stone these days," I panted.

Conan snickered. "He certainly crawled under it in a hurry. Shy, probably." He lifted his voice to address the foe. "Don't take any stones off that carrion; pile more on!"

But Oliver apparently wasn't carrion yet. In a few minutes they picked him up and carried him to the shade of a tree, where he lay motionless. We couldn't judge how badly he was hurt, but we hoped for the worst. He would at any rate be in no mood to enjoy our downfall.

Seeing them all so interested in their injured chief, Conan took a dead man's steel cap, leaving me on guard while he went back to the spring. The water he brought me tasted as only water can at such times. It revived me to a degree and helped to quiet my breathing. As I looked up from drinking I saw that his eyes were on me intently.

"Finnian," he said after a moment, "it may seem foolish to say this now when we have no more time belonging to us; but you've played a friend's part even though you didn't know me, and—"

"I wasn't keen for it," I interrupted to confess.

"Who would be? Nevertheless, you did it, and because you did it there are good things between us. Moreover, we are men that would have taken to each other anyhow."

I merely nodded at these accepted facts. It was too bad we'd never had a chance to put our legs under a table with wine on it. Oh, well.

"Finnian," he used my name again, "if you don't want it, say so, but I should like to swear blood-brotherhood with you." He smiled. "We don't have to go to any bother about opening veins."

I was more than willing to seal our hectically brief intimacy. That act of ritual seemed eminently suited to the moment, at once exalted and desperate. Besides, as the imp that is seldom absent from man's mind on even the most solemn occasions whispered, any obligations that the bond ordinarily entailed would soon be liquidated. "You're a good man to stand with," I said, with something of the formality the situation called for, "and I'll take pride in mixing your blood with mine."

So we did that and took oath. "I see they're through fussing with Oliver, brother," Conan said. "If you've got any last prayers to make, now's the time."

I thought about it but shook my head. For any retributions or rewards to follow, my rate of pay was already assessed; and it didn't seem likely that a prayer squeezed in at the last minute could change things much. I crossed myself and let it go at that.

Conan, however, made some sort of prayer. That interested me, because it seemed so appropriately in character. For such a definite mind Christianity supplied adequate answers with no vague nonsense about them. It not only explained life here but told all about the next world, complete with instructions as to the procedure on arrival. A final prayer was the requisite introduction to that new life, so a prayer he would give. I had an instant's quiet mirth at the vision of the capable aplomb with which Conan would take up flying and other angelic properties.

"We're for it now," I said, seeing a group making toward us. "Good luck in whatever happens."

"Good-by, brother."

We knew how near done we were, but they weren't sure and approached warily. They were not happy about being leaderless, but they knew that if they went away without finishing us they would never forget it. Oliver would have been enraged at the way they crowded each other, but we could no longer take advantage of it. Loss of blood was abetting my general weariness. After a few minutes I felt dizzy and could not see too well.

How long we held them I don't know. I only remember that a song I'd once made started running through my head, and I sang it over and over again as best I could with the little breath I had. After a while I was down with Conan standing over me. Then as I tried to rise he fell to squash me down painfully, and when I pushed out from under him everybody was gone.

It was puzzling, and I was annoyed at being puzzled. With some dim notion of finding out what had happened I tried to climb over the wall, but when I'd got as far as straddling it I bogged down from weakness. I was bleeding badly high up on my chest, and I sat in a sullen stupor watching the gore well and spread.

Somewhat later, however, men were standing around, staring at me. I spat at them, making the only attacking gesture of which I was capable. "Well, come on and get it over with!"

"Who are you?" one wanted to know.

This infuriated me. "Does a man have to have a formal introduction to get killed around here?"

"He's got a leg on each side of the wall, but I'm damned if I know which side he belongs on," another said. "Any of you fellows ever see him before?"

"Of course not!" I raged. "You never saw me before, and I didn't kill any of you and carve up a lot more. Next thing you'll be saying you never heard of Conan, and it was all a mistake. Get it over with, I say!"

"Somebody helped Conan," a voice said, "and as he's the only one alive we'll give him the benefit of the doubt—for the time being. Better look to that wound."

A young fellow started fussing with my chest. I was too feeble to push him away, but I glowered. "What are you doing that for?"

"To save your life."

"You mean to say you're not going to kill me?"

"No," he said patiently, "I'm trying to help you."

I had been keyed for mortal enmity, and now that I was on the way to delirium I wasn't going to be placated by anybody on any account. "You bastardly busybody!" I cursed him. "Go to hell and drink toad sweat! Here I've been killed all day, and now you say I can't die. I'll show you whether I can die or not, because I wouldn't stay alive for any of you snake fangs!"

After pronouncing that dictum I don't recall any ensuing events until I was being lifted off a horse. My head cleared enough to let me know I was in great pain and that I was being carried into a small house. "We're leaving you here," a man said. "It'd be bad for you to go any farther with that wound."

"What did you bring me this far for?" I asked testily. "It

was bad for me to go anywhere with this wound."

"Conan shouldn't travel any more today either," a voice remarked.

"Yes, but there'll be hell raised if he isn't brought home," another said.

"What for?" I butted in. "Conan's dead."

"Oh, no. He's still alive."

"I suppose some Conan is still alive," I conceded, "but the one I know is dead." I looked up sourly at the one who seemed to be in charge. "Are you ever going away so I can sleep?"

"I don't know who you are," he said thoughtfully, "or how you got mixed up in that business, but Fulke says he heard you—or somebody—singing when he located Conan."

"Damned good singing," I said complacently, less annoyed with him then.

"Well, anyhow," he concluded, "you won't be in a state to make a getaway for a while to come, so I'll let Conan decide what to do with you when he gets around to knowing what's what again."

He left, and I slept.

Chapter
Six

IT was a few days before I knew anything much, but when clarity and recollection returned I was in bed in a tiny wooden shack. I hurt in quite a few places, I was weak, and the wound in my chest stabbed me as I pulled myself up to look outside. There was nothing in sight except trees and nobody came when I yelled, so I lay back, trying to reconstruct what had happened and calculate what was liable to happen to me.

In an hour or so and after I had dozed off once or twice a man, a woodsman by the look of him, came in. He was a compact, quick fellow, quiet but pleasant.

"Are you my host?" I demanded when we'd exchanged greetings.

He scratched his head and chuckled as if I'd said something funny. "Well, I guess I am at that. I live here."

"Could you get me some food please? I'm hungry as a bitch werewolf with pups. What's more I've got the money to pay you with—or I did have."

"They left you everything they found in the vault," he assured me, "but you won't need any money. They're figuring you may be the fellow that stood by Conan, and anyways food don't cost me nothing."

I watched him catch a spark on tinder and nurse it to a blaze. "When they brought me here I couldn't get it out of my head that Conan was dead, but now I remember that they claimed he was all right."

A shadow took his face. "He's not all right, but he's alive. He got a bad cut on the head and still sleeps."

It was bad news, but we were both fortunate to be alive at all; and there was no use in mourning yet. "How did they happen to rescue us?" I inquired.

"Oh, we had every man and boy out looking for signs of Conan when he didn't show up after the wolf hunt. Fulke the minstrel was sent to scout around the Old Farms. He saw that armed men had somebody treed and guessed that Conan was there, too, though all he could hear was somebody singing about cats and rats." My host grinned at me. "Maybe you were the one, though nobody will be sure until Conan comes to."

The head of the rescue party, I recalled, had said almost the same thing. "And if Conan doesn't come out of it?" I asked.

The woodsman's face sobered. "I don't know what will happen," he said quietly, giving me something to think over with great care.

"Well, anyhow," I said by way of shelving unpleasant subjects until my meal was ready, "Fulke wandered into the neighborhood. Oliver's men were too entranced with my song to spot him, and he rallied Conan's men?"

"Leaving out a couple of words I ain't so sure of, why, I guess the answer's yes. Our men were scattered, and it was a while before we could get word to a reasonable number; but Rainault led twenty horses there. They'd had enough fighting by then and were glad to reach their mounts in time to get clear."

"What about Oliver?"

"Oh, they all got away except the corpses. Rainault was too anxious about Conan to waste time following them. Besides, counting two we sort of put out of their misery, they lost nine men, and some of the others looked well chewed. Oliver and his crew won't forget that fight in a hurry, and Fulke has seen to it that the song is sweeping the countryside. He's a real minstrel, that boy; he memorized your whole song. Everybody's laughing at it, and Chilbert will hear about it.

"Of course," he added solemnly. "He'll have the last laugh if Conan dies, though we've given out word that his wounds don't amount to much."

The stew he heated for me was tasty and contained plenty of good venison such as I needed to replenish my drained blood supply. By the following morning I was able to hobble out-doors to lie with comatose gratitude in the warm summer shade. It did not seem possible to me that I had ever been or would ever again be capable of violence or swift movement. Not that I wanted to be, then. It was the ultimate luxury to lie still so that my wounds wouldn't hurt and sense the richness July has to offer in blossom-flecked grass under a tree. Every time I thought of anything, which wasn't often, I fell asleep.

It is strange what things can satisfy a man when his cosmos is thus reduced, with emotion and action all but deducted from life. The small dramas of birds and insects could suffice to absorb and amuse me while I soaked up strength from earth, sun, and air, waiting for the rents in me to mend. At night the woodsman was adequate for my curtailed conversational needs. He seldom offered anything, but he could answer intelligently if I asked him a question.

His name was Thomas, he had lived thereabouts always, and, unlike many another, he knew his country. From him I learned that I had strayed west and south again toward the Loire after having got lost, that Thomas' house stood not a hundred yards from a stream that ran into the Loire, and that it was possible to follow the creek all the way down to the river in a small boat. I heard that possibly useful information without comment.

Thomas may have had arduous duties at other times of the year, but just then his labors consisted of hunting and fishing, and I seldom saw him during the day. When I was capable of a little more exercise, however, he took the trouble to show me an old stone bridge where I had the choice of lounging or spearing fish. In view of my condition I was not quick enough to stab anything, but clear, shadowed water is soothing to watch.

The old bridge had in fact been nothing but a couple of stone pillars for a long time, maybe since Rome. There was a ford near it where a horse could wade across, though, and a small barge which could be yanked to either shore by leather ropes for the convenience of walkers or horsemen who didn't want to be splashed. Sometimes I'd sit in the barge and try to spear the fish that would pause to mark time in its shade.

I was so engaged in the afternoon of the second day's fishing when I heard horses *chop-chopping* along toward the op-posite bank. As there was still a truce between me and Conan's men I was not alarmed. Nevertheless, they might want to use the barge, so I got out and sat on the bank to wait till they'd passed.

First two men came, then a girl; and behind her four other men. In spite of the fact that she looked hot and tired she was lovely. In addition she was the first woman I had seen since the fight, and I looked at her with that intense appreciation of the world's beauties that is the property of one who has come very near losing sight of them forever. She dismounted, stepped to the fore, and then looked across to where I sat.

No doubt my comfortable coolness annoyed her as much as my staring. At any rate she snapped an order at me with obvious assurance that I would obey and like it. "Hurry up and bring the boat over."

I picked out a tasty-looking bit of grass and stuck it in one corner of my mouth, "If one were observant," I said out of the other, "one would see that it could be pulled across by a rope, wouldn't one?"

She looked startled at my snub but didn't apologize for the manner that called it forth. She turned away from me to watch one of her followers haul the barge into position, but she hadn't forgotten me. Just as she was preparing to step in she threw me a queenly glance plainly designed to show me the infinity of my unimportance. In doing so, however, she misjudged her footing, and the man helping her in could not save her from plunging knee deep in mud and water.

It was a perfect anticlimax, and the laughter I could not restrain—not that I tried—put the finishing touch to her own consciousness of it. Furiously she stepped to the other end of the barge and was therefore the first one ashore. Without waiting for the others she strode over to glare down at me, beautiful with anger and elf locks. I understood what a gorgon was like then.

"What were you laughing at?" she demanded.

There was going to be trouble, and I was too busy wondering what I could do to get out of it to waste breath answering her. "Come here!" she called to her men who were busy getting the horses out of the water. "Come here and make this fellow say what he was laughing about."

It would make no difference whether I attempted to resist man-handling or not. In either case my wounds would open, and though I might not die I'd have the long travail of con-

valescence to start all over again. Four of her followers were
moving toward me briskly, and I acted with swiftness. Reaching for a belt she wore, I pulled myself to my knees, at the
same time thrusting the prongs of my fish spear against her
stomach.

"Call them off," I said, "or I'll jam this in you and turn
it."

The men, at least, were convinced I meant it and stopped
abruptly. She merely stared at me with shocked disbelief, too
astonished even to be scared. "You wouldn't!" she challenged.

"Maybe I oughn't to," I admitted, "but it so happens that
between my life and yours I'll choose the former every time.
What makes you think I'd be willing to die just because you're
in a bad humor?"

"Nobody said anything about dying," she protested.

"No," I snarled, indulging my anger a trifle now that the
situation was somewhat under contol. "You only wanted
your bravos to bully me into apologizing for your rudeness. It
so happens I wouldn't have stood for it. I'd try to finish one
with this," here I exerted a little pressure on the spear, "and
then they'd end me."

She saw I was right, and I knew she merely hadn't been
thinking. Still she no more than myself liked to be menaced
and scolded. She maintained a sullen silence, and I went on,
more plaintively this time. "I've never seen such a country.
Every second person I meet tries to kill me."

"I don't blame them!" she declared hotly.

"But I do," I pointed out. "I blame them a lot, especially as
all I've ever asked here is to be let alone while I go on through
as fast as possible. Now shall we call the whole thing quits?
I don't want to hurt anybody, but I don't want to be hurt,
either."

There was an uncomfortable moment of waiting while her
men fidgeted in the background. I found myself noting
abstractedly that her blue eyes and clean features rimmed with
dark brown hair could make a very sweet picture were she less
enraged. In the end she again looked through me.

"I was at fault for noticing a serf's laugh. There will be no
more of this scene." Taking hold of my hand as if it were
something slimy she removed my relaxed fingers from her belt
and turned away, a tall, graceful girl. Not once had she shown

any nervousness, and considering how nervous I had myself felt I admired her.

She rode away without looking back, but one of her escort lingered behind. "We'll be around to look for you," he said, and I knew that was what they would do. The rights and wrongs of the case were of no interest to them. They had not liked to see their charge threatened, the which was natural enough.

When they were out of sight, therefore, I sighed and headed for Thomas' house, seeing clearly that it was time to be pushing on. Even if the girl's bodyguards didn't find me, there were other considerations. I was a half suspect figure and only not a prisoner because they thought I couldn't get away, weak and horseless as I was. But if Conan died without exonerating me there was no telling what the attitude of his grieving friends would be. As likely as not I'd be not only suspect but convicted and hanged.

Thinking mournfully of the loss of the bay, I took my harp, sword and personal accessories down to the barge, together with a slab of venison and a bearskin. Then I cut both tethers and pushed off downstream. I hadn't the energy for sculling, but the current was stiff; and unless there were other boats around of which I knew nothing they would have a hard time catching me.

As there were no rocks to worry about I soon sat back, exerting myself only when the barge caught on a jutting bank or low bough. At that time I was making several miles an hour, and the mode of travel was perfect for an invalid. I could generally relax to take leisurely stock of the ever-changing scene, and there was mild warmth with no glare. On the whole I congratulated myself that this trip had been forced upon me.

It wasn't till the soft dusk had all but passed that I tied up and snuggled into the bear rug to watch the sky deepen richly. Not long after the stars had taken on their full lustre I dropped off, soothed by the faint motion of the boat and by the faint swirling of water around it.

Some animal, attracted, I judged, by the salt savor of human sweat, chewed through the rope, which I'd carelessly looped at too accessible a spot. I awoke during the night to find myself adrift, but I was much too sleepy to be willing to do anything about it. And when I opened my eyes on the day I saw that no obstacle, contrary to expectations, had acted as more than a temporary check. Now broadside to the current, now one end or the other first, downstream the barge went, and I went contentedly with it, making no effort to move until I thought the morning chill must have been thoroughly routed.

The creek was a bit wider, I discovered when I sat up; otherwise the general outlook hadn't altered. The banks were still thickly wooded to give the impression that no place at all was at hand. Nevertheless, I knew because of the slowed current that the Loire could not be far away. Before the morning was half gone, indeed, I was swept around a bend to behold the bridge that yet carried the old Roman road over the stream.

It was hardly more than two weeks before that I had ridden over that bridge, a whole man who regarded himself as a peaceful wayfarer. Since that day, I reflected moodily, I had scarcely met either man or beast, ranging from pretty girls to wolves, who hadn't proved actively hostile. So after all I had been through I was back where I started, without a horse, badly hacked, and averaging one enemy *per diem*.

Not much beyond the bridge the creek joined the Loire, and directly across from where it did so there stood a monastery. Though some of it was in ruins it was obviously inhabited, and I nodded to myself. Here was where I would finish recuperating.

I was a good half a mile below it before I managed to work myself across. Leaving the barge for who would have it, I hobbled along a narrow road back to the abbey and knocked with the hilt of my sword. I had to repeat the summons, but eventually I heard somebody fumbling with the shot window.

Mean, little eyes set in a flabby face peered out at me. "What do you want?" the porter asked with an abruptness that annoyed me.

"Entry first of all," I answered.

He continued surveying me, and I was conscious that my clothes, though clean, had had to be liberally patched after the stand with Conan. "Why should I let you in?" he wanted to know.

This was not a man to talk to like Father Clovis. Reaching into my wallet, I extracted a couple of coins and waved them before his widening eyes. "Because I'm a distinguished scholar," I told him with an abruptness to match his own.

"Oh," he said. "Come in." He opened the door and held

out his hand; but I brushed past him, closing my own fist on the money.

"This goes to the hospice," I declared, determined to get credit for my donation where it would do me some good. "I shall give it with the stipulation that some later and less learned guest," and here I chinked the money under his nose, "shall be entertained for the asking."

He was both disappointed and miffed, but there was nothing that he could do then. Turning without a word, he led me across the court, which I noticed was paved almost as much with grass as with flagstones. In transit we passed a stout monk with a fringe of gray around his freckled dome. Noticing that he had stopped to stare after me, I looked back.

"Aren't you an Irishman?" he asked in Gaelic.

He was a benevolent-looking old man. I smiled at him. "Yes, Father: like yourself truly ex-isle," I punned.

He wasn't interested in my sword or my war-torn raiment. His eyes went to my harp. "You are a bard, my son?"

He was hoping, I could see, that I was not just a minstrel, "I like to think so, Father," I answered.

He came toward me eagerly. "Have you been trained in the schools? Are you a scholar?"

"No, Father, just a lover."

"That's all any of us are." He was almost afraid to ask the next question. "Have you any books with you?"

"A few," I replied, pleased to be able to make his eyes light up.

"Could I see them?" he cried, but before I could oblige him he put his hand on my arm. "I am sorry, my son. I see that Father Paul was about to conduct you to the hospice. You're probably tired and hungry."

"Having recently slept and eaten well, I am neither, Father."

His face grew eager again. "Could you spare me a few minutes to show me what you have?"

Considering my plans concerning the monastery that was a trifling request. "Gladly, Father."

Taking me by the arm, he bustled back whence he had come, asking questions about schools and scholars in Ireland which I answered as best I could. His study, a small room on the second floor, was cluttered with scrolls and sheaves of parchment and vellum. "Nobody else here cares to read," he confided in me, "so I just moved into the library."

"I'll take pleasure in looking over your collection," I told him. I meant it, too, for he had the look of a man who might possess items I had never seen before.

"Splendid!" he beamed. "Does that mean you're going to remain with us for a while?"

"If I may, Father?"

"Of course, you may. You see, the Abbot's gone to Rome to try to get money for us to rebuild; and I'm Prior, so if I say you can stay it's all right." He looked at me anxiously as if he wasn't sure I'd believe he held such a position of importance.

"That's fine," I applauded.

"I'm not a very good prior, I fear, because I spend too much time with the books. But somebody has to. Nobody else cares," he said again.

Opening my scrip, I drew forth the tiny collection I carried with me: the *Georgics*, a miscellany of Latin poems and songs, Horace's *Ars Poetica*, two tales of Finn, a lay of Walter, a ballad of Roland, and assorted pieces of my own. With the exception of the latter he was familiar with almost all that I had to offer, but just to be able to handle them and to talk them over with someone who was interested was ecstasy for him.

Only in the miscellany did he find a couple of items that were new to him, and those he promptly scooped into his mind. As to my own compositions, though I warned him with an unwonted humility that he might find nothing in them to interest so informed a person, he protested his anxiety to read them also.

"Virgil was not born with the *Aeneid* in his hand," he told me. "Nor was it famous till men had read it." He put my poems in a compartment of his cabinet. "I'll read these when I have the time to give them a considered perusal."

To see that devotee handling my work with the same loving carefulness with which he touched the books of the provedly great moved me a great deal. "Father," I said, "as a token of my appreciation of your courtesy in permitting me to stay here, I hope you'll accept the Latin anthology for your library."

"Oh, thank you very much my son, but—" I saw him resolve to refuse my gift and saw the resolution break down. A new book didn't come his way every day, and the thought of one swelled his heart.

My spontaneous offer won him, just as he had already won me by his passion. From then on we talked in the knowledge that a friendship we would both enjoy was taking on stature while we spoke. Then a bell sounded, and he rose regretfully. "I have other duties to attend to, but you can stay here and read if you like." He paused at the door. "I hope you'll eat with us at the refectory, though perhaps you'd really prefer the hospice where you can have silent meditation during the meal."

"Oh no," I assured him, "I think it would be sinful pride to feed on my own thoughts when I could be sharing those of one so much wiser."

He blushed. "I'll see you at the table then, my son."

He left, and I stretched contentedly before picking up a scroll. I was home.

Chapter
Seven

THE Monastery of St. Lucien was very different from the last one I had visited. It had been looted and burnt by the Danes twice within the past thirty years, and since the last attack it had never been fully rebuilt. Nor had it regained more than half its original complement of monks, and this remnant was an ill-organized body without impulse toward either religious or social achievement. The disorderly times had cut them off from the inspirational nourishment that could come from the sense of being a unit of the Pope's great organization; and they lacked the man to make the abbey strong by itself.

As for the monks, most of them had been frightened out of the world into a life which called for a mysticism they had not. It was a definite place to be in a land that offered them no other comfortable one, but though a few took to the life the rest remained in a state of relieved puzzlement. They had a way of living that in general was less harried than that of other men, but they didn't know quite what they were supposed to be doing.

Discipline was not there to supply some sort of substitute for feeling, and ritual itself had inevitably become debased in the hands of men who didn't understand it. Only a handful could read better than haltingly, and an untrained mind cannot be expected to grasp the philosophic rewards of self-denial. In consequence they were neither citizens of the world nor dignified exiles from it. They were just slovens of life.

There was one in particular, on the other hand, who made himself an exception by the hardy practicality with which he viewed the monastery and ascetic vows. Not bad company when it was too hot to want to think, he was an ardent fisherman, and I often joined him. Drowsy with repletion, I'd dangle a line from the bank or lounge to troll from a drifting boat. The heavy heat of midsummer made me disgruntled when fish caused me the effort necessary to haul them up, but to do them general justice accidents of that kind were rare.

Father Gaimar, however, was a highly successful angler, although he never allowed even fishing to interrupt for long his inexhaustible flow of narrative. The pole star of his wit was concupiscence, and his reminiscences, too, were salty to a degree. Even making allowance for the heroic lying symptomatic of the promiscuous he must have been a man of varied experience.

A fish nibbled, and I made a dutiful effort to hook it. I failed, smiled contentedly, and yawned. "What's a whoremonger like you doing in a monastery?" I asked.

"Keeping out of trouble. You don't got to marry 'em, and you don't got the temptation of telling 'em you're going to. They know what the set-up is, so everything is fair like it should be." He was quite serious, for once, a man who had found the ideal existence and was giving the key to a friend. I had an enchanting vision of the whole mighty structure of the Church being created through the centuries by the martyred saints so that Gaimar could fornicate with a clear conscience, but he couldn't see why I laughed.

If the food at St. Lucien was nothing special it was sound and plentiful. I thrived, healing and taking on weight again, but I didn't push on. My mind was still set on faring east, but the attendant difficulties were great. I had neither horse nor sufficient money to buy one and yet have anything left over for traveling expenses. As for going afoot, it was dangerous everywhere and too perilous even to consider there. To get anywhere I wanted to go I'd have to cross the Loire and use Charlemagne's highway. That would take me directly through Chilbert's territory, and I was a marked man, known personally or by description to the count and his followers.

Chilbert himself, I heard, was moving everywhere trying to procure strengthening alliances. His power already extended north a considerable ways and west along the river to the stream down which I'd drifted in the barge. That meant, I mused, that he had St. Charles Abbey in the crook of his elbow and reached along the southern border of Conan's holdings. My friend was mentioned a few times, but they didn't seem to know that he was or had been in mortal danger. I didn't dare to betray the knowledge implied in asking any direct questions, for as the monastery stood near the sphere of Chilbert's influence he might have a man or so there in his pay.

I would have given much to see Conan again before leaving that section of the country, but the risk of seeking him out, granted he would be alive to make me welcome, was only one drawback. War was imminent, and if it broke out in the course of my visit I couldn't gracefully avoid doing my part against our common enemy. But there was no gain for me in that, and it struck me that I had already lost enough blood in his behalf to satisfy all reasonable demands of friendship.

All in all the river appeared to be the best means of getting out of the corner I was in. I saw none but local boats, yet I learned that sea fishers came in the fall to sell salt stock, working their way upstream as far as Tours. As that exactly fitted into my plans I determined to wait and buy passage on one of their ships.

I enjoyed the first month I was there, alternately loafing with Father Gaimar and working with Father Michael. The latter was articulate as well as knowledgeable, and he inspired me to refurbish some of the worn patches in my education. In turn I was able to do a few things for him.

I early found that he blamed himself for not being able to fire his fellow monks with his zest for reading. In post of fact he could not get through to them, being by nature incapable of dealing with an uneducated mind. He could say nothing in a way they could understand, and to them he was half a wizard and half a joke.

Sitting in one of his classes I observed how he was openly flouted. They yawned, fidgeted, and talked to each other; and his pathetic eagerness to teach was met with a stolid determination not to learn.

It angered me to see him helpless and pitiable before such oafs. "Father," I said when he had forlornly dismissed them, "why don't you let me take the class tomorrow?"

His very desire to get out of it made him refuse. "No, thank you, my son. It's one of my duties."

I feigned great disappointment. "I suppose you don't think I'm learned enough to instruct others in even the rudiments of knowledge."

"Oh, I didn't mean that!" He was distressed, as I had known he would be, at the thought he had hurt my feelings.

"Then why don't you let me take the class?" I wheedled. "There's much more valuable work you could be doing in the library, and I really think I might be able to teach them something."

"It would not be hard to do better than I," he said humbly; and because of this alone he surrendered to his own wish.

The next day I marched before the students and laid my sheathed sword on the desk. "Father Michael has asked me to help you to read," I announced, gazing from one to another with a challenge they instantly recognized and resented. "I expect your attention."

That wasn't true, and I didn't get it at first. They started gabbing as usual, their eyes everywhere but on me or their wax copy plates. "Shut up, damn you!" I shouted.

For an instant they were startled into silence. "Fathers of the Church are supposed to have two things you midges lack," I said belligerently. "They are grammar and courtesy, and I propose to teach you both." I fixed my eyes on a young man who looked more intelligent as well as more insolent than the rest. "Can you decline *mensa?*"

He smirked. "No, but I can decline to answer."

I rose when his mates had finished laughing. "This," I stated, picking up my sword for him to see, "is a thing. Its name is a noun, which can be declined but not conjugated."

He pursed his lips mockingly. "Oh?"

"The act of moving a thing," I pursued, "is a verb, which can be conjugated but *not* declined." I hit him over the head with the sheathed blade, and he sagged in his seat, almost out. "To confuse one with the other," I concluded as I resumed my seat, "is a shocking fundamental mistake."

After a few more such incidents interest in literacy waxed. All were attentive, and the better minds began to take hold. Not that I could claim to be popular with my class. Some resented my methods, but more were displeased because I, a non-cleric, was presuming to instruct monks. The fact that instruction was needed only aggravated the sting of the point. Even though they might not want to take the trouble of knowing more, by rights I should have known less.

Father Michael would have been dismayed at some phases of my technique, but he was overjoyed at the results. "You are a real teacher, my son," he said happily, and I could see that he already had visions of the abbey swarming with eager students. Perhaps in other days, like many another house, it had been; but the great age of learning had passed. A saint of scholarship himself, he could not believe this, and it would not have flattered, but instead pained him, had I pointed out how wonderfully alone he stood.

A teacher of bare fundamentals I might have been, but he, awkward as a swan on the ground, was as splendid when allowed to soar. He had a flair for making the magnificent real that could stun the intellect with dreams.

Piety of a true sort he had. But though he was unaware of it he was no more a theologian than myself. I'm sure that Virgil was a much more vivid and beautiful spiritual reality to him than the banded Twelve Apostles, and I know, if he did not, that he viewed the loss of the Garden of Eden as a trifling tragedy compared to the sack of Troy. Rome and Greece in truth formed his paradise, and even the most despicable rogues in it had a glory that made their villainy inconsequential. Naïveté of a kind it might have been, but such was his love for it that he could put you in that dead world and take you through it, breathless at its wonders.

At the end of five weeks, however, our association was interrupted when some species of fever to which he was apparently subject sent him to the infirmary. While waiting for him to recover, I spent more time with Gaimar than ever. By then I had all but regained my full strength and felt so good about it that I usually took the oars for the returning upstream pull. I was well sweated getting my back into it on a scorching day when Father Gaimar stopped telling me and a boon companion of his who had joined us about the Mother Superior who had found a fiend under her bed.

Reprieving the fiend from ravishment, he said in a startled voice: "What's that?"

I gazed where he was pointing, then stood up the better to see. The head and shoulders of what appeared to be a man, the rest of him trailing in the water, lay on the north bank just down river from us. "It's a basking nicor!" Father Gaimar said in an awed voice.

"Let's get away quick!" the third member of our party whispered.

Ignoring them, I let the boat drift until we were directly parallel with the figure. It didn't move. "It's a nicor, all right," Gaimar said authoritatively. "Make for the other bank!"

Notwithstanding the heat, I felt gooseflesh, but I wasn't entirely convinced. "Nicors hang out in the sea," I objected. "I never heard of one in a river."

"It's come up to catch fish," he opined. "Row like the devil!"

"It'll put a spell on us!" the other monk cried.

"Let me take an oar!" Gaimar urged, but I pushed him away. Their panic had had a steadying effect upon me.

"Why don't you two holy men exorcise it?" I asked, half ironically and half wishing they could.

"I never got the hang of it," Gaimar said, "but I'm going to learn if we ever get back safely."

I had been studying the thing carefully. The hair was fair, which is true of nicors, and what of the torso could be seen was naked. Still there was nothing in his appearance to disprove he was human, either. "I think it's a man," I announced.

"It's not!" the odd brother said angrily. "If you don't want to row, give us the oars."

I sat down and put the sculls between the thole pins once more. "I can't and won't leave without finding out whether that's a man or not. If it's a man, why, we can't just go off without seeing what's the matter with him."

They didn't agree and jumped me, trying to wrest the oars away. I stopped Gaimar by putting my foot in his stomach. His fellow struck me, and my reciprocating shove landed him on his back. I caught up my sword and drew it. "This can put a spell on you as quickly as a nicor," I warned them. After a moment I laid the weapon on the thwart beside me and so began pulling toward the creature.

Had I not been myself somewhat nervous I would have derived more amusement from the sight of those bawdy monks kneeling and stumbling through the Latin of their prayers.

About ten yards from the thing I stopped. The river was too roiled from recent rains to let me see whether the lower extremities took the form of legs or not. The face was that of a man right enough, but it was so colorless that it might well have been something kept from the sun by deep water.

I almost weakened and consented to leave without pushing the investigation further, when to my excited fancy the face suddenly looked like that of the Saxon youth I had let Chilbert kill. "I'm going to find out exactly what's what," I told my wildly babbling companions. "You can come with me or you can jump ashore."

They preferred the latter course, so I rowed them to the south shore and let them scramble up the bank and away. They had no intention of waiting to see what happened, either, but bee-lined home to the sanctuary of holy ground. Gaimar, it occurred to me as I pushed off, had at last found a spiritual use for the monastery.

Rowing backwards so that I could see better and be in a better position for flight, I approached the figure slowly. Reassured by closer inspection, I grounded the skiff near him and sprang ashore. His body was chill but not death-cold, so I rolled him over to get his face out of the mud. It was then that I saw his trouble, a deep gash in the shoulder. I examined it and whistled.

Unless I was much mistaken that wound had been made by an arrow, since pulled out. Bows aren't used much for war purposes, although an occasional Dane is dangerous with the weapon. Leaving the man for a minute, I climbed the bank to look around. He had come from the west, the road, which ran quite near the Loire at that point, showed me, and had turned off to the river, no doubt desperate with thirst. Apparently the steep bank had been too much for him to negotiate, he had fallen in the water, and had fainted in the course of his struggle to get out.

His wound had stopped bleeding but recommenced a little when I put him in the boat, so I bound a press of leaves over it to keep the flies off. On the way back I devised gibes for Father Gaimar and planned to entertain my fellow diners with an epic account of his prayers and panicky retreat. But when I walked up to the monastery to get help in carrying my foundling the door was not opened at my word. Instead, as on the morning of my first arrival, Father Paul peered at me through the shot window. He closed it a second later but still did nothing about the door.

"Open up!" I said irritably.

"You can't come in," he retorted, and I could tell that he was enjoying himself.

"Quit playing jokes," I told him sternly. "I've brought in a wounded man that needs looking after."

"Father Gaimar told us how you picked up a nicor. You can't come in."

With the hilt of my sword I knocked the shot window loose from its grooves to glare at him through the small opening. "I tell you it's a man. Hell! I've been with him an hour, and he's done no harm to me."

He swung the key on his finger and smiled. "Well, my distinguished scholar," and by those words he as much as announced that he was avenging the snub I'd given him at our first meeting, "nobody knows anything about you except that you suddenly appeared. You may be a fiend yourself."

He would not call any of the others when I asked him to, so I began shouting. When they appeared they did not come singly but in a group. They had been talking about me. "Father Raoul," I addressed the sacristan, "I have a man in need of attention here who should not be made to wait while this gnat-brained fool plays bad jokes."

He was a well-intentioned old nincompoop, but he was of the kind to be thoroughly taken by Gaimar's story. "You can't defile a house of God by bringing in devil's spawn," he said uneasily. I could see that he did not relish even talking with someone who had associated with that spawn.

"Gaimar," I said to my former friend, "tell them you lost your nerve and ran away before you could find out whether it was a man or not."

"Father Gaimar saw he had a fish's tail when you took him out of the water," another monk volunteered.

"Tell them you lied, Gaimar," I said ominously, but he just looked at me sullenly. In part he was a bearer of exciting news who balked at publicly confessing its falseness, but I believe he also now thought he had witnessed what he so vividly imagined.

I was losing my temper, but I was still making an effort to be reasonable. "Come out and see for yourselves that he's just a harmless lad who's had a bad time of it. Look. I've lived here over six weeks. You all know me and can see that being near this fellow has wrought no change in me."

"I've always thought you were a devil anyhow," one of my students spoke up. "Nobody ever caught you praying."

Some of them were smiling behind their hands, and then I knew. They had more or less believed Father Gaimar's story until I had returned with evidence to refute it; now it was an excuse for satisfying the enmity aroused by their jealousy of me and of the Prior's friendship for me. From the beginning they had resented my post of authority, and with Father Michael ill they could turn on me with impunity.

"All right, you ticks," I said angrily, "I'll find another place for him—one with no monks around to make his wounds fester. Now send out my things, and make it fast!"

"We're keeping them to pay for your board and lodging," Father Paul informed me impudently, and at that I lost my self-control.

"Bring out my things!" I yelled, "or I'll wait around and kill the first polecat of a holy father that tries to leave. Bring out my harp carefully and every coin of my money or I'll kill two! Bring them right away or I'll kill three!"

They ceased smiling then. They weren't fighters and didn't have the gumption to organize against me, so unless they stopped all outside pursuits, be they of business or of pleasure, I could lurk in the neighborhood and easily waylay enough monks to make my threats good. "Will you leave us in peace if we return your property?" the sacristan asked.

"If you hurry," I snapped. "But you'd better keep a certain fat slug inside while I'm around or I might forget my agreement."

Once I'd held his unwilling eyes, Father Paul had had all the jesting he wanted for one day. He scuttled away, and it was another monk who undertook the task of gathering and surrendering my gear. Still burning with rage, I went in search of a peasant's shack where my charge could be housed.

Chapter
   Eight

HIS eyes were partly open when I returned with a fellow whose hospitality I had bought. I had succeeded in finding a fairly clean shanty, and beyond cleaning his wound there was not much more I could do for him. Though he had lost quite a lot of blood I judged his condition not serious, and I sat by his bed on the chance he'd revive enough to talk. I had plenty to think about while waiting.

I would no longer have any of the pleasant things—companionship, a library, decent quarters, or good food and wine—which the abbey had offered, so it seemed foolish to remain in the vicinity. Moreover, I didn't have much money, and unless the injured man should unexpectedly convenience me with a speedy demise I would shortly have no funds. There was no way of acquiring any more money where I was, and no reasonable means of traveling anywhere but west, whence I had come.

An hour's consideration was sterile of good answers. Finally the man stirred and looked at me. "Water?" I asked.

His eyes were feverish, but he was clear-headed enough to understand. He nodded, and I held his head so he could drink. "What happened to you?"

"Danes."

That was interesting. "It looked like their work," I said. "How far away are they?"

"I don't know now. I broke through their attack and

escaped. I was going to try to find help and have another crack at them, but I got fever. Lost track of what I was doing, though, so I guess I just kept right on going nowhere in particular.''

"Yes, of course." I knew how it was with fever. "I found you in the water."

"I don't remember that." He closed his eyes tiredly, and I went outside. The fellow had given me something new to consider. Down river were vikings who might solve my transportation problem. Once or twice in the past they had gone all the way up to sack Tours, but only a very strong force of them would dare that. They might not proceed any farther than the ten or fifteen miles below us they then were.

At the moment, with the drab work of piracy finished for the day, they should be gathering for drink and talk. As I visualized their bustling camp my own lot seemed a drab one. I thought about that a minute and made up my mind. I'd join the Danes and go whichever way they'd take me. If they wanted to thrust on east, well and good. I'd leave them at Tours. If they were returning west, on the contrary, I would accept it as Fate that I was not to make my trip to the Isle de France—at least by the Loire route. I'd see where they'd take me, hole up somewhere for the winter, and possibly go by way of Normandy in the spring.

Pleased at having an actual course to pursue, I retired early to the haystack that provided me with bedding and was up at dawn. Leaving the remainder of my money with the peasant to reward him for harboring the invalid, I started walking toward Nantes. I had thought of taking the skiff; but Gaimar had suspected that I might think of that, so it wasn't there.

In so far as my impedimenta would allow, I walked fast. It was possible that the Danes would decide to go no farther inland, and I wanted to make sure of arriving at their camp before they turned back to the sea. Around a sweeping bend four or five miles downstream I first saw the smoke rising. It was not from a cooking fire either, and I nodded to myself. Arson was the national pastime of the Danes. If they couldn't carry off a thing they had to see whether it would burn.

Not much past sunrise I met the first wayfarer, a worn man on a disinterested mule. "Don't go any further," he warned me. "There are Danes down river."

"How many ships?" I asked.

"Seven," he said, but I wasn't impressed. They'd never reach Tours with just those few.

"Anybody making a stand against them?" I inquired next.

"No," he said disgustedly. "There's no leader, and all anybody thought of was getting out of the way. I'm just riding to let people know they're coming."

He went on, and after a moment I followed him. He'd warn them at the monastery, and they'd escape all right; but there was something I had to do for Father Michael. But when I got back I went first to see if my waif had been taken care of. As I had half suspected he had been deserted.

He was awake and knew me. "What's all the excitement? The Danes coming here, too?"

"Yes," I told him. "I'm sorry, but I've got to move you."

When I picked him up he gasped, but he made no other sound while I struggled the short distance to the abbey with him. The monks were all busy loading wains in preparation for flight out of reach in the forest. I put my burden down and looked at them grimly, but they weren't inimical any longer. Calamity had temporarily cured them of pettiness, and they met my eyes sheepishly.

"Father Raoul," I addressed the sacristan, "this man has already been wounded by the Danes. If they find him here they will finish what they started. You will take him with you?"

Though a fumbler, he was a good-hearted old man, and I knew that he was one of the few that had not been actuated by malice the day before. "Certainly we'll take him," he said hastily. "Are you coming with us, too, my son? You're welcome."

"No, thanks. Where's Father Michael?"

My friend was in a horse litter, shrunken and pale. It looked to me as if he might not survive the rigors of an overland journey, but I could help him a little. "I'll see that the books aren't burnt, Father."

His drawn face lighted with pleasure. "That's splendid," he whispered.

"I'll hide them and leave word where they are." I hesitated while I thought of a safe place. "The message will be in a box under the northwest corner of the wheat field. Good luck, Father."

He had no more strength for words, but his hand squeezed mine slightly. As I left him to enter the abbey they were placing the wounded man on a part of one of the wains where piled bedding would soften the joggling for him. "Who are you?" he asked.

"Finnian, an Irish bard."

"I'll remember," he said.

I hadn't told Father Michael where I was going to put the books, for the idea would have worried him. An old burial vault was the place I had in mind as being at once weather-proof and safe. The Danes would never look there because they had long ago learned that Christian priests, at any rate, didn't bury valuables with their dead. It took me well over an hour to accomplish my task, then I returned to await the vikings.

The monks had taken things of practical worth and the more portable valuables, but there was still some loot. The Danes wouldn't be too pleased, but at the same time they wouldn't be put out of humor by complete disappointment, which was good for my purpose. I filled a couple of demijohns with wine, gathered a bunch of cups, then put them all on a table I'd dragged out into the court.

After a while a dragon came into sight, swiftly legging it up river, and I climbed down from my perch on the wall. No Dane could resist a monastery, so I knew there wasn't any danger of them passing me by. When I heard them beaching a ship I filled a mug with wine and walked over to open the replaced shot window just enough to peek through with one eye.

A powerful, squat black Dane led. He had horns on his helmet, carried a huge axe and walked with a bow-legged swagger. About twenty warriors streamed after him, and I heard other ships landing. Marshaling his followers, the chief roared for the door to be opened. He himself apparently expected no results from this order, for he called out for those just arriving to bring a ram. I unlocked the door, slipped a chip of wood between it and the jamb to hold it closed, and went back to my wine.

"Get your weight behind it," the leader was urging. "Hard now!"

I've never seen more surprised-looking men than the ten Danes who breezed through that door carrying a heavy, utterly useless log. Braking, they stood there, looking foolish and gaping at where I sat on the table idly swinging my legs.

"Why don't you put it down?" I added to their astonishment by speaking to them in their own language. "It's a pretty hot day to be running around with that sort of thing."

The bandy-legged viking had followed them and was leaning on his axe in the doorway, glaring at me uncertainly. I was obviously no part of a monk, and what's more I was grinning at him good-humoredly. I felt friendly, too, and not a bit concerned. It's perfectly easy to get along with Danes when you haven't got anything they covet. He began truculently enough, however.

"What are you doing here?"

"Drinking," I illustrated.

"Why didn't you open the door when I spoke?"

"Get your own men to open a door for you," I told him calmly. "Of course, you did, but it shouldn't have taken that many. When a door isn't locked one man can move it quite easily."

The log plumped to the ground. It takes a little time for a Dane to see what jokes he can see, but he gets a lot of fun out of one when he does. They roared, and finally bow-legs as well as the other vikings who had crowded to the door to peer in whooped with laughter also. I laughed with them and slapped the demijohns invitingly.

"Work first and drink later," the commander said sententiously. "Anybody here but you?"

"No," I replied offhandedly. "They got wind of you and cleared out last night. I happened to be passing by and moved in as there was no other decent place to sleep."

He thought of something, and his voice grew edged again. "I suppose you've taken everything."

I smiled to myself. Nothing hurts a Dane's feelings like prethieving him. "There's a lot of junk in there that you might like," I reassured him. "The only thing I wanted was this. Skoal!"

After directing his men, who went about the business of pillaging like the old hands they were, the chief decided to join me. "I'm Thorgrim Gunnarson," he said when I filled a mug for him and introduced myself.

Looking at both him and the big axe, which was not Danish made, though I had seen others like it, I thought a minute. Wherever Danes gather they tell about those among them who have distinguished themselves, and it's part of my business to know such things. This was not a great viking leader but none the less a man who had won himself a name.

"You're Thorgrim the Varanger," I said. "Sweyn Bucktooth killed your brother, you returned west, called him to a skerry, and slew him."

He was delighted at being recognized, and from that point on I was in a favorable position to deal with him. "How far up are you going?" I asked.

He smacked his lips ruminatively. "That depends on what there is to take and how much trouble there's likely to be in the taking. Do you know anything about that?"

As I knew how small a force he had and as long as I was counting on going with him, I didn't want him to go any farther. There would be hard, fruitless fighting in which I had no lust to take part. "There's a man just up the line called Chilbert who is considered very tough," I informed him. "He doesn't like anyone but himself to do the thieving, and he has a lot more men than you have to back him up."

Thorgrim nodded. "I'll go up and take a look at him. If it doesn't seem feasible I won't land."

I'd pressed my point as far as I could. "How's the luck been treating you?" I inquired.

"Oh, not so bad," he said cheerfully. "We're not strong enough to attack any really fortified towns, and the Loire has been pretty well picked over; but there are always slaves. They're the most valuable thing next to gold itself."

"Everybody around here seems to have cleared out," I said.

"We'll round up some though," he responded confidently. "These Frankish villeins seldom run far. They're more afraid of a territory they don't know than they are of being caught."

The miscellaneous booty from the abbey, consisting largely of sacramental appurtenances, trimmings, and assorted items of personal property, was being piled up outside. Then inevitably they set fire to the place. The abbey was soon burning furiously, and the Danes watched, pleased.

Others, meanwhile, had been sent inland to capture any people and commandeer any livestock that hadn't fled or been driven out of reach. Thorgrim and I took a demijohn to the shade of a tree so that we could loaf in comfort until the foragers returned. "I was told you had seven ships," I remarked. "Where are the other three?"

"I sent them to scour the north shore," he answered.

"They're supposed to meet us back here before dark."

Wine in quantity in the middle of a hot day put me to sleep.
By the time I'd waked, the raiding parties had started to sift
back; nor was Thorgrim's optimism unfounded. Between
them they had seized enough cows and pigs to feed the pirates,
in addition to one horse which Thorgrim sacrificed to Odin,
hanging it and cutting its throat. There were, too, nine
assorted peasants, of which none was old or a very young
child. The latter is too poor a risk, being liable to perish on the
voyage to the slave market.

Nobody injured them, because slaves are valuable, but they
grouped together weeping or staring around with piteous eyes.
A man who travels with Danes has often to harden his
stomach, but I didn't look at the captives any more than I
could help. Not that they could be physically much worse off
than in the life France allowed them; indeed, it was probable
that they would be much better fed, plus being infinitely better
protected. Moreover, in so far as slavery is concerned a
villein's status is only nominally above it; but at least here they
could suffer among their own kind and with their own families.

When the meat was eaten and the wine drinking began it
was time for me to make my bid. For though I was on good
terms with Thorgrim nothing definite had been accomplished
toward accompanying him when he left. It was up to me to
show that I would be an addition to the voyage, and I rose
with my harp. "Shut up and listen to the scald!" others
echoed my roar for silence.

Danes only want one thing, a lay to satisfy their concept of
adventure. Nevertheless, a certain amount of care was necessary as to the exact choice of subject. There are so many feuds
and factions among them that it is well to know a band's leanings and connections before praising a leader or recounting a
battle. I avoided this risk by choosing an incident from the far
past.

"I'll sing to you," I called out, "of how Hogni got the
Odinsword."

"That's fine!" one raised his voice above the general mur-
mur of approval.

"Silence for the scald!" another took it on himself to command.

Merry and on the way to being drunk, they were in the

mood to hear any fast-moving tale that didn't step on their toes. Hogni was a popular figure with Danish poets, and his whole story was well known to everyone present. An incident of his life could, therefore, be told without preface. With one motion I swept the strings and flung out my arm dramatically.

> *"The king of the trolls caroused at yule,*
> *Whiling winter with wine from the south,*
> *Never fearing a foeman's coming*
> *To pierce this hill, piled high with snow.*
>
> *No gloom was there, for glowing gold*
> *Roofed the room where rang their songs,*
> *Driving dark from deep in the caves*
> *Where trolls hide well the treasure they win.*
>
> *But one-eyed Odin entered the sleep*
> *Of Hogni, telling the hero a sword*
> *Of Wayland's making might be his*
> *If he forbore to fatten on rest.*
>
> *Up rose Hogni to run on staves,*
> *Skimming the drifts on skis, as petrels*
> *Skim the waves of the wife-bereaver,*
> *Swift on slopes as a sliding otter."*

I glanced to make sure that I was holding Thorgrim's attention. He was manifesting interest, though I couldn't be certain how much. There was a nice but important point involved in the extent of his enthusiasm. Should I be forced to ask for inclusion in his company I would be consigning myself to the position of just another one of his followers. If, on the other hand, he should be moved to issue an invitation, I would be going along as a guest and an equal.

> *"The cold mirk-wood might cast no terror*
> *On such a man. His mood was baneful.*
> *He'd slake his longing or sleep forever,*
> *Win the weapon or waste in his howe.*
>
> *He found the drift his dream had showed him,*
> *Winnowed the woof of winter's loom,*

Found the rift in the rocks behind it
And entered the earth there, eager for plunder.

A fearful fire-drake formed by Loki
Was there to watch but winter had lulled it;
Certain of safety, sightless with sleep,
Traitor to trust, the trolls' guard lay.''

Thorgrim was watching his men. His own judgment of the poem was of less moment to him, naturally, than their reaction. If I proved someone who could help to keep them good-humored, and therefore easily handled, why that was all he wanted to know.

''No man-made sword could mar its life;
Steel-hard scales were scornful of axes.
Woe was Hogni's should he wake it,
As well he knew; but he never wavered.

Hardy the hero who held his course
Past such a monster, mocking the peril!
Boldly he passed it, bored through the hill—
A dangerous mole in that dark passage.''

I was using every trick of harp, voice and gesture in the trade, and at the next line I caught up my cup with a flourish.

''Soon he heard 'skoal!' from skinkers by hundreds,
And, following further, found the cavern
Glorious with gold and glittering jewels,
Splashes of fire in a splendor of colors.

Careless the king sat, cracking jests,
Proud of his thanes nor thinking of evil;
But Hogni was grim and gripped his axe.
He would not turn with his task undone.

Wild were the warriors, wine-sodden trolls!
When Hogni harried the hall of their monarch.
Fierce was his onset, fast as an osprey's.
He made no pause to ask pardon of any.''

They were with me now, exhilarated by Hogni's swift daring, and laughed at the understatement. Downstream I saw the other three galleys pulling toward us. Fortunately all the rest had their eyes on me and failed to notice. I twanged my harp loudly to announce the climax of the lay.

> "Before the ruler could roar for help
> Hogni's axe was high above him.
> Keen was the edge the king saw then;
> Trapped in his hall the troll sat moveless.
>
> 'What will the hero have for my ransom?'
> The ring-bestower wrathfully asked him.
> 'I'll give you gold or gorgeous gems
> Craftily hewn from the hold of the earth.'
>
> Loud laughed Hogni. 'Leave it for dragons
> Sour with aging to sulk over treasure!
> Let cowards be misers—a man is before you!
> I want no baubles, but Wayland's sword!' "

They cheered the sentiment, but I was wry in my mind. Catch these or any other Danes I'd ever met turning down loot in favor of honor! Still the fact that they knew how they ought to feel was sufficient for my purposes.

> "Not gladly given, the glaive was his
> And warriors ran for weapons, raging;
> They were all fain to follow Hogni;
> Who leaped to leave them, laughing his triumph.
>
> The noise unknotted the noose of sleep
> That bound the fire-drake, fiercely it reared;
> Sure no sword could shear its armor,
> It deemed then Hogni was done with life.
>
> But Wayland forges no false weapons—
> They're valkyries with vampire mouths,
> Brands that none but the Norns can break—
> And Hogni carved to its cold heart.

> *Maddened with anger oncoming trolls*
> *Rushed to catch and kill the riever,*
> *But skillful on skis he skimmed away,*
> *Bearing his booty back to his steading."*

They roared cheers, and Thorgrim himself refilled my cup. "Have you any particular plan?" he asked when we had toasted each other.

"Why?" I inquired offhandedly.

"We've a long voyage ahead, and there's not a scald in the company. It ought to be a pretty interesting trip for you, too. Why don't you join us?"

I made as if to consider. "Where do you go now?"

"To the Spanish slave markets," he answered. "Maybe?" and he tapped the Varangian axe, "I may even decide to go back to Miklagard after that."

Constantinople was a place I had long wanted to see, and Spain I had only visited once. "Thanks. I'd like to join you."

"Good," he nodded, and we both turned to watch the galleys land.

Chapter
Nine

I WAS feeling good. Here my life was all arranged once more, and the prospects were excellent. If we made the great journey to Byzantium it would be strange if I couldn't find the makings of some good poems. Moreover, if the expedition was successful I should return with pelf to spare. Triumphant chiefs are generous in their gifts to scalds.

Best of all was the thought of getting out of that accursed country where nothing ever turned out well for me. I shook my head cheerfully at thought of the Pictish priest. He had made good his threat, and I was glad to get out from under.

The first boat contained the plunder, including a half-dozen newly made slaves. With drowsy compassion I watched them being herded ashore. Then the roof of hope fell in. "Holy St. Patrick!" I breathed. But I knew that neither he nor anyone else would help me.

The fourth of the lot was the girl I'd met at the ford. It wasn't that I cared for her as such or had the slightest concern for her personal welfare. She and her bravos had given me a bad scare, and I hadn't wanted to re-encounter her. And at that moment I would have given all Charlemagne's empire, had I owned it, for the privilege of not seeing her again.

Or if I hadn't seen her before it would have been all right. I could think of her what was probably true of all the others. They were wretches whose lives it would take a deliberately sadistic master to make less endurable. And if the women were sold to Moorish harems, why, they would lead a sheltered existence compared to that to which they were accustomed, with outlaw bands periodically subjecting them to gang rape. The alternative for their kind was becoming some leader's doxy.

But I had looked on this girl in her pride, and I could not so classify her. She was of my own sort, and whatever else she was she was no man's whore. So though we had met as enemies the fact that we had met at all before placed an obligation on me. I shivered, feeling sick.

Her frightened eyes glared hate as the vikings cheered her beauty, but Thorgrim came between her and a couple of drunken youngsters. "Who takes prizes first?" he asked them dangerously, nor were they too crazed to remember he was chief.

Mustering a guard, Thorgrim sent the prisoners to join the others in one of the ships. "One good thing about getting older," he said as he resettled himself comfortably, "is that you don't let lust interfere with the profits. When I was the age of those boys I would have had that girl, and very likely she would have knifed me for it as soon as she got the chance. That kind doesn't take to man-handling. As it is I'll get a good price for her from some Moor, and let him get killed instead." He stretched. "Feel like giving us another song?"

"No," I said. I didn't yet see what I could do.

I gained nothing but a headache and a morosely fatal feeling from that night, and I took ship the next morning with only the knowledge that I'd made some sort of gesture toward freeing the girl. Thorgrim, as I had taken for granted he would, had arranged that she, as his most valuable prisoner, should voyage in his galley. He took the tiller to steer up river, and I stood silently beside him.

It was just after we had started that she recognized me for the first time. I saw her eyes widen, then her mouth set in a yet harder line of hate. No doubt I was in just such company as she would have expected. I looked away from her, sweeping earth and sky in an aimless reach for courage.

My mouth was dry, and my hands started to sweat. If I was to help the girl, now was the time, before she was borne too far from kinsmen or friends who might take her in. Otherwise I'd have her on my hands, and the last thing I wanted was somebody to look after in that land where I wasn't able to keep any decent footing for myself.

When the ship had straightened its course to head upriver I got behind Thorgrim. In addition to being jumpy with nervousness I disliked so repaying his hospitality, but there was no other solution. "Thorgrim," I told him, letting him feel the point, "there's a knife at your back. Move or yell, and you die."

He stiffened, but that was all. "Well?" he queried; and his whisper carried his anger as well as a shout could have done.

"It's the girl there. I want you to put us both ashore."

"I might have known she'd make trouble," he said bitterly. "Why didn't you say you wanted her? Maybe I'd have given her to you."

I paid no attention to that. Nor was there any use in telling him that I didn't want her. He would merely have considered that incomprehensible meanness. I was sorry I couldn't make him understand, for we had been friendly.

"Put us on the north bank," I ordered.

He was too surprised and furious to stop arguing and make up his mind. "Why didn't you fight me for her openly?" He was still pursuing the ethics of the case. "Only a bastard Irishman would drink a man's wine, then knife him when his back was turned."

Not bothering to point out that the wine in question was really the property of St. Lucien Abbey, I pricked him a little harder. If it came to the pinch I'd decided to kill him, too. He showed no mercy to any, and my last act would be to see that he got none. "Well?" I said in turn.

"No!"

He meant it. A Danish chief will do anything rather than compromise with his own sense of dignity. He'd let us both die and be damned before he'd accept the ignominy of being forced to surrender a valuable prize in the presence of his own men. I sought desperately for a sop to his pride.

"Look!" I urged. "If you'll give her to me and let us go free I'll make a lay about how Thorgrim the Varanger fared back from Miklagard to avenge his brother." That had actually been a notable exploit, because Sweyn Bucktooth had had a great reputation as a warrior. "I'll sing the tale in every land I visit," I continued persuasively, "and I'll write it in runes for men that live after us to read."

It was that last touch that won him. A Dane is as desirous of having his name and exploits known by later generations as a

saint could be of securing a place near the throne of heaven.
Every man to his own immortality.

"Do you give your word that you'll do this?" he asked, and
the burden of death started to skip from me.

"I swear it by Christ and by Odin," I answered earnestly.
"If I don't make this lay within three months and sing it in
every country I fare to may my bones be dug up and mouthed
by cur dogs."

That apparently satisfied him. "Sheathe your knife," he
whispered. "I give my word to the bargain." Gulping with
relief, I stepped forward to stand in friendly-wise beside him.
Signaling for the remaining galleys to proceed, he swung the
tiller of his own to head it for the shore.

"Vikings!" he cried when the oars were dipping just enough
to hold the dragon's nose on the north bank, "my friend the
great scald is going to make a hero-lay about how we fought
our way through the Middle Sea to Miklagard. He'll tell of the
treasure we won and how word came that my brother was
slain. He'll tell how Sweyn's blood paid the wergild when I
followed him to the Western Isles; and now how we return to
Miklagard for more honor and wealth!"

His men cheered him, themselves, and me. All that Thorgrim had promised them hadn't been specified in our contract,
but I nodded my acceptance. He raised his voice again, now
carried away by magnificence of his own gesture. "For reward
I am giving him the lovely Frankish maiden."

He made the statement with telling directness, and the applause was great. Generosity in requiting service is one of the
hallmarks of a Danish chieftan of standing, and this was a
princely gift. None of his followers dreamed that Thorgrim
would turn over such a prize to them, so they didn't begrudge
me my supposed good fortune.

"Scalds make fame, the only good thing a man can have,"
an older man quoted. "No gift is too fine to exchange for it."

It was a high moment for all of them. I could see the
younger ones a-dream for the day when their adventures
should be sung and the singer rewarded with a hero's magna-
nimity. Of all those there, as he himself had temporarily
passed beyond the point of caring, I alone knew how
Thorgrim would soon regret his loss.

Forcing myself to appear pleasurably excited, I made an appropriately grateful speech in answer, told them how for-

tunate I thought they were to have such a chief to lead them, and wished them luck in all ensuing exploits. Then I hastily strode toward the girl.

Up till then, being ignorant of Danish, she had naturally been unaware of what had been taking place. "You're free," I said in Frankish as I took her by the wrist. "Come on ashore fast!"

But all men seemed enemies to her then, and she did not remember me kindly. She snatched her arm away and backed from me. "Let me alone!" she screeched.

Her delay in the face of the urgency for haste suffused me with wrath. "They'll sell you to a Moorish brothel!" I thrust it at her bluntly.

It might only be a private brothel, but it was the same thing as far as I could see. It got home to her, her eyes wavered, and I seized her during that instant of uncertainty. Picking her up, I stepped forward and dropped her overside in the soft mud. I was standing beside her by the time she had risen.

Panic and loathing had rendered her incapable of making distinctions between grades of bad situations, and my rough-ness had aroused furious antagonism. She struck me hard, and the vikings peering over the gunwale laughed uproariously.

"Better trade it in for a tame one," a man counseled me sagely.

"What odds on the scald?"

"No takers!"

"He hasn't got a chance!"

Even without their gibes I was keenly conscious of the ridiculousness of my position. Moreover, Thorgrim might take advantage of her obvious unwillingness to go with me to rescind this gift. Shifting my harp out of the way, I ducked under her next swing, grabbed her around the knees, and heaved her over my shoulder. Then by sheer force of will I bore her up the bank in spite of her kicking, hitting, and scratching.

The Danes were overjoyed at my difficulties, but a glance showed me that Thorgrim wasn't joining in the mirth. Pleas-ure at his gesture was already past, and he was remembering to what an extent it had been compulsory. It would be bad luck for me to meet that man again.

As soon as we were out of sight in the trees I dropped her unceremoniously and put my foot on her throat. "Move and

I'll step down," I warned her. Her nails had made some uncomfortable gouges in my back, and I was in no mood to humor her. "Now," I went on as she lay still, "let's get a couple of things straight. The only thing I want or ever have wanted to do with you is to get rid of you. Do you know how to get home from here?"

It took her a minute to receive the import of what I was saying. Her eyes grew dazed then, and I took my foot from her neck, certain she would cause no more trouble. "There is no home," she finally said. I could see her thinking about it and, as she thought, emotion emerging from the depths where it had been driven by overwhelming horror. Soon she was sobbing terribly, but I was no one to comfort her. I walked a little apart to review and face my own problems.

The night before I had been the chosen companion of a successful chieftain and bound on a voyage that promised to reestablish my fortunes. Now he had become my enemy, as all men seemed to be those days, and I was moneyless as well as horseless in a country marked perilous for me. Worse than all, I had a charge I must somehow dispose of before I could get around to the much more desirable business of improving my personal circumstances.

It had been my hope that all that would be required of me would be to take her home. She had stated that she had none, and I assumed that the Danes had destroyed it. If there was anyone else who would undertake her care I piously prayed that he didn't live far away. It was not only the disinclination to be inconvenienced which inspired this wish; there was the downright danger of being with her in that disordered land where marauders abounded. Any such would try to help themselves to such a beauty, and it would be up to me to try to do something about it.

Some while later she was quiet and slept, exhausted by emotional stress. I let it be so on the theory that she would be more rational after some rest. Bored, nervous, and fuming with impatience, I alternately paced and sat till at length she roused herself. Gloomily I returned her dull stare.

"Who are you?" she asked; and it occurred to me that a woman is never too hard put for personalities.

"You say you have no home," I brushed the questions aside. "Is there any other place where it would be good for you to go?"

I thought she was going to break down again, but she controlled herself and shook her head. "No place near here. The Danes—" She spread out her hands and stopped.

"I can guess," I put in. "They killed everybody that got in their way, looted your home and burnt it."

"My mother didn't fight them, but they killed her as well as my father and the rest. Why?" She was like a hurt child trying to find out about the world.

"Too old to be a useful slave," I explained somberly. I knew Dane ways. They had killed the woman for that mysteriously exciting moment when life ceases to be.

"Most of our people ran away when they heard the Danes were coming. Only our household men stayed with us. We beat off the first batch, but lots more came. Now I'm the only one left."

She had to talk about it to get free of it at all, so, though restless and annoyed, I let her go on. It was not that I felt no pity for her, but the necessities of the future were then too imperious for me to be interested in any phase of the past.

"All right," I said when she had finally paused to give me an opening, "there's nothing left you around here. True?"

"It's true," she muttered, "but—"

"Never mind," I interrupted before she could get started again. "Is there any place at all where friends would welcome you? You've got to go somewhere, you know," I elaborated when she failed to show interest.

"Yes, that's so, I suppose." She passed a hand over her eyes. "A cousin of mine is married to a man north of here. It was she I was visiting when I met you at the ford."

As she said that I had an ironic mental picture of the stout lads that had been with her and how angry they had been with me for menacing this girl. Now they were all dead, and I had their job. "How far away would that be?" I asked her.

"About forty miles. More if anything."

"Any chance of finding a couple of horses around your place?"

She shivered. "The barn caught fire during the attack, and we were too busy to save them."

I grunted. It would be a dangerous trip on foot, but it had to be attempted. I wished then that I had more of an appetite at breakfast. "If you know how to find the road to your cousin's we'd better get started," I suggested.

But now she was sullen about a remark I'd made two hours before. "You said you only wanted to get rid of me," she pointed out. "You don't have to come."

Exasperation choked me. "You were a slave, and I overpaid them buying you for a song!" I snarled when I could think of anything else to say. "If I want to go some place with you, why that's my business!" Then the absurdity of it all took hold of me, and I laughed.

"What's funny?" She was more sulky than ever.

"You wouldn't see it," I told her. "Now listen carefully. I don't like to stress the fact, but I was of some assistance in getting you out of the hands of the Danes. It's possible, too, that I could be of help in case you encountered local bandits. Shall we stop the foolishness and get under way?"

Theretofore I had doubtless appeared to her in the light of being one more irritant in a nightmare world. Now at last it was borne in upon her that I was a man who was putting himself to some inconvenience on her account. She was as yet too upset to order her mind, but she made an effort to place me in the scheme of things.

"Why do you take the trouble?"

"I don't know any better," I said wearily. There was no use in trying to explain what I myself but hazily understood.

She got up, staring haggardly around as if she had never seen anything before. "You're trying hard to do something for me." She looked at me again. "You had been going somewhere in that ship, hadn't you?"

"That had been my intention," I said drily.

"You got off for me. Thank you." Then she added, quite irrelevantly: "I'm sorry I was rude to you then."

She was referring to our encounter at the ford. "At my age I should know better than to laugh at a woman." I apologized in my turn. "There's always trouble in it."

Making no answer, she started to pick her way through the woods, and I followed. In a short while we came to a path which soon led us to the road to Tours. There was no one in sight, and I reflected that the Danes had been of service to us by clearing the district of other marauders. Not until we were well inland should there be any special need for cautious faring.

A half mile west on the highway we found a narrow road

running north into which she turned. I was glum enough, and my knowledge of the despair my companion was in didn't help to make the journey more cheerful. She said no more about her grief, but every now and then I noted that she was weeping silently. She didn't care enough either to walk well or to rest, but I made her stop about once an hour. Not only was she tired to begin with, but I guessed that she hadn't eaten since the previous day.

Having no food, I could see nothing for it but to forge ahead as swiftly as the adverse circumstances would permit. But it was sultry, even in the forest, and toward late afternoon the high heat of the day began to tell on the girl. She was asleep almost as soon as I suggested that she lie down, but, though I stretched out, I was listening alertly to make sure we wouldn't be taken by surprise. In the end I was reluctantly forced to sacrifice comfort to keenness.

She had rolled over on her back, I saw when I sat up to drive sleep away, and was slumbering soundly. With the drawn, lost expression smoothed from her face she looked appealingly sweet and young. I shrugged. Life never cares to whom and how precociously its most terrifying phases are shown. Things happen, and there are but two responsive choices—acceptance or death.

A deer almost stepped on us, got panic-stricken when it noticed our presence, and crashed away through the under-brush. Awakened by the noise, she opened her eyes. I looked away, having no words to offer, but I could feel her studying me.

"You don't make any more sense to me than the Danes did," she accused suddenly.

I was startled by this sudden attack. "Why?"

"It puts me just as much at a loss to be under the wing of a perfect stranger as it does to be warred on by somebody that's not an enemy. They weren't enemies, you see. They weren't even angry—just businesslike. On the other hand you're doing me a great favor without having any kindness for me."

"Oh well," I said, thoroughly taken aback.

"You're not even doing it because you disliked the Danes," she pursued. "You knew they were all thieves and murderers, and yet you were willing to travel with them."

"There are thieves and murderers everywhere in France," I

reminded her. "Slave owners, too. Danes make good friends, as far as that's concerned, if you don't allow yourself to be bothered by their morals, and personally I've always found my own about all I could rightly handle." I stood up by way of ending the discussion. "It'll be cooler walking now."

Chapter
Ten

IT WAS almost at the point of night when our luck broke down. There was a shrill whistle off to the right, and immediately afterwards I heard a bunch of men running toward the road. I didn't need to be told what was happening. Unless I was much mistaken, the thing I had most feared had come to pass. We had walked into the clutches of one of the roving outlaw bands.

I grabbed the girl's arm and shook her for emphasis. "Hide off there!" I commanded, shoving her toward the woods to the left.

She hesitated. "But—"

"Get going!" I whispered fiercely, "and don't come out unless I call you." When I shoved her again she complied, and I commenced singing loudly to cover the sound of her movements.

"Hallo!" I called out jovially when the men were almost upon me. "Anybody there who has food for a hungry man?"

There were eight or ten of them, their truculence the more disturbing because of the dark, and I couldn't see just how ready they were to act. They were, however, seemingly surprised by my friendliness, so they started off by asking questions instead of getting rough.

"Who are you?"

"A strolling minstrel," I answered, shifting my harp into line of what vision was left.

"I thought there was a couple of 'em when I gave the signal," another spoke up.

"I wish to hell there had been," I said. "It's been so lonesome on the way that I felt like a fellow left on the world by mistake after Doomsday."

"Aw, everybody's hiding from the Danes!" a third complained with professional envy. "There's nothing left for us when they've passed by."

I was feeling a little more easy. "If you're robbers," I laughed, "you're wasting your time with me. Not a coin to my name."

"What are you doing up here where there's no one to pay you then?"

"Oh, I ran from the Danes, too," I answered with some measure of truth, if not too much. "Moreover, I didn't have a lot of breakfast, and I've had no food since. What do you say to giving me a meal in exchange for a few songs?"

They frisked me expertly but found I was as poor as I said I was. "Let's take him to Piers and see what he wants done with him," an outlaw suggested.

I didn't like the sound of that, but there was no choice, so through the forest I went with them. We were striking directly away from the girl, leaving her a free trail which I hoped she had sense enough to make use of promptly. Now that we had met one band the odds were in favor of a safe road ahead for her.

Before us there was much loud talking and laughter, and in a minute I saw the flicker of fire. Quite a large one it proved to be, a high blazer with about eighty men, women, brats, and assorted in-betweens lounging in its warmth and glow. The sight of them amply confirmed my forebodings. I had fallen into bad company indeed.

This was that part of the people who had enough strength to refuse the role of serf but not enough to establish a natural and healthy place for themselves as free men. They were far more savage than the Danes, who at least preserved certain dignities of life among themselves, however prone they might be to force chaos on others. A man cannot live with the narrow directness of animals, because he is not satisfied with eating, sleeping, and mating for one brief period of a year. The only thing that stands between his surplus energies and dangerous madness is the recognition of values. Even what these values are and what the sources they are drawn from are questions of minor importance. Without them a man is senseless; and these people had none.

Piers, their leader, proved to be a ruddy, flat-faced man of about my height, though a little more powerfully built. He was fairly drunk, at which I'm not the one to cast a stone, but he didn't hold his face together the way a proper drinking man should. Having energy and strength without purpose, he personified the whole lot of them. I was very nervous as I stood before him, because there is something peculiarly horrible about persons who don't act casually.

His initial moves were direct enough, though. "That's a fine sword you're sporting," he remarked after my captors had passed on the information I had given them.

"It's not bad," I muttered, "considering I got it just for being in a house when its owner wasn't." I was trying to invoke the old law of thieves respecting the loot of colleagues, but he wasn't moved.

"Easy come, easy go," he said and laughed as he took it from me. "You wear pretty nice clothes, too," he went on after looking me over again.

I didn't think so much of them myself, although as compared with his own they stood for finery. "We'll swap," he announced, starting to strip then and there.

Silently swearing vengeance if ever the opportunity for it should come my way, I imitated him, while his unkempt following aggraved the indignity by cheers, laughter and meaningless insults. As I had feared, he no longer had as many fleas as he had nourished before the exchange, and his clothes were greasy. I gulped to control my temper and achieved a smile.

"Your friends forgot to tell you this," I said, "but in addition to being poor I'm hungry. Will you feed me if I give you a song or so?"

He was delighted with himself because of his new possessions and started to give good-humored acquiescence. Then it evidently struck him that I hadn't been sufficiently hazed. "I'll tell you what I'll do," he said, with a wink at his audience. "If your song's good I'll let you eat and drink, too. If it isn't good I'll slit your throat to make sure I won't have to listen to you again."

He led his rabble's noisy appreciation of his wit by slapping his thigh, but I lodged one more score against him in the event I lived to meet him again when I had a chance to hold up my end. Actually I was not afraid of disappointing a group it was so easy to please. All that I had to do was to make them laugh, then Piers would have no grounds for fatal practical jokes; and I knew what to give them. Like Gaimar their kind really saw no humor except in bawdiness, and there was no phase of it, so convinced were they that it was always funny, that wouldn't convulse them.

Swallowing my wrath again, I decided upon a ballad I'd heard at an inn in Paris some years before. "I'll give you a very sad song of a monk who met a maid," I announced, and as I'd foreseen they were agrin before I began. Lust on the part of those vowed to chastity was a jest whose bloom never withered.

> *"A sleek, round monk once saw a maid*
> *Off in the woods so green:*
> *There never was a lustier monk*
> *And fairer maid was never seen.*
>
> *He looked to east, he looked to west;*
> *She had no kin or friend in sight.*
> *The father licked his lips and smiled;*
> *The maid was in a sorry plight.*
>
> *Now she was kneeling by a spring*
> *To fix her hair, which was unbound.*
> *The monk came stealing up behind*
> *And pinched her where she was most round."*

Out of the corner of my eye I saw a couple of the outlaws making pinching motions dreamily. Several of the women giggled. I scratched a flea bite and went on.

> *" 'You're caught, you're mine, my pretty maid!'*
> *He cried and gripped her well.*
> *'Rather than lie with a monk,' she wailed,*
> *'I'd choose a fiend of Hell!*
>
> *'A fiend of Hell will sometimes rest—*

Sorrow that I was born!—
A monk will wreck a maid in a week
And leave her old and worn!'

But still he vowed by all the saints
To have her maidenhead.
'If it must be,' she said at last,
'It's better done in bed.

'My father is away all day,
My mother died last year;
And feather beds are snugger than
The cold, hard ground is here.

'So if you'll take me home to where
It's soft and warm indoors,
Why ask me then and I will say
My maidenhead is yours.'

But when they came to where she lived
The maiden gave a shout:
'A lusty monk would force his will!'
Then four stout men came out."

Some were already laughing. The holy father should not
only be unmasked, proving no better than anyone else, but his
lot must still be harder than that of other men. Punishment
must fall for the merely contemplated sin, not one accomplished and enjoyed.

" 'My father is away,' she laughed,
'And mother died last year.
You never asked of other kin:
These are my brothers dear.'

They beat that monk until he howled.
'You lying wench!' he said,
'You swore that if I brought you home
You'd give your maidenhead.'

'It still is yours,' she answered him,
'Though where I do not know;

> *But when you find it, keep the thing—*
> *I lost it years ago!'* ''

Piers, I was relieved to note, laughed as heartily as any of the others. "Give the man food!" he commanded as impressively as though he were an emperor decreeing a new law. "Ale here for the minstrel!" Then he snapped his fingers in salute to an idea. "Can you make poems as well as sing?"

"Sometimes," I said cautiously.

"That's great!" he commented, irritating me by throwing his arm around my shoulder. "From now on you'll be my own particular bard."

That wasn't a suggestion; it was a statement of ordained fact. He meant to confer a favor, and I murmured my recognition; but that didn't alter my status as prisoner. That such a wild cur should think I'd let him be my patron annoyed me, but I didn't let it spoil my appetite for good venison. The ale was heavy and bitter, yet I reasoned that my new fleas would otherwise keep me awake and so drank at large.

"You've come along at a lucky time for you," Piers roared confidentially. "I'm going to claim all the land around here and set myself up as baron."

"Yes?" I said with mild interest. With food and ale in me my resentment was more or less quiescent.

"Sure. There'll be fighting, of course, but they'll have to give me what I want."

"Who will?"

He frowned. "There are three fellows who've been rowing about who's going to run this part of the world. I'm making myself the fourth. They wouldn't listen to me a while back, but they'll have to from now on. You see, I've not only got these of my own crew, but I've lined up other outlaw gangs."

I knew how hopeless it was to try to get such bands to act in concert, but, of course, I didn't tell him that. "I've just arrived in this locality," I lied. "Just what's going on?"

"Like I told you," he answered, "besides me there are three men who count hereabouts. There's a fellow called Chilbert to the south and east, there's a fellow called Conan to the north, and the Abbot of St. Charles is sandwiched in between."

Perforce their local politics had come to be a matter of real interest to me as one by one I had encountered the figures he had mentioned. "Who's top rooster?"

"They don't know it yet," he smirked, "but I'm going to be. I'm smart enough to wait for the right time, though, see? But just now the Abbot's got the best grip on what he has, and Chilbert has the most land and people."

This was my first chance to get definite word of Conan. "How about the other fellow? Is he getting frozen out?"

"He's newer come than the others and harder to figure, but he's got quite a name as a fighter." He chuckled harshly. "A whole bunch of Chilbert's men ran Conan and another to earth and were damn sorry later. Conan and his partner stood them off, killed plenty and left their marks on a lot more."

Now I had the opening to discover what I really wanted to know. "You mean to say he did all that and got off scot free?"

"Not exactly but near enough. He was carved up quite a bit himself, I hear, although he's as good as new now. As a matter of fact the business turned out swell for him, because it made him famous and made the others look like ninnies. Conan rubbed it in, too, sending his minstrel around with a funny version of the story that had everybody laughing at Chilbert. A lot of men who'd been getting ready to join up with him decided to hold off after that until they can be surer about just who's who."

That was an interesting development. "What do you think is going to happen now?" I inquired.

"Oh, Chilbert and Conan will have a showdown soon. One will beat the other, but even so the winner will get too much fighting for his own good, see? So I'll jump on the winner before his men get a chance to rest up, and I'll beat him. Then I'll tell the Abbot he can keep his land if he pays me for being nice." He beamed at me as if my face in reality mirrored his self-approval.

I wasn't at all impressed by these drunkard's dreams. "Suppose Conan and Chilbert settle things peaceably," I suggested by way of removing a prop from under his tower of wishes. "Where will you be then?"

"I'll make 'em split the loaf four ways anyhow," he swaggered while sitting, "because I'll take my share without asking them whether they like it. Pretty soon, when I get around to it, that is. But Chilbert won't settle without war. He wants everything in reach, and besides Conan has made too much fun of him." He barked laughter. "I bet Chilbert could chew rocks every time he thinks how he had his fingers on Conan and let him slip away." With an inebriate's emotional vagaries he suddenly ceased to be mirthful. "Conan would never have worked out of my hands," he said grimly.

"No?"

"By God, no! He had his chance to be my friend and passed it up. When the time comes I'll remind him of that."

"What happened?"

"Well, he came along about when I was getting ready to make my bid. I figured that neither of us was as strong then as we might have been and offered to team up with him and split what we could take. He sent back word that he'd just missed hanging a pig the day before, thinking it was me."

Piers glared in indignant recollection, and I shook my head, making deprecating sounds. "He said," the outlaw went on heavily, "that he'd apologized to the pig when the pig explained the difference, and that the next time he'd get the noose on the right neck. He meant mine by that," Piers concluded unnecessarily.

I was pleased with Conan. "What do you think could have given him an idea like that?" I wondered.

"Aw, he thinks he's better than anybody else because his people have been chiefs around here since before God started teething. But men and forts make a lot more difference these days then who your old man was. I'll show him, and I'll show the others, too. Chilbert wouldn't have me for his ally either, because he wants to run everything all by himself. He had the nerve to tell me I could fight for him, though. Can you beat that? Why, if anybody should follow anybody, he should follow me!"

"Obviously," I said. "How do you get along with the Abbot?"

Piers damned the Abbot. "We've been enemies from the first, so I never tried to team up with him. I made a raid on his territory once when I first got in power just to let people know I was around." He looked thoughtful as if contemplating the memory.

"Did you give him a lesson?" I prodded, being certain he had done no such thing.

"No," he admitted grudgingly, "but that was before I had the following I have now. I'll show him the next time I fight him."

Thinking of Father Clovis and the other soldierly priests I'd dined with, I looked around at his frowsy, undisciplined outlaws and doubted him. Some were already nodding, and all would soon be asleep. I didn't believe for an instant that any who might be on watch would make an all-night vigil of it, especially as I had noticed that the fellows who had got wind of me had never returned to their posts. If an organized body could have been made of those men it hadn't been done.

Not that I disapproved. I was elated with the assurance that escape could be easily achieved by refraining from drink the next time they went in for it heavily. At the moment, however, I was very tired and sleepy myself, and I was wishing that Piers would let me rest.

But drink had expanded his natural tendency to brag, and I as the one person present who hadn't heard it all before was his inevitable victim. "They all think I'm no smarter than the other outlaws," he informed me, "but they're wrong. I know what's got to be done to hold my land just as well as any of 'em. You've got to build stone forts. Not wooden halls with dirt walls around them that anybody can climb over, but high, straight-up-and-down stone walls. That's the only way you can be safe from attack and have a safe place to attack from."

"How many have you built so far?" I was mean enough to want to know.

"None yet, but I'm going to. Come to think of it, I guess I'll start one tomorrow. How's that for a good idea?"

"Excellent," I granted, "but if you're going to do that we'd better get some sleep."

"Yeah, that's right." He roared for somebody to keep the fire going and lay down where he was. I followed his example gladly, even though I didn't anticipate a hard day of fort building. For, improbability granted, if Piers should happen to remember and persevere with his scheme, those men of his would abruptly leave him for a less ambitious leader. They weren't spiritually geared for long-term hard work.

I yawned, scratched, and adjusted myself to the ground as comfortably as I could. Even for that country it had been something of a day, and I wondered at the turn of events. Was I ever, I wondered somewhat wildly, going to be permitted to leave, or was I forever doomed to be jerked back like a training hawk just when I was certain of freedom? Fortunately sleep stopped such futile speculations until I waked with a grouch, stiff muscles, new flea bites, and the taste of too much bad-quality ale sour in my mouth.

It was cool, early morning, and the fire had died to ashes. I shuffled over to benefit by what heat was left and stared at the recumbent figures distastefully. They might not look as savage as they had by firelight, but they looked a great deal fouler, especially the women. One, a hag at less than thirty, lay on her back not far from me, with a dirty breast swelling shapelessly from her torn bodice. A man from among a group of six rolled over and commenced copulating with the woman next to him. The little boy in the crook of her arm cursed the man for waking him and was smacked into silence.

I was appreciative of the causes that had contributed, but the fact of what they had become could draw no more warmth of pity than could a long-dead fish. They had become too alien and would so remain until law, if it ever did, should come again to restore a little of the pride in human dignity without which man is not. I spat and waited for Piers to wake.

Chapter
Eleven

WITH them it was gorge or go hungry. There was no ale left, and Piers, who had seen to it that there was no ale left, was much aggrieved. He kicked the cask, hurt his toe, then took vengeance for it by booting a little girl who had the misfortune to be passing. She did no harm to his foot and screamed satisfyingly.

After a grumpy breakfast he decided to move south in hopes of intercepting men straggling back toward the Loire with what possessions they had been able to keep out of reach of the Danes. I walked with him at the head of the mob, and as we reached the road I noted with relief that the girl's tracks showed she had gone on.

That was the only thing I had to be glad of for three days more. I might, indeed, have escaped any one of the nights, but I wasn't going to leave without my sword, and Piers was too sober to make its retrieving possible. It was not only that it would have been stupid to go anywhere alone without a weapon in the country, but I valued that particular sword. It was an excellent blade whose weight and balance exactly suited me, and I strongly begrudged its use to a mean, shiftless braggart.

He tried me to my limits of control by giving me what passes for friendship with such a man. That is to say he talked about himself continuously, and it was my business to chime in with applause at appropriate intervals. Volubility unalleviated by a sound worldly outlook, scholarship, or humor is a sin for which I have no charity. I don't mind a man being a fool if he has but the grace not to rub it in. My chagrin was aggravated, moreover, by the fact that I could neither avoid his company nor voice any of the cutting remarks that crowded into my mind.

The other men were inclined to be sullen because I basked in the great man's favor, and the women were inclined to be vulgarly arch for the same reason. The first I didn't mind because I could pay no attention, but an aggressive wanton is harder to snub than a month-old puppy. Though not pure, I'm particular, and there was certainly no woman in that blowzy lot for whom I would have risked a quarrel. Two fellows did slash at each other to the delight of the young slut who had caused the contention. They left the loser unburied by the side of the road.

We never went more than a few miles in a day, for when nothing happened everybody got tired of walking. Then, too, they were living largely on game, and hunting took a great deal of time.

It wasn't till the third day that they netted their first windfall. To my intense satisfaction as well as theirs, a group of their foragers had run across a wain loaded with wine casks. It wasn't very good wine, but I was confident that Piers would oblige me by getting drunk on it. He started pouring it into himself at a great rate, and all but the youngest children followed his example. Drunkenness was attained all the more speedily for that they forgot all about supper, which had been in preparation when the wine arrived. I rescued a part of one joint of venison, but the rest of it was allowed to burn up.

In an hour the camp was a scene of rampant sordidness. No one sought privacy to urinate, vomit or fornicate, and there was much activity along all three lines. Men, women, and children in varying stages of inebriety and sickness fought and cursed according to their respective abilities. Of course, there was also considerable merriment in the form of songs, good-natured insults, and obscene practical jokes.

I kept out of trouble by playing my harp and staying close to Piers. Music has more power over the drunken than over the sober, and by playing gay tunes I was able to keep him in a good humor most of the time. As a result he was greatly pleased with me and shooed away any man or woman who showed an inclination to interrupt or otherwise annoy me. The drawback to the arrangement was that he kept filling my cup, and I did not, for once in my life, want to drink very much. Ultimately my only defense against his hospitality was feigning tipsiness on an amount I'd scorn to have affect me.

"Drink up!" Piers yelled, though I wasn't two feet from him.

"Had enough," I said thickly and yawned.

"Aw, you ain't had enough to get a baby lit."

"Haven't had enough for you," I said ponderously, "but I've had enough for me. I wish I could drink as much as you can, but I can't." I shook my head as if in wonder. "I never saw anybody who can drink as much as you can."

He was delighted at this tribute to his prowess and immediately became sympathetic toward my frailty. "Everybody can't expect to drink like I can." He hiccoughed kindly. "Why don't you go sleep it off?"

I rose falteringly. "Guess I will. Don't see how you do it."

He laughed, and I made my uneven way to the edge of the firelight. Being on the opposite of the fire from the wine cask, the spot I had chosen was comparatively free from traffic. I sat down awkwardly, then sprawled to watch and wait.

It was some hours before Piers gave up, and I began to fear that he would drink the night out. He was, in truth, nearly as capacious a drinker as he thought he was, and he kept filling his cup as soon as it was emptied, which never took him long. Even in sottishness magnitude is awe-inspiring, and I half admired him as cup after cup found him on his feet, his zest apparently undiminished.

Eventually the only thing that could have helped me came to pass. All the rest had given in to the wine, but Piers and two fellows still worked at it, not certain of thought, speech or movement but undaunted. The smoke from the dying fire prevented a clear view of the cask itself, but I saw one of them walk toward it, then heard him swear plaintively.

"What do you know? The goddam thing's empty!"

Considering the enormous amounts that had been drunk, plus the quantities that had been wasted through tipsy clumsiness, I was not surprised. Piers, however, was outraged. "It can't be!" he declared.

"Well," the other presented his grounds for belief, "you turn the spigot, and nothing comes."

"Maybe you don't know how to turn a spigot right," the third man said hopefully.

"Hell! I guess I can turn a goddam spigot as well as the next man. It's empty, I tell you! Shall we start on another?"

I held my breath, but Piers saw an insurmountable objection. "It'd be too much work getting it off the wain. Besides, I'm getting kind of sleepy."

"Yeah, I'm about ready to call it a night, too," one of the others confessed.

Piers lay down about thirty feet away from me, and I gave him a half hour or so to find the depths of sleep. The wine's victory was all the more complete for being belated, and I saw as I stood over him that nothing short of violence could rouse him. I looked around. Nobody was paying any attention to me, though one man nearby opened his eyes. The sight of me seemed more than he could bear, for he closed them again and rolled over.

In another minute I had unbuckled my sword from around Pier's waist. It surely felt good to have a weapon, particularly that one, in my hand again after so many defenseless hours. In a great rush of relief I realized I was free of those graceless churls, free of Piers and his inextinguishable boasting, and free, best of all, to go my own way, I felt so good about it that I almost let Piers off, but just in time I remembered the little girl he had kicked. Drawing back my foot, I gave him all I had. I didn't hear any ribs crack, but he'd be sure to find them sore the next morning. At the moment, however, he only realized that something had waked him up.

"What's the matter?" he asked, raising up on one elbow.

"Nothing," I responded cheerfully.

"That's good," he said and went to sleep again. Humming to myself, I picked my way through the woods til I came to the road. The southern route was still closed to me, and by Danes perhaps as well as Chilbert, so I shrugged and stepped out north with humorous fatalism. I had become used to the knowledge that such things as where I myself wanted to go or what I wanted to do were now factors of negligible importance in my life. I didn't like my predicament, but it hadn't begun to pinch me yet, so there was no use in getting depressed about it.

I traveled briskly, thus keeping warm as well as putting distance between myself and Piers. I had little fear that he would bother to pursue me, as far as that was concerned, but there was no sense in making it easy for him if he should happen to. Two wolves, needlessly suspecting competition, looked up from the dead outlaw they'd been sharing and snarled at me as I passed; but otherwise nothing happened for several hours.

When the sun was high enough to give genuine warmth I sat down by a stream and finished the joint of venison, the remnant of which I'd taken the precaution of putting in my scrip. From that point on, I reflected as I tossed the bone away, I'd be living off the country. My immediate problem, though, was sleep, not food, so I followed the brook into the woods, looking for a likely place to rest. Not fifty feet in, but yet out of sight of the road, was a little open patch with the sun full on it, and I stripped happily.

"You should have stayed on Piers," I told my fleas. "He would never have done this to you." I dunked my greasy garments, scrubbed them with clay, rubbed them on a flat rock, rinsed them, wrung them, and spread them to dry. The water felt marvelous when I got around to immersing myself, and the clay took the grime from me. It was wonderful to feel the cleanness as I lay down, sunwarmed. I slept soon.

It was fine to wake as I did a couple of hours later, thoroughly refreshed and with the knowledge that for the moment, at least, everything was as it should be. I was in the shade by then, but the little breeze that ran over me from time to time was just the right temperature. The stream was casually musical and quiet about it, the forest was sultrily aromatic, and the trees individually were high-reaching and clean-cut. I was suicidally imbecilic thus to signal my presence in that pot of factions, but I started to sing.

After finishing the first song it struck me that I was in excellent voice, and others were rendered as they came to me. Finally I thought of a poem I'd written when I was quite a youngster, and out of pure, good spirits I boomed it forth at the top of my voice.

> "I'm older than God, but gay and frisky.
> I'll never die,
> Which may seem odd
> Till I tell you why:
> I drained off my blood and put in whisky.
> Yes, by damn!

> *Dram by dram*
> *And likewise bottle by bottle,*
> *I poured it in*
> *To fill my skin*
> *Through an ever-ready throttle.''*

It had been a long time, I reflected wistfully, since I'd had any whisky. It is strange that only the Irish and the Scotch have the sense to make that excellent drink.

> *''I had a young wife, both fair and frisky:*
> *But what the hell!*
> *A wedded life,*
> *As you know right well,*
> *Can play the devil with drinking whisky.*
> *I was strong:*
> *Wrong is wrong,*
> *And surely duty is duty.*
> *I ditched the hen,*
> *For I scorn men*
> *Who'll scamp ideals for a beauty.*
>
> *Death called for me. He was feeling frisky.*
> *Sure of his kill;*
> *But wait and see—*
> *He guzzled his fill*
> *And a whole lot more, of good, strong whisky.*
> *Fool to think,*
> *Drink for drink,*
> *That he could better his better!*
> *I watched him fold*
> *And, passed out cold,*
> *Crouch at my feet like a setter.*
>
> *Oh, what a head! Death didn't feel frisky*
> *When he came to.*
> *'Can't I be dead,*
> *Not feel like I do?'*
> *He groaned—''*

If I hadn't been bellowing I would have had warning earlier. As it was they were almost on me before I heard the horses.

Having time for nothing else, I dove for my sword, and that was the nearest thing to a garment I had when the woman rode into the clearing. The dozen or so men behind her could have ridden me down if they felt like it; therefore I didn't try to run. Instead I put my back against a tree and looked them over for enemies.

It was typical of the locale that I found one forthwith. The first man to range himself beside the woman was the fellow who had chased me off my road and into Conan's life. A second later he recognized me.

"That's a spy of Chilbert's, Ann!" he told her. Then he looked at me, and I couldn't imagine why I'd once thought he had a merry, likable face. "Will you hang peaceably or are you going to fight?" he inquired.

I had no answer for him in my despair. If they hanged me, naturally I was going to see to it that they hanged a corpse. But as I was considering rushing them to get it over with, the woman amazed me by interceding. "Wait a minute, Jean," she said, and I saw to my incredulous relief, that she was in charge. I'd been giving all my attention to the men previously, but now I wanted to know something about her. She was as blonde as myself, a neatly but strongly built, sweet-faced woman who knew her own mind.

"Why don't you put on your clothes?" she suggested.

"Are your dogs called off?"

"My men," she corrected me. "For that long anyhow."

My ragged garments weren't quite dry, but I was glad to get into them. Clothes, even though they're of no real use in a fight, make a man feel more protected.

She gazed at me searchingly when I had finished and was facing her again. "You were singing a song," she reminded me.

Her unexpected remark gave me hope that we could conduct negotiations on the friendly basis I earnestly desired. "That's right. Did you like it?" I asked, brightening.

"No," she said.

"Oh well," I shrugged, "it's not a woman's song." It seemed to me that the conversation had reached a dead end, but she opened the way.

"My husband's very fond of it."

"Your husband seems to have good taste in all things." Nevertheless, I was wildly searching for an explanation. That song, appropriate to its subject, had been written in Gaelic.

My puzzlement, I could now see, was giving her a great deal of amusement. "My husband can, fortunately, only recall snatches of it," she teased me further, "but he sings it all the time. He says it was made by his best friend."

Dumb with bewilderment, I was convinced that I was in reality dreaming. The other men couldn't make any sense out of her words either and stirred restlessly. Not very hopeful that there was a rational explanation for the woman's improbable statements, I began trying to remember on what occasions and with whom in France I could possibly have sung that song.

Promptly and stunningly it was clear that there could be but one solution to the problem. The song was the one I had been mumbling over and over during that last hour or however long it was, of the stand at the vault.

She saw I had the key and smiled. "You're the man he was talking of," she told me rather than asked.

"Why must I be?" I countered. "Once the song is made anybody can sing it."

"Yes," she conceded gaily, "but I don't believe, as far as that particular is concerned, that anybody but the maker and my husband, who happens to like him, would bother."

I laughed, as I could well afford to do, seeing that enemies had turned out to be allies. She laughed back, and from that moment we were friends. Her companions were still mystified, naturally, and the man called Jean spoke for them. "What's so funny about a song nobody can understand?"

"Oh, but I can understand it," she contradicted him. "Conan studied in Ireland, and he told me what it means. Jean, this man you were going to hang if he'd be nice about it is Finnian who was with Conan in the fight at the Old Farms."

I had been correct in my original estimate. Jean's face could be very jolly indeed. He was off his horse in an instant, offering apologies and pledges of friendship, and all the others followed his example. Conan, it was understandably clear, was well liked by his men.

Being a little shaky from reaction, I didn't have much to say in return, but I grinned amiably. After my experiences of the past few days it was good to be with people I could respect again.

"It's my turn now," Ann told them after a minute or so,

and they drew aside to let her stand before me. Conan, as I would have expected, had used sound sense in choosing his woman. She was clear and honest and laughed when she could. Her face was very serious then, though, and she had great dignity as she looked at me. Beneath her scrutiny, perforce, I looked at myself and wondered what, if anything, there was for her to see. A man can feel very humble when a woman is considering him, and one corner of my mouth twitched down in self-derision.

She saw that and quite simply took my face between her hands and kissed me. "You'll come with us, won't you?" she asked, letting her palms fall to my shoulders. "Conan will never forgive me if I don't bring you along. He's away now, but we expect him back within the week."

If, as it seemed, I was condemned to be mixed up in the troubles of that country whenever I happened to be in it, it was well to be among friends. And it would be grand to see Conan again. "Thanks," I said. "Who'll ride me?"

"Take my horse, and I'll double up with somebody else," Jean offered. "I owe you that for running you that day." He chuckled. "Nobody told me that you took Conan up on Chilbert's horse."

"Didn't you know that?" Ann asked. "Why, that was the top of the joke."

"I was away when Conan got well enough to tell just what had happened, and I only got the story second hand." He scrambled up behind a comrade. "Let's get started. I want to have a drink with this man."

I rode next to Ann at the head of the Cavalcade. "How did you happen to be passing by?" I queried.

Her face became sad. "Word of a Dane raid on the Loire came to us," she said somberly. "I have kinsmen there. That is, I had. The house had been burned when we arrived."

"Maybe your kinfolk escaped," I suggested, but she shook her head.

"They would have come to us, I'm sure."

My unfortunate, if inevitable, question had left her in a despondent mood I didn't try to break. She would have to have it out with herself, and the sooner the better. I on my part had enough to occupy my mind. My hosts had imminent war on their hands, and there was no telling when it would break upon them. To what extent a friend's war is one's own is a question of some delicacy. Rationally I could justify non-participation, but there are so many times when obeying the dictates of common sense makes a man feel like a louse. My strongest hope was that a lull in action would give me the chance to leave gracefully. Conan, I knew, would give me a horse to replace the one I'd lost on his account.

In a couple of hours we came to the ford, and I saw that the barge I had stolen hadn't been duplicated. It was the tag end of summer, however, the water was low, and we crossed easily to the banks where I'd first seen the girl I'd extracted from the Danes. I hoped she had emerged from her subsequent difficulties as fortunately as I.

Chapter
Twelve

ABOUT fifteen miles beyond the ford we came to Conan's stronghold. It was only partially completed, but it was of solid stone. Except for church work or where Rome or Charlemagne had passed I had never seen a stone edifice before, and I halted to admire it. This was what had inspired Piers with the longings he'd never try to satisfy.

"Conan got the idea for it somewhere," Jean said with satisfaction. "It'll be thirty-five feet high when we're through, with plenty of room for men to maneuver on top. What's more, it's ditched, with water around it deep enough to drown a man. That fort will need some taking."

I agreed and rode on, noting that although there were wide fields under cultivation all the horses in sight were clustered in the shelter of the fort. There could be no surprise attack which could prevent the villeins from taking refuge, intact with families and food. These lands could be defended with a minimum of loss, and attackers working out from such a base could do so in the confidence that all would be well with their own when they returned. To possess such an island, one which the floods could sweep by and leave comparatively untroubled, was to have the upper hand in the world.

We crossed the ditch, and a wide one it was, over a wooden bridge which had been let down for us by a man on watch. The hall, not to mention the other buildings within, was an old Frankish wooden structure, but Ann told me that that, too, was to have a stone substitute in case by any chance the wall should be successfully stormed.

"I'll arrange for dinner to be served as soon as possible," she told me when our horses had been led away. "Jean will show you where you sleep when you've attended to the wine he was talking about."

She smiled and turned away, but as she did so a girl came out of the hall and rushed to meet her. I knew that girl, and as the women embraced it came to me that she was one of the kinfolk whom Ann had mourned for dead. About the others, I was aware, she had been sadly right.

Jean and the other men, naturally interested, forgot about me, so I stood to one side watching. They all asked a lot of questions and had many bitter things to say about the Danes. But the fact that even the girl herself was alive was better news than they had expected, so on the whole they didn't feel so bad.

Then one of the men happened to shift his position, and she saw me. Her mouth closed on a word, and she stared with no sign of welcome. The others turned to see what she was looking at, while I smiled uneasily.

"Oh, do you know Finnian?" Ann asked.

That was exactly the wrong thing to say. "He wouldn't tell *me* his name," the girl replied austerely, "though I asked him civilly."

"I was busy," I muttered lamely, wondering how it was that even the most brainless women had a genius for making a man feel like a fool. Not that this one was by any means brainless.

"Where did you meet him?" Ann pursued, and I mentally crossed myself.

"Down by the ford. He threatened to kill me with a fish spear."

"Oh, no!" Ann's voice was horrified.

"Oh, yes! And the next time I saw him," the indictment went on remorselessly, "he was with the Danes. Friends with them," she emphasized.

The men were scowling doubtfully, and I saw with regret that the bridge had been pulled up behind us. There were no readily understandable explanations, and I didn't attempt to present them with feeble excuses. "Well, what's going to happen?" I inquired shortly. "Are you going to let me go in peace or not?" That I would not longer accept their hospitality, even if for Conan's sake they should continue to offer it, was a foregone conclusion.

But having made a dent in my peace of mind, she was satisfied. She had paid me back for the cavalier way in which circumstances had forced me to treat her. "Of course," she said in a small, reflective voice, "he did save me from the Danes when they were getting ready to sell me for a slave."

"Marie!" Ann's tone contained a mixture of relief, amazement, and indignation. Jean threw his head back and shouted his mirth. I bitterly wondered what I had done to deserve meeting such a girl. Marie smiled, pleased with herself.

"I'm sorry, Finnian," Ann apologized contritely for their doubt of me. "Why didn't you say that in the first place, Marie?" She shook the girl, still partly angry with her. "Tell me what happened."

"I don't know exactly what did happen," her cousin answered truthfully. "They were taking me away in one of their ships, then all of a sudden they landed, he threw me over the side, and carried me away."

"How did you manage to shake a Dane loose from anything valuable?" a man asked respectfully.

"Poetry," I replied. "He liked mine." I could see they thought I had actually used some sort of spell, but they didn't say anything.

I was tired and anxious to get at the wine Ann had mentioned, but that girl was always in my way. It was embarrassingly evident that something was expected of her, and an uncomfortable silence fell upon us. She flushed, thinking a moment, then went at it bravely. Coming quickly to me, she smiled, though half fearing I might rebuff her. "I don't know you or where you're going. Maybe after today or tomorrow I'll never see you again. But at the worst time for me you were the best friend I could have, and that was good of you. Very good."

It was well done, and, remembering how bitterly I had resented having to put myself in danger for her, I knew it was better than I deserved. Nevertheless, I could not in graciousness say my service was nothing. I winked at her. "I couldn't bear the idea of so much Christian beauty being wasted on buzzard-faced Moorish infidels."

"Naturally," she grinned, and the tension vanished.

My own face sobered. "And," I went on, "I couldn't help

but be moved with pity at the thought of those poor Danes trapped at sea with that baneful tongue of yours.''

Jean, who evidently never missed an opportunity to enjoy laughter, roared with it again to drown out her own appreciative chuckle. ''Who were the men who captured you?'' she asked when she could be heard.

''A crew of outlaws led by a fellow called Piers,'' I answered, looking at the others to see what reaction the name would enduce.

Ann frowned, and Jean whistled. ''That's a bad bunch, and Piers is a mad dog. You're lucky he didn't kill you just to see the flies gather.''

''We saw their camp as we came north this morning,'' Ann said, ''but as they weren't on our land we let them alone. How did you escape?''

''There was no trick to that. They finally got hold of enough wine to get them all drunk at once.'' I turned to Marie. ''Did you have any trouble after we parted company?''

''Not a bit. I was afraid to travel on the road except by dark, though, and as I found nothing but berries to eat I wasn't strong enough to walk very fast. It took me a couple of nights to reach the ford even.'' She turned to her cousin. ''I hid out in the woods during the daytime. That's how I happened to miss you, Ann.''

With that last sentence she recalled realization of the tragedy that had driven her there. Ann put an arm around her, and the two women walked off together to resolve the matter of death in the family, no doubt at the poor best possible.

Our eyes followed them commiseratingly. ''Let's have that wine,'' Jean said after a moment.

''Fine,'' I agreed, and we made for a table in the shade of the hall.

At Jean's shouted order a flagon and two cups were brought. It was good wine. The first gulp spread a healthy interior glow, and I relaxed contentedly. ''How soon do you expect Conan?'' I asked.

''Tomorrow or a week from tomorrow.'' He shrugged his nescience. ''It all depends on how long it takes the man he's seeing to make up his mind. He's kin to Conan, and we think we can get him as ally, but he's a canny bird, who won't be hurried. I take it that you know pretty much all about our political divisions?''

"My education may not be complete, but it's thorough enough," I said ruefully. "I know a lot more than a stranger has a right to."

He nodded cheerfully. "You have had a pretty rough time of it, haven't you? Well then, Gregory, the man in question, holds land directly north of the abbey's which also borders on the northern reach of Chilbert's territory. Chilbert has the abbey on two sides as it is, and if he won over Gregory, as we assume he'd try to do, he'd have it on three. The Abbot wants to remain neutral, but under pressure of a squeeze like that he might feel forced to join the count.

"Well, you see from that." Jean sloshed the wine in his half-emptied cup thoughtfully. "The fellow's damned important to everybody, and he's smart enough to know it. Conan's been sounding him out for months but has received nothing but evasions. Finally, since we need Gregory so much and as long as nobody will risk large scale hostilities until the harvest is fully taken care of, Conan decided to go himself. He left just before we got word of the Dane raid two days ago, and, knowing what a horsetrader his man is, he said not to expect him for four or five days or more. Still he might come tonight."

"Did Conan go alone?"

"He took four others," Jean scowled. "I wanted him to take a good-sized troop, but he maintained that when you're asking a man for help you shouldn't burden his hospitality with an army. Then, too, he didn't want to take either men from the harvest or from work on the walls."

"I see." It was remarkably pleasant sitting there. Bees buzzed soothingly up and down a flowering vine and drank in unison with us. The fine day grew finer as it cooled with the waning afternoon. The wine was even better than I had first thought. I was sure that nothing ill could befall Conan.

"Rainault! Fulke!" Jean called out suddenly. "Come here!"

I roused from dreamy contemplation of beatitude to see a chunky, wedge-faced man of about forty approaching in company with a tall, freckled youth.

"Rainault," Jean said to the older of the two, "say when you saw this man before." He leaned back, happy over the puzzle he had presented, while I met the newcomer's dark-eyed scrutiny blankly.

"I've got it!" He slapped his companions in vigorous delight. "It's the one, Fulke! Don't you recognize him?" He turned to me once more and laughed. "Lord! how you cursed us."

He didn't seem to mind, so I smiled vaguely, not quite at my keenest. "Interesting but not true," I told him. "You're thinking of somebody else; I'm—"

"Finnian," he silenced me. "I didn't expect you to place me, but I found you at the Old Farms and took you to Thomas' house. You weren't for being nice about it." He grinned reminiscently. "It was good cursing."

I concentrated. "I remember a little of it now. At the time I couldn't get it through my head that everybody I saw wasn't a man of Chilbert's."

"You made that plain." He jerked his head toward the lad, who had been staring at me fixedly. "Fulke here is the one who first got wind of you and Conan that day."

"It was when you were singing the tirade," the latter burst out excitedly. "I couldn't get near enough to see without risking certain discovery, but when the song indicated there were two of you I felt sure that the other must be Conan."

I looked at them with interest. One was the young minstrel who was said to have memorized my song on the spot and sung it all about to deride Chilbert's power. The first man was he who had led the rescue expedition. I rose. "I am in debt to you both," I announced with a formality that was perhaps a trifle heavy. "If you'll call for cups I hold it fitting to toast the reunion."

That was done, and for the next hour the four of us drank and talked with benevolence enthroned among us. No one was drunk; but on a warm day it doesn't take too much wine to soothe a man, and all of us were soothed.

We broke off wrangling good-naturedly about something or other to grin at Ann, who was smiling at us with the special tolerance a woman reserves for the harmless follies of men she likes. "Dinner's ready if you want to eat," she informed us.

Jean rolled an owlish eye at me. "Do you think it would be wise to abandon such good wine?"

"The full weight of my opinion is against it," I replied. "We might never get any like it again. Consider that possibility before you make any rash decision," I concluded warningly.

"There will be excellent wine with the meal," she humored us, "so you'll be quite safe."

"Lots of wine?" Rainault asked with a shrewdness I admired.

"Yes, lots."

We four looked at each other. "It seems all right," I said cautiously. "Shall we take a chance?"

Jean rose boldly. "Let's risk it."

The next few days were enjoyable ones during which I was left to my own devices until late afternoon and enjoyed good company during the evenings. Daytimes the men were busy with the harvest and the building of the fort, while Ann had her double job of chatelaine and housekeeper. Marie assisted her in every way possible, proving she was wise enough to see that work was the best panacea for her griefs. Outwardly she gave little evidence of what she was enduring, and I took a mildly proprietary pride in her.

As for myself I took advantage of the free time on my hands to pay my debt to Thorgrim. Locally nobody but Conan, who had done viking work, would understand the poem, but if and when I got to Otho's court men could listen. It wasn't bad as poems to order go. It lacked the heat of inspired conviction, of course, but there was nothing I could do about that. Thorgrim got the best craftsman's job I could produce for him and would have to rest content with it.

When not so engaged I rode around the countryside to see what Conan was accomplishing. He was doing a magnificent job. Even quite far afield no villain scuttled away like a badger making for his hole at sight of me, and many had found sufficient confidence and human poise to return a cheerful greeting. I saw no burnt houses, no hungry children, no casually left corpses in all that locality. Everywhere men were engaged in reaping full, unspoiled crops to tide over the winter. It was a rare and marvelously wholesome sight such as I had seldom seen, especially in France.

On a couple of occasions Fulke managed to get away from the work in hand to go with me. He was a pleasant, clever lad without swank, but I found his conviction that I was a great poet—arrived at solely because he wanted to believe it—somewhat embarrassing. I knew I wasn't yet if indeed I was ever to be such; but I also remembered the vast, amorphous yearnings of an apprentice and did my best to fulfill his expectations of me. He longed, I found, to be himself a maker; and by precept, if not, perhaps by example, I could be of help to him. It was pleasant to talk craft to so eager a listener, and by this indulgence of both him and myself I won a good friend.

Day by day, however, the tension began to grow, although nobody said anything much. There was no definite cause for alarm in the fact that nothing had been heard from Conan, for he had left prepared for somewhat lengthy negotiations. But everybody was experiencing concern, none the less, as each night fell without news. Ann ceased to smile as much as usual, and a general air of sober, if unvoiced, speculation pervaded the place.

Dinner on the fifth day was an unwontedly subdued affair. As there was a precocious nip of autumn in the air as soon as the sun went down we took our wine indoors. Jean and I attempted facetious chatter to keep the spirits of the gathering high, but we weren't doing very well at it, and nobody joined in our own unconvinced laughter. At the same time nobody felt like sleep, either, so we sat up later than customary, growing progressively more silent and drinking without pleasure.

Ann was the first to hear anything. "The watchman's challenging," she said, starting to her feet. Then I heard the horse's hoofs.

We were crowding hurriedly to the door when it was opened by what was left of a man. Aside from being weary to the point of dissolution he was badly wounded. In three separate places his clothes were stiffened by large patches of dried blood. "It's Francois!" Rainault said in a taut, hard voice. "Wine for him! Quick!"

It was a minute before this man who had gone forth with Conan and returned in such bad case could get strength to be articulate. While we waited the rest of us fidgeted, feeling the pressure of ignorance unbearable. None of us would meet the others' eyes. There would be plenty of time for that ordeal of recognition when our dread was substantiated.

"What is it, Francois?" Jean was almost whispering. "Conan! Where's Conan?"

The fellow made a great effort and raised his head a little from Fulke's supporting arm. "Hostage," he managed hoarsely.

The worst had not yet happened then. We let him rest a little longer while Fulke gave him wine in small sips. "Tell us!"

Jean finally commanded. "We've got to know."

"Gregory's holding him," Francois mumbled hoarsely. "He's sending to find what Chilbert will offer."

Ann gasped, and Rainault began cursing with smothered violence. I didn't know how I felt, but it wasn't good. My teeth clenched till my jaws ached. Jean meanwhile went on patiently and inexorably worming the story out of the exhausted man, and finally we had it all.

Even though not certain of his kinsman as an ally Conan had trusted him for hospitality. Not unreservedly, however, as he had taken the precaution of leaving Francois in hiding several miles down the road from Gregory's fortress with orders to return home and report if he received no message by a certain time.

"Sunrise today was the time he said for me to beat it back, but I couldn't leave without knowing something for sure, see?"

We saw.

"I started for Gregory's place, and part way there I met a fellow riding like he was going somewheres. I figured he could only be coming from the fort and would know about Conan, so I waylaid him. He cut me up some, but I finally got him so's he'd talk."

"You killed him, of course?" Rainault said.

"Yeah, but it wasn't any use. His horse headed back home while we were fighting."

That would naturally have given the play away. Ann had the man carried to bed and promised that she herself would shortly give attention to his wounds. The rest of us stood where we were, thinking hard.

"They found the messenger's horse in a couple of hours, say," Rainault offered as an opener. "Another man was on his way before noon."

"But Chilbert may take a little looking for," Jean took it up.

"Yes, and Chilbert won't send. He'll gather riders and come himself for game as big as Conan."

"No moon tonight," Jean agreed. "We'd never locate the trails without light."

"And there are no through roads. We'll have to wait till morning to ride."

There was an oath that Conan and I had sworn. I stared at

the floor, growing wearily disgusted as my grasp of the situation enlarged. Although I wasn't yet sure what could be done I did know that I couldn't leave it for Jean and Rainault to bungle. Why, they didn't even see what they were faced with!

I moistened my lips and spoke with toneless authority. "Forget about your riders. An expedition won't do any good." For the first time I raised my eyes, and I saw to my surprise that Ann had been looking at me, waiting for me to speak.

"What do you mean it won't do any good?" Jean asked roughly. "Do you think we can save him by prayer?"

I paid no attention to his understandable rudeness. "You get there with a troop," I diagrammed. "Gregory says stay put or he'll kill Conan. You wait around to swear at him. Chilbert arrives with *his* army. He and Gregory have you sandwiched. You probably lose your troop, and they've certainly still got Conan. No, it's one man's job."

"Mine, then!" Jean and Rainault chorused.

"No, mine," I contradicted them.

"Damn you, no!" Rainault shouted. "Who the hell do you think you are telling us—?"

"He's Conan's sworn brother," Ann told him quietly.

They were abashed then and listened. Next to Ann herself I had the most right to speak.

Chapter
Thirteen

SOMEWHERE in the back of my mind I could see that infernal Pict grinning triumphantly. In recent months I had stepped into sufficient trouble but always at times when circumstances had me cornered, leaving no loophole. Now I was outbidding eager scapegoats.

"One reason I'm better suited for this job," I explained to Conan's lieutenants, "is that I'm a stranger to Gregory and all his men, not to mention the fact that I'm obviously not a native. You're both known by reputation and, I suspect, personally."

They nodded glumly. "Moreover," I gestured toward where my harp hung on the wall, "that will give me entry and a reason for passing that way on the loose which demands no explanation."

"All right," Jean gave in. "What are you going to do once you're inside?"

"I don't know," I answered frankly. "Anything that seems indicated. I'm not guaranteeing I'll be of any use even, because they've got us on the hip and no mistake. But it's our only chance."

"Yes," Ann said after a long moment, and that settled it.

"You'll need a guide," Rainault said hopefully.

"I will," I agreed, "but it can't be either of you. You'll both be needed to save what's possible if Conan doesn't return."

I didn't want a companion that would pound me with advice and suggestions. But there was one among them, who, I felt sure, would follow and obey me blindly when, as, and if I conceived a plan. The youngster, Fulke, had a bad case of hero worship which he'd get over in time, being a sound lad. Now, however, I could make use of it.

"If you know the way, I'd like you to go with me, Fulke."

His face lighted up as if I'd just given him something of immense value instead of inviting him on an expedition to get his throat cut. "Sure, I know the way. Thanks, Finnian!"

I grunted sourly. Everybody except myself seemed to think that extricating a man from a well-garrisoned fort was some sort of delightful pastime. Had I chosen to stay with them, the other men would have gone on discussing the project, but I wasn't in the mood for useless gab. "I'm going outside for a while," I announced. "Try to get some sleep, Fulke."

He had the saccharine docility of a child with a treat in store. "I'll go to bed right away," he promised.

Ann's face was stiff and white. "I'll have food ready when the night starts to change." With an ineffably poignant gesture she touched my arm, then turned away. I nodded to the others and strode to the door.

It was a star night, cool and quiet. Ordinarily I might have found it too chilly without a cloak, but trifling discomforts could make no impression on me then. I walked slowly over to a low, unfinished portion of the outer wall and after first notifying the watchman of my presence sat down to consider. I had vaguely hoped that inspiration for a course of procedure might come to me, but the more I thought about it the more convinced I became that I would have to wait and improvise plans after I'd looked the scene of action over.

I had no inclination for sleep, but I was on the verge of forcing myself to attempt it when I heard a low but urgent voice just below me. "Would you help me up, please?"

The voice was Marie's, and I assumed its rightful owner was using it, although the figure in the heavy shadow of the wall was unrecognizable. I reached down a hand, hauled her up, and waited to hear what she had to say. I didn't object to her company, but I was considerably surprised that she had sought mine. While we had been quizzing the messenger and afterwards I had been hardly aware of her, for she had kept sensibly in the background. And had I since thought about her at all I would have taken it for granted that she had retired when Ann did.

"I'll go away if you wish," she said with a hesitancy I had not learned to expect from her. "I know you've got important things on your mind."

"Both obliging and flattering," I murmured. "You haven't always so pampered me."

"No," she admitted, and I could sense that she was more at ease. Nevertheless, her tone remained serious. "You may not come back, and I wouldn't like to feel that I had never talked to you. You happen to have been a crucial factor in my life, and I'd like to realize you a little. Do you see that?"

I nodded and then remembered the darkness. "It was nice of you to come out," I helped her. "I'm too restless for sleep."

"Thanks, whether it's true or not." She hugged herself, fighting off the chill. "Everybody takes it for granted that you're willing to go for Conan. They're so wrapped up in what they're trying to do that they think you're part of it. But you're not, are you?"

"No,"

"And suppose you save Conan—what'll you do then?"

"Hadn't figured."

"Oh yes, you have," she astonished me with contradiction. "If you can help it you won't come back to get mixed up in troubles here any longer."

I didn't bother to argue the point. "I'm only catechizing you to find out some things for myself," she apologized when I didn't answer. "You see, I don't belong to this, either. I don't belong to anything now, and I don't know what I'm going to do. I'm talking to you because you seem to get along without everything most people want. Or have you got them somewhere else?"

"I haven't got much," I admitted.

"Well, I had a home and people. Things belonged to me. I was going to marry a man."

"What stopped you?"

"The Danes. They killed him, too."

"I'm sorry," I said. "Did you want him much?"

"Some. I don't know. But as a wife I'd be a person doing everything about life that I could. I wanted that, and now I'm not sure that I can ever have the chance again."

I knew a girl without property couldn't often make the sort of match she desired. "You've still got the land," I suggested.

"Yes, but there are no men to rebuild the hall and hold it

now, and none can be spared for long hereabouts. Besides, what's the use in building something for more Danes or some other batch of thieves to destroy? No, that's gone, and now if Conan dies everything here will fall apart, too. I think," she continued after a brief pause, "that if I saw that happen I could never hope again or believe that men have any power against evil, any choice but to live in bestiality like Piers and his kind."

Anybody who has lived in France in our time has necessarily seen too much of the harsh side of life, and this girl had just been forced to look long and carefully at horror. I wished that I could have been some use to her; but her problems were involved with the social conditions, and there was nothing good to say about them. "The game isn't over," was the most I could offer.

"Not yet," she said without optimism. "If Conan lives, why—Well, I've seen what he has done, starting out with almost nothing but himself. He knows what we all must have and has the strength to bring it about. He has all our hope in his hand; and that's what is so queer now. If one of the others were going for him he would be desperate with the knowledge that his whole world would collapse if he failed. But you don't care."

She couldn't be expected to know how I felt about Conan. "Oh, I do in my way."

"What is your way? That's what I'm trying to find out in case all the props I know about should fail me utterly, as they seem likely to do."

"Don't look to me for any guiding philosophy," I told her uneasily. "I have none. There's a thing I possess which pleases me. It's poetry, and by and large it is a spacious enough kingdom in which to move. In situations where it isn't adequate there aren't any rules. Things just happen."

"You're being very patient with me," she said, "but you never have made any sense."

"This is more like old times," I cheered her, but she refused to be shaken out of seriousness.

"You're deliberately taking a trip to do something which is apt to prove disastrous for you. If it doesn't, you and Conan will get drunk and talk a lot of nonsense together, then you'll go off as unconcernedly as a dog that's stopped to scratch a flea. What you're trying to do is hard and good, and it should have great significance for you. But it hasn't."

"Maybe I'll have time for it later," I said, amused alike at her diagnosis and arraignment, "if a bunch of Franks don't stick swords through me. So far as I know now there's only one significance to that."

She laughed apologetically. "I'm sorry, but now that it's been taken away from me I see that what I want most is a continuity of experience, the building up of associations with both people and things. But as you're trying to be the answer to necessity I was wrong and silly to scold you for whatever nonessential things you are not. And maybe you have your reasons. In times like ours it must be as hard to be a man as to be a woman."

A bachelor of any maturity may be sad or glad about his singularity, but shelve the problem he cannot. Even churchmen have to fortify their vows of chastity by slandering womankind, the shrill petulance of the vilifications betraying the sense of wrong. Perforce then when she was still after that remark I thought how I might die the next night without ever having undertaken a male's ultimate responsibility. I looked at Marie's shadowy profile and wondered if I would ever talk to a girl again. Feeling half fey, as I did, I had no passion, but I experienced the tenderness a man occasionally knows for women in general seen as the embodiment of fineness and beauty.

And with that feeling came a sort of weary resignation. "I'm glad you came out here," I told her again. "I'll sleep now, and I can use the rest." I jumped down and reached up. "Here, take my hand."

I eased her descent, and we walked toward the hall quietly, our fingers still locked. A couple of torches were still burning to light the main room, but no one was about. I filled two wine cups and looked at her face, a lovely and always changing pattern in the flickering light. "Good luck!" I toasted her.

She looked at me with compassion. "Good luck, Finnian." It was the first time I had heard her use my name, a thing I have always found compelling on the lips of a sightly woman. We smiled warmly and parted.

I got into bed, and the next thing I knew Jean was shaking me vigorously. "It's still night!" I protested.

"First light's showing," he insisted and threw the blanket on the floor. Dumb with drowsiness I reached for my clothes, but he handed me a cloak. "Take a dive in the moat," he ordered. "You can't be sleep-walking now."

The cool water first, then the cooler air on my wet body waked me thoroughly. I dressed on the bridge, whither Jean had followed with my clothes, then returned with him swiftly to the hall. Fulke was before me and greeted me enthusiastically, but Rainault told him to shut up and eat. The meal was adequate but briefly handled. Nobody shared it with us but stood watching, their anxious expressions and subdued whispers adding to the cheerlessness of the dimly lit hall.

"Come on," I mumbled to Fulke over my final bite, and led the way out to the court. The sky had perceptibly lightened by then, and I could see the three horses being held for us by the gate. The third, destined, we hoped, for Conan, was loaded with my harp, such trifling supplies as we would need, and a sword. That, too, was for Conan.

"Now you do exactly what Finnian tells you and nothing else," I heard Rainault warning Fulke while Jean was giving me a leg up. Marie was not there, having said her farewell the night before, but every other member of the household and garrison was astir; and there was a half-hearted attempt to give us a cheer.

Ann, who had been taking leave of Fulke, now turned to me. I was glad the pre-dawn murk made our faces unreadable. "Finnian," she said, and that was the most she could manage. I reached down my hand, she held it to her cheek an instant, then pushed away through the crowd.

"Don't drink all the wine," I told Jean. "Watch him, Rainault."

They made valedictory gestures, and we trotted across the bridge. The fields were smoky with mist, but the pallid sky was cloudless. We were going to have a good day for it, which, as there had been no recent rains to muddy the trails, guaranteed us prime traveling conditions. It proved good for our morale, too. In the early chill we rode in moody silence, for even Fulke had been depressed by the lugubrious attitude of our well-wishers, but when the world became fair with light we drew a measure of gaiety from it. Fulke, especially, having recovered his pristine zest for the undertaking, joked and sang continually. As he was doing it for his own amusement he put no burden of conversation on me, although I occasionally interjected comments and jests of my own. At other whiles I wrestled with the problems of our venture, assuming possible contingencies then trying to answer them with sound courses of action.

When the sun had been up two or three hours I saw that we rode a little south of east. We were heading, my calculations assured me, into territory I had visited before. "Pull up," I ordered Fulke, and while he fidgeted with curiosity I considered what had just occurred to me.

"Aren't we heading toward the abbey?" I asked after a minute.

"More or less, but not quite. We'll cross the road several miles north of it."

"How soon could we reach it?"

"In about an hour, traveling fast. But what would be the use of going there?"

I thought a little longer. It was a chance, but it was a good chance. It was, in fact, the only useful notion that had so far occurred to me. "If we can see the Abbot he may help us," I said. "He's the only man I know of who can."

So it came to pass, just as it had a little over two months before, that I sat in the saddle looking up to where Father Clovis lounged above the abbey gates. "God the Father!" he chuckled. "Here's our poet and scholar back with a new steed."

"The other was taken from me," I said, sighing, as I thought of that splendid bay.

"He begrudges a man his own horse," the monk said to no one in particular. He chuckled again. "I saw Chilbert on it not three weeks back. I could have kicked myself for not having recognized it when you first came. How have you been?"

"Fine, thanks." I jerked my head at my companion. "Father Clovis, this minstrel is Fulke, a man of Conan's." I uttered the concluding phrase pointedly, and the monk straightened, cocking an eye. "I've heard of him. So it was you who helped raise Cain with Oliver. I often wondered."

"We'd like to talk to the Abbot," I said when he paused questioningly. "It's important."

"All right," he nodded. "I'll see if he has any time to spare for horse thieves."

We rode into the court, and a couple of minutes later the Abbot himself came striding toward us. He looked at me keenly as we exchanged greetings. "Well, my son?"

"Chilbert's about to score a coup, and we're trying to stop him. Would you be interested to hear?"

"Yes. Will you come to my study?"

Fulke and I dismounted. "Thank you, Father. I'd like

Father Clovis to be there, too."

Knowing something of my man, I came to the point directly the door was closed. "You once suggested that I join Conan. I have done so, and now in turn I've come to ask help for him from you."

"That sounds just," he admitted. "What's Conan's need?"

"Gregory's got him."

"His kinsman?"

"Yes, and his betrayer. He's holding him to see what Chilbert will bid. One of our men intercepted a messenger."

Clovis whistled, and he and the Abbot exchanged glances. The latter shook his head, and I allowed him to ponder in silence. I knew that he would quickly see what could and could not be essayed.

After a while he raised his eyes to look at me. "What do you yourself plan to do?"

"I don't know any to well, but as an unknown harper I'll probably be given entry."

"Not much but something," he remarked. "What do you want of me?"

"First I'd like to know if the abbey is on good terms with Gregory."

"Not cordial but good. Politically speaking we're friendly."

I had thought so and nodded, well pleased. "Now am I right in assuming that in the current mess of affairs it is no extraordinary thing for a powerful faction like yours to send legates to check up on the position and leanings of minor chieftans?"

"You are right," he said slowly.

"That's what I want then," I leaned toward him, calling on all the powers of persuasion I could command. "The abbey need not be committed to anything, Father; but a neutral diplomatic representative arriving to investigate rumors and all that sort of thing could ask questions a wandering minstrel could not. He might discover where they have Conan imprisoned, and as a priest he might be permitted to talk to him where a layman wouldn't be. Then he could find occasion to tell me what's what, and step aside. I ask no more of you or him."

He met my urgency with unhurried calm. "If Conan's being sold the abbey's interest will, of course, be vitally affected. All right. I take it that you wish Father Clovis to be the man?"

"If he's willing. Are you, Clovis?" I asked, dropping the "Father" and appealing to him as a man and a friend.

"I'd like to. Will the Father permit?"

"The Father will," the Abbot answered, "but remember that your part is that of one obtaining information only. You are to do nothing that will give the minutest inkling that the abbey is taking sides in this matter."

"Certainly, Father. I suppose you're in a hurry, Finnian."

"Well, I want Conan, not his corpse."

"It won't take me long," he promised and left us briskly.

"I'm greatly obliged to you, Father," I told the Abbot fervently. With this added help, I felt with a surge of relief, there was some trifling grounds for hope.

He waved away my appreciation. "It was very little but the most I could afford," he stated, and he was speaking simple truth. Since the odds were in favor of Conan being killed and the power of his people broken it was no time for any outsider to espouse his cause. Yet the Abbot would see that Conan's fall would upset the balance of power and dangerously enhance Chilbert's lust and hopes for empire.

"If I'm not successful," I said, "the count may promptly strike to take over everything in sight. Do you know what you will do?"

"I hope it won't come to that, but the abbey will be tributary to no one. If necessary we'll form alliances, but while I live we'll be vassals to God only."

Some men speak of how they will behave during perils not yet reached either to boast or to convince themselves; but this man spoke in the calm knowledge of how he would in truth act. He rose as Father Clovis returned and shook my hand with the vigor he brought to all things.

"Goodby and all the good luck you'll badly need, my son."

"Goodby, Father." I nodded to the others. "Let's ride."

Chapter
  Fourteen

WE didn't travel in company. Clovis at my request pushed on as fast as possible in order to be able to obtain the information I wanted before I arrived. About mid-afternoon I separated from Fulke.

We had been riding single file on a little-used woods trail, the spare horse between us. "The road isn't far from here," Fulke said over his shoulder. "Not more than a mile, I should say."

"And how far to the fort?"

"Say ten miles to be safe."

"Stop then." Sliding to the ground, I hitched my horse to a sapling. He imitated me, and we approached each other on saddle-stiffened legs. "Ten miles" I said. "I can make that on foot by sundown." That was important because few places admit strangers after that.

"What about me?"

"You'll follow with the horses later."

I knew he had been counting on going almost to the fort with me, and another man might have argued. He merely looked pained. "Do you know the place well?" I asked.

"I was there fairly recently to sing your tirade."

"Tell me which side is the best for our rendezvous, bearing in mind that we don't want to be cut off from this path."

He closed his eyes the better to bring out his mental picture. "It's on a hill, Finnian, and a by-road leads up the gate, which faces west. That would be our quickest route, but the peasants' houses line the road, and I couldn't get very near on that side. From the south, though, we could slant across open fields, and if we have any sort of start we could beat them out.''

"That's it then. Work nearer in the dusk, and when it's dark get as near the southwest corner as you think you safely can.'' One good thing about a lawless land, as far as our purposes were concerned, is that everybody who can holes up by twilight. Fulke should run small risk of meeting any of Gregory's people. "I'll count on your being on the grounds within an hour after nightfall. And no matter what excitement you may hear going on in the fort stay where you are unless Conan or I give you a yell.''

"I'll stay put. What'll I do if you don't come by dawn?''

"Return to the trail here and wait for Father Clovis. If there's any use in your sticking around longer he'll give you instructions.'' There was no need to tell him what to do if the news was absolutely bad.

I took the extra sword and my harp from the lead horse. Fulke was a thoroughly saddened youngster as he watched me sling the instrument over my shoulder, and I grinned at him to cheer him up. "Sorry you're not joining us at dinner. See you later.''

He smiled wanly. "Don't get killed any more than you have to.''

In a couple of hundred yards a good deal of the stiffness had worked out of my legs. When I reached the road, I took care to obliterate the tracks that showed whence I had come, then turned north, walking swiftly. At that it was more than two hours before I got my first view of the fort.

As Fulke had said, it was on a steep little hill. The walls were of the usual kind, earthworks topped with a low stockade. There were open fields all around the base of the hill, of course, and I was pleased to see that those on the south side had already been harvested. There were no obstacles to fast moving if we ever got under way.

I had been carrying both swords wrapped in my cape, with the hilts showing, so that it would be evident that I was trying to conceal nothing. That was not only a politely peaceful gesture; I wouldn't be allowed to wear either of them inside the fort anyhow, and it made the walking easier. Rounding into the byroad to the gate, I cut my pace to slow trudging and ascended the hill. From now on, I realized wryly, I had no plan of procedure.

Well, I was going in, and what would happen would happen. On the way up I had been trembling with nervousness and the foretaste of action, but as I halted before the fort I was suddenly calm again. "I'd like housing for the night," I confidently informed the warder. At harvest time when food is plentiful few chiefs will refuse that to an unsuspect person, especially if he is geared to give something in return.

He took in my harp, ordered the gates open, and called down to one of a number of men loafing around the court. "Hey, Henri! Take this fellow to Gregory and find out whether or not he wants his head cut off."

As my guide took charge of me I looked around, albeit not too pointedly. The place was quite strongly garrisoned, with a number of watchers stationed at various points on the walls. The buildings within were not remarkable, none looking especially as if it might be a prison. There was just the hall, a rambling composite of wings and leantos, and the ordinary assortment of barns and outhouses. At the door to the hall I was ordered to wait while my arrival was announced to Gregory.

To my surprise he came out instead of waiting for me inside. Father Clovis was with him. "Good evening; good evening, Father," I saluted them in turn.

The monk held up his hand in an elaborate gesture of benediction. "Peace be with you," he intoned in Latin. "They won't let me get a word alone with him, but he's right in the hall here."

"Where are you from?" Gregory cut in impatiently on the tail of this. He was a broad, cold-faced man with a suspicious mind, and I saw what the porter meant. If my answers weren't right, he'd have me finished without hesitation.

"I came up from the Loire."

"Born south of here?"

That was a trap, because anyone listening could detect the accent in my speech. "No, I'm Irish, I've been playing for Louis and am on my way home from Paris."

"What are you doing up this way then?" he asked sharply.

Strolling minstrels were common enough, and I wasn't much afraid that he would connect me with the bard who had helped Conan and dropped out of sight months before.

"They were having Dane trouble along the river"—I knew he would have heard about that—"and I wanted to get well out of the way. The Danes may be gone now, but once I was in this country I thought I'd look it over. I'm in no hurry as long as there's business, and this time of the year it's always good."

"By business I suppose you mean singing and playing." He didn't suspect me, I saw; he was merely being thorough. "Why do you carry two swords?"

"One because a traveling man needs one, and the other because I was lucky with the dice at Angers." My story should hold until he had any reason to doubt me, but he considered for another lengthy moment while I fought to keep from showing my anxiety.

"Take him to the barn, Henri," he said curtly, and I stopped sweating. "And see that he leaves his weapons there."

"Thanks!" I beamed, relief lending as authentic note to my gratitude. Then, while Henri was showing me to the loft, I could at last give consideration to what the priest had said. Conan was apparently in the main hall, and the implication was that by day, at least, he had a certain amount of freedom. If we dined inside, then, I might casually encounter him. I grimaced. But suppose that, in his astonishment at seeing me again, he should betray the fact that we were acquainted.

I thought about that while I climbed a ladder to a loft and stowed my belongings, my harp excepted, under some hay in one corner. "You'll have lots of company, even not counting the rats," my cicerone called up to me. "It's harvest time, and we got a full house."

"I don't mind the rats," I matched his genial tone, withal saying exactly what I meant. Men might turn out to be fatal bedfellows.

He was gone by the time I'd descended. Tables, I saw, had been set up at the rear of the hall, and the call for dinner was imminent. While the others were engrossed with the meal-time rush it seemed a good time to make Conan aware of my presence. Or if he wasn't given liberty to eat with the assembly I wanted to be in evidence in case Clovis could elude his host long enough to tell me anything he might have found out. Making a business of tuning my instrument, I strolled across the court.

I had barely taken my stand near the door of the hall when it opened for a man whose blinking eyes took me in indifferently before he ambled toward the tables. Gregory, right behind, nodded curtly in answer to my affable greeting. Clovis smiled with ecclesiastical benignity, and there were more following. I struck a chord to cover the oath I muttered. That first man had been Conan, and his non-recognition hadn't been simulated. Emerging from the gloom of the hall into the comparative brightness of early twilight, he simply hadn't seen who I was.

The rest of the men started drifting toward the food, and I did likewise, seating myself as far from the chiefs as possible pending another opportunity for letting my friend know I was there while nobody was noticing us. But when the food was brought, Father Clovis pounded on the table and rebuked those who would have pounced on the viands immediately. "We are Christians, and we'll give thanks for what we are eating," he told them sternly. Some grumbled, but under his eyes all bent their heads.

Oh, the good Latin, which only he himself, Conan, and I understood! I had liked that monk from the first, but then I loved him. "The rat king has been sent for, but there's an Irish bard you'll remember at board with us now. He has horses beyond the walls." That was for Conan. I didn't want to be caught looking up at the priest; but there was all the unctuousness of professional piety in his voice as he went on for both of us. "The mean-eyed mongrel's game is to have the enemies bid against each other, the one for his freedom, the other for the former's death. I think the hell-damned bastard had decided that the man from the south will win, but he thinks he can exact more from him this way. I couldn't find where they keep the cat at night, but he won't be there another. The butcher is expected in the morning."

"*Dominus*." Father Clovis concluded loudly. "Amen." He sat, the unleashed men commenced gobbling their victuals, and I took a needed pull at my wine. Conan now knew that I was not only there but that my arrival had not been accidental, as he might well have thought after having been so completely out of touch with me. Also the predicament had been defined for both of us. All that was good, but the most important item of information was missing. I didn't know where Conan was kept during the night.

Knowing I must maintain my strength, I ate quite a bit, but I had no appetite for it. The only man there who had alike the ability and the willingness to tell me what I wanted to know was Conan himself, and my chances of getting a word alone with him were non-existent. Nor could our knowledge of foreign languages be of any more use, for they'd surely choke him off and as certainly grow suspicious of me, the stranger, if he should suddenly start saying anything in tongues they didn't comprehend like Danish, Irish, or—

I twitched. Conan knew Gaelic because he had studied at a monastery school in Ireland, and therefore he should know a trick I'd learned at a similar place. For the first time I looked to pick him out where he sat next to Gregory, and even under the circumstances, or perhaps because of them, it was heartening to get a good look at him again. A moment later his gaze wandered listlessly in my direction, and I saw that he had already found me. Then he dropped his eyes and sat slumped, epitomized resignation.

At harvest time men begin early and work hard. When the day is finished, consequently, they demand drink and song, and a chief with any wisdom lets them have it. These were labor-hungry fellows, not epicures to linger over their food; but even so it was nearly dark when they had done, and a great blaze had been started in an open fireplace to one side. There would be an hour or so of relaxation, and benches were dragged to ring the fire. Now was my time, and I claimed it.

Most of them applauded beforehand when I stepped forward, my harp a guarantee of entertainment.

"A minstrel!"

"Swell! Let's hear him!"

"How the hell can we unless you shut up?"

Gregory knew his business and smiled tolerantly as he held up his hand for silence. No doubt, with triumph envisioned for the morrow, he was feeling fairly jovial himself. I bowed to him when they were hushed. "I should like to repay your generous hospitality with a few songs," I told him.

"Make it something gay for the season," he suggested.

Conan, sitting beside him, could now look at me in the natural order of things. He knew that I would speak to him if I could, and his eyes were alert in a still face. While I looked around, smiling acknowledgment of the audience's cheers and suggestions, I scratched one hand with the other, then flexed the fingers of my right hand before I touched the strings. That, I reasoned, would serve to show that I would signal rather than give verbal cues.

At the monastery where I had been schooled it had long been a tradition for the boys to communicate with each other by hand ogham, and I was banking on the probability that its usefulness was known at every school in Ireland. The ogham alphabet was originally designed for cutting words on stones or wands, letters being formed by combinations of one to five dashes in relation to a horizontal or vertical line; but an adaptation of it was eminently suitable for silent communication during classes or the interminable prayers that make up so large a portion of monastic routine. During prayers the nose was used as the transverse line while the fingers of the supposedly worshipping boy, his hand held reverently to his bowed head, would nimbly move back and forth to signal insults to some watching mate. In the classroom the forearm could be used for the transverse, or the stylus. The harp strings would serve me. I was no longer adept at sending, and he would be rusty at receiving, but a thing at once so simple and so carefully practiced for years could never be forgotten. If I went very slowly he must be able to read.

When all had quieted to listen I strummed a brief prelude and commenced singing. Thereafter my voice carried the burden of the tune, the harp supporting it with only occasional chords and runs of music between the stanzas.

> *"Oh, Jacques met Ann*
> *And found her crying.*
> *'Pretty little Ann, say why do you weep?'*
> *'I'm wedding a man,*
> *And I'd rather be dying!'*
> *'What would you marry—a mule or a sheep?"*

Meanwhile my hands had been at work. "Where?" I had spelled. There was no response from Conan, and for a panicky moment I thought my scheme had failed. As I began the next strophe, however, my friend casually crossed his legs to sit, ankle over knee. He could thus use his shin bone for the transverse, his signaling fingers looking as if they were tapping time to the melody.

> " 'But Robert's gray
> And mostly belly
> And stinks like a fish in the noonday sun.'
> 'Then why not, I pray,
> Pick a fellow less smelly?
> For one so pretty it is simply done.' "

"Northeast wing," Conan had spelled. I looked at Gregory, but he wasn't an attentive member of my auditors. His mind was on Chilbert's visit. Father Clovis was smiling lazily, but I saw his eyes roll to take in Conan. He knew that something was being accomplished between us.

> " 'But Robert's rich
> And Dad likes money
> Better than a heathen is loved by Hell;
> Ah, an old bear's itch
> For to guzzle new honey
> Makes Robert pay high, so Father will sell.' "

"Door?" I had asked. "No," Conan had sent. That meant no egress except through the hall, which was bad.

> " 'Would you wed me?
> I haven't a penny,
> But I will love you well, I swear, my sweet.'
> 'But, Jacques, how could we
> Get along without any?
> All we pretty maids rather like to eat.' "

"Window?" I had spelled. "Too small," had been the answer.

> " 'You'd rather bed,
> Come, dare confessing,
> With a lad like me than a fat, old cluck.'
> 'But I'll never wed
> Unless I have a blessing
> Given by my father, for that's bad luck.'
>
> 'Don't, pretty Ann,
> Be broken-hearted;

> *I'll get a blessing for us out of hand,*
> *And as I'm a man,*
> *Stinking Robert, outsmarted,*
> *Will buy us a house and acres of land.' "*

"Guards," Conan had been telling me. "Two. Lights. All night." That was very bad. In fact, the more I learned the worse I felt.

> " 'Sir, do you know
> *That in the hollow*
> *Kings buried treasure in the swamp of old?*
> *Now if you will go*
> *Down there tonight and follow*
> *Where the folly fire leads you'll find much gold.'*
>
> *'I'm in a bog*
> *And stuck fast, sinking!'*
> *'Sir, will you let me wed your daughter dear?'*
> *'Why never, you dog!'*
> *'Then go on with your shrinking:*
> *I'll stay around and watch you disappear.'*
>
> *'Oh, help me, Jacques!*
> *My neck's in the water!'*
> *'Hard on the turtles, but it doesn't hurt me.'*
> *'I take it all back,*
> *You can marry my daughter;*
> *But first make sure that I'm alive to see.' "*

"Best wall?" I had asked. Having been there for some while and having, perhaps, visited the fort before he became an important enough figure to be worth a kinsman's betrayment, he might know not only which steps up to the wall could be reached and climbed with the greatest chance of privacy but also, and even more important, where we could jump down with the least chance of breaking a leg. "North," he had answered, which wasn't good, either. That meant we'd have to circle half around the place before we could reach Fulke and the horses.

" 'If there's a maid
For whom, sir, you're pining,
And you put your head through the bridal stone,
She will be displayed
In the moon's shining
With no clothes on her—just herself alone.'

'My head's stuck now!
The devil's in it!
I can't pull away so I'll starve and die!'
'Don't fret, sir, I vow
I'll free you in a minute
If you'll buy this oil—though the price is high.'

'I'll grease the hole
And free you gently
With no wounds left you by the rough, hard stone,
Or shove a live coal
At you incontinently,
And you'll jerk back then, ripped to the bare bone.'

'The oil, Jacques, pray!'
'Where is the money?'
'Here in the belt I wear around my waist.'
'You're kind, sir, to pay
For the luscious, new honey,
All for me and which you will never taste.' "

There had been one other thing to find out. What about the three men who had accompanied him into the fort? Once outside, Conan might be able to do something for them, and I knew, the odds being what they were against even Conan himself escaping, that that was their only chance. Still he might refuse to leave without them. I had asked about them during the stanzas, and, to my great relief, his answer had been: "Later."

" 'Sweet Ann, let's run
To church for wedding;
Your father's overjoyed that we are matched.
And when that's done,

Then it's ho! for our bedding
In our own fine house that Robert has thatched.' "

For one of the few times in my experience I took no note of the applause. I remember giving two or three other songs, then I excused myself and pretended to be very busy with the wine. Though as a matter of fact I drank almost nothing. I had many things to think over in a very short time, and I wanted only solitary silence; but Gregory might start thinking about me if I abruptly took leave of the company. It was he himself who came to my rescue. He had an eye on the harvesting and sent his men to sleep early.

Chapter
Fifteen

A DOZEN men, it turned out, were sharing the loft with me, but I got there first and gained the corner where my weapons were hidden. Those who straggled in after me had had enough wine on top of weariness to bring sleep suddenly. It would be a sound sleep, too, so that when I got ready to move none of them was likely to challenge me.

I lay on my back, open-eyed in the black dark, and methodically worked the problem over. I had pictured Conan as being in some convenient guardhouse out in the court, watched over by no more than one man at a time. Such a sentinel could conceivably be slugged in peace and quiet, but as it was there would be no such easy means of getting at my friend. Aside from the two who stayed in a lighted room with him—they were taking no chances, sure enough!—there would be men bedded down in the main room of the hall, my point of entry, who'd rise at a word from the guards to overwhelm me.

The only solution was to have the garrison's attention otherwise and thoroughly occupied. Well, there was a means of doing that, though it would beget noteworthy dangers on its own account. After a while I was sure that the risk was worth it because there was no other way possessing even a smell of feasibility. Then I considered where to begin and concluded that I could do no better than to operate in the barn where I then was.

Well, now it was coming. I used one of my old tricks for

handling myself, running over some lines of amusing poetry to clear my mind of doubts and hesitations, then I sat up. Snores muted the rustling of the hay as I felt along the wall carrying the two blades still wrapped in my cape in such a way that they wouldn't rattle against each other. My harp I had left behind. If I survived Conan could buy me another; if not, its loss would be a matter of no more concern to me than anything else. I was too intent on the business in hand even to regret the destruction of a fine and prized instrument.

I felt as stealthily feral as my movements. One great thing about action, once it is thoroughly entered into, is its self-containment. It believes thoroughly in its power to complete itself. Nothing else seems possible, let alone logical.

By listening carefully to the snoring and heavy breathing, I avoided stepping on anybody, though I came near falling out of the loft when I reached the edge. A minute later I located the ladder, however, and descended to stand in the litter of hay on the floor below. I could see a little there, but neither my eyes nor my ears could detect a possible watcher. Soft-footing it to the door, I saw that the court looked deserted. There was no sign of anyone being awake, but I knew there were guards on the walls. I stole back.

It didn't take long to make a pile of hay several feet high against the inside wall of the barn. The men above, I thought with hard humor, had better not sleep too soundly or they'd know all about Hell before they got there. Striking sparks to my tinder, I blew the glow to a flame.

The hay smoked heavily, then burst afire. I threw more on, and the blaze stretched, reaching up to the hay drooping down from the loft. One pendent wisp caught but dropped harmlessly. Another took fire and did not drop. The little flame crept upward, got a grip on the main bulk of the hay, and spread like something spilled. A moment later there was the crackling of burning wood, and I waited for no more.

As I ran from it I could hear a man coughing between drowsy curses. I spun when I had gone a few paces and made sure the glow was apparent from the outside. "Fire," I yelled, running again.

"Where?"

"Look! It's the great barn!"

"Oh, my God!"

"Fire!"

The watchmen shouted the dread word repeatedly as they came down from the walls. Possible danger from without was dwarfed by the archfoeman within. I hid in the shadow of the woodshed and watched them finish the rousing. There were frantic shouts from the barn itself now, and a frightened horse screamed horribly. The fire had eaten through the boards at its original starting point and was climbing up the outside.

As I glanced toward the hall again, men began scrambling out, each pausing for an instant for a look then dashing either for the barn or for the well. Gregory was one of the first, for I heard his angry voice yelling commands. I had little fear that any of the men who sped by would look my way. They had serious business on hand.

That barn housed horses as well as winter food for stock. The loss of either, let alone both, would be a crippling one. Then there was the chance that the fire would spread to the rest of the buildings, maybe all of them. There were none so far away as to be out of imminent danger. Prompt work should save the horses and, conceivably, part of the hay and other fodder, but I didn't wait to watch. When no more men came out of the hall I skirted all around it and approached the door from the side away from the barn. Already the radiance reached half across the court.

"Everybody out! Fire!" I shouted as I stepped inside.

"Is it very bad?" a man called nervously.

The voice came from a corner of the east side of the great room. I started to fumble my way toward it in the dark. "Everybody out!" I repeated. "Gregory says every man's needed!" I bumped into a long table and guided myself by it. A streak of light, I could now see, showed under the door. Carefully I drew both swords, leaving the scabbards and the cloak for whomsoever would find them.

"Get moving!" I commanded angrily. "You can't skulk there and let us do all the work!"

"Gregory's orders were to stay here," one of the men inside told me sharply.

I was by then in front of the door, and I pounded it imperiously. "That was before the fire, you fools! Two other buildings have caught now! The whole shebang is likely to go, the hall included!"

I could sense their hesitation and I was about to spring on it with more unnerving arguments when I heard scuffling sounds. "In, brother!" Conan grunted, and I hit the door with my shoulder. It shook but didn't yield, so I stood back and leaped, smashing it with all my weight. There was a slight opening now, I shoved the spare sword through it half to the hilt, and pulled savagely. The sword broke; but its work was done, and I whirled into the room.

Conan had one man under him and a grip on the other's neck. The close quarters had forced the guards to drop their swords, but the man on top was working his knife loose. I killed him with a cut across his back. Taking the dirk, Conan finished the other and rose, panting.

"They forgot and turned their backs," he explained as he bent to help himself to a sword.

Gregory's men had done some shouting before they died, but there was far more noise out in the court. I handed Conan a torch when he straightened up. "Fulke's in the woods' edge off the corner nearest home," I said. "You know how you want to go."

He nodded, and I could see his eyes gleam with the energy of fighting hope. "It'll take several to stop us."

Up to that point my plan had worked, with some luck to help, as well as could be wished, but just ahead were the dangers I had foreseen. By the time we had reached the court the flames were so high and bright that a book could have been read almost anywhere within the fort. Moreover, the heat—for the barn was past the point where there was any chance of saving it—was such that it had driven people back toward the hall.

Having saved the still excitedly snorting horses, all of the garrison except for a group engaged in wetting down the thatch of other buildings was waiting idly, if alertly, for the moment when a threat of more damage should call them into action. Indeed, some, seeking a cool vantage point from which to enjoy the terrible fascination of a destructive fire at night, had joined the women and children on the walls. A few were weaponless, but most had instinctively caught up their arms when roused from sleep.

Whether or not Conan had had any more reasons, strategic or otherwise, for advocating the north wall, I had observed that the steps leading up to it were the nearest to the doors from which we now burst. Tossing away his torch, he led me full tilt around a knot of gabbling men, and we were half way to the wall before anyone was struck by our haste. Then some-one shrieked: "Jesus! It's Conan!"

After that plenty of things happened. A bunch tried to cut us off, still tugging to get their swords out as they rushed us. We in turn, with our advantage of momentum, blasted through them without bothering to strike. Just before we reached the stairs one man with more hardihood than brains got in our way. Conan parried his outstretched sword and mowed him down by the force of his charge. I ran over him, feeling one foot sink in his belly, and then we were at the wall.

The steps were short logs imbedded in the packed dirt, and we took them by threes. But men were concentrating to wait for us at the top, so that was where our real difficulties began. They were coming up behind us, too, naturally, and I turned to hold them back while my friend cleared the way as best he could. Men in the fort had stopped their fire-prevention ac-tivities to watch; others were mounting the walls at different points and running toward us; and Gregory was bawling orders to both groups. All this I noticed in one flash, and then I had no time to notice anything except who was trying to kill me.

There were some few so minded; but only two could be ef-fective at a time, and I was in a strong position steeply above them. Conan had much the harder task. After a moment I nicked one of my opponents, drove his mate back, and stole a peek over my shoulder. Two men, incapacitated or dead, lay at Conan's feet. He had seized footing on top, and I backed up to stand just below him.

"Shall we shove and jump?" I barked.

"Whip 'em down, then come fast, and we'll try," he gasped.

By tremendous exertion I backed them down four steps. The sounds told me that Conan still kept his place on the wall, so I yelled to let him know and came leaping. The weight of my drive carried me past him into the melee, and a man in the rear rank toppled over the waist-high palisade with a cry. I gutted one but wasn't fast enough in drawing back my blade to ward a stroke from another. I shifted but not far enough, and his sword sliced across my ribs. It wasn't a bad wound, but avoiding a worse one had made me break my rush. Still I held my ground, and Conan surged along the little swath I had left.

"Don't stop!" he cried.

They gave a little before the sweep of his weapon, and I piled after, stabbing one and kneeing another in the groin. The trick was to make it across the wall before they could take us full in the back. But I don't think we ever would have succeeded if Gregory hadn't spoiled his own game.

Not that it was stupidity on his part. His dilemma was that Conan dead in advance was an asset that Chilbert would appreciate but one for which he wouldn't pay. "Take Conan alive!" Gregory was howling. "Kill the other, but capture Conan! I'll hang you all if he's killed!"

Their chief's threat left them undecided, and Conan grasped the moment. Knocking two more men off the wall as he charged, he beat through the wavering swords, spun, and braced. I was after him on the instant, but I hesitated beside him, and he snarled at me. "Over!" he ordered, so over I went. Ducking beneath his swinging blade, I flung my own sword where I wouldn't land on it—there was plenty of light in which to see where it fell—vaulted over the palisade, and dropped where God put me.

Unlike the stone walls Conan was building, earthworks though steep, cannot be perpendicular. I hit with a jolt and tumbled swiftly to the bottom, but my descent didn't have the absolute force of a fall. I was well bruised, but neither my wind nor my sense of direction was knocked out of me. I rolled completely over before I could jerk myself erect, then I lunged for my sword.

The men who had been shoved over before me, not being prepared for the fall, had in general not fared so well. One was nursing an arm, and another was holding his head dazedly. The third, however, was seemingly uninjured, and he had preserved the presence of mind to mark my weapon. He had just stooped to pick it up when I landed on his back, my knife in my hand. I pulled my brand from under him and turned to look up at Conan. His sword was flashing to the ground, while he himself was on the outside of the palisade. One of the men that gripped him he pulled clean over, and the remaining arms could not hold the double weight.

Catching up Conan's blade I ran to meet the two bodies skidding groundward, ready to stab one of them if necessary. But my friend had ridden the other man like a stone boat, and he lay inert after rolling. I pulled Conan to his feet, noting that he was bleeding in a couple of places. Then I handed him his sword, and we sprinted.

The men who were dropping down the wall after us were danger enough, but inside I could hear Gregory yelling for horses. It wouldn't take them long to cut down our lead, and there was light enough for them to keep us spotted as long as we stayed near the fort. Escape would take us longer, and we wouldn't find it easy to pierce the dragnet it would give them a chance to throw out; but our only hope was to try to reach darkness. I didn't have to waste time or breath explaining this to Conan. Having got off in the lead, I dove downhill, and he followed a half a pace behind.

"Down the hill north! Straight down from where I stand," somebody on the wall was directing. Foot runners were pounding along right behind us, and, further away but more ominous I heard the rumble of a cavalcade. The sky-searing flames were roaring and crackling, there were shouts and squeals from all ages and sexes, and dogs yapped. But above all the din I could hear Gregory promising to hang everybody if we got away.

I was beginning to feel the pace more with each stride. After all, the hot work of the past few minutes had been prefaced on my part by a long day of riding and walking. I felt generally used up, my wind was going, and my side ached where the sword had slashed it.

Conan was running easily, seemingly in no great distress, and as I could still manage considerable speed we were giving them a good race. Two men, however, had the legs of us; and the horses had rounded the corner of the fort to thunder down the slope. I was no good to help, but Conan sidestepped to let the leading pursuer pitch over his leg, then jammed a foot on his back to wind him. The second man tried to stop without slowing. He found out his mistake when he landed hard on his knees and my friend booted him in the solar plexus.

I watched that over my shoulder. Tiring as rapidly as I was, I couldn't spare anything from my lead. We were well down hill and out of the light then, but though we were keeping ahead of the other runners they were near enough to keep us in sight and point us out to the oncoming horsemen. I peered ahead, and it was then that I saw at least one point in favor of that particular side. We were descending on a field full of cut and drying grain.

I knew it must be that, albeit in the confusion of darkness the stacks could just as well be taken for swine or sheep—or men on their hands and knees. Gazing at such a mass by night, a man will see it change size and shape, yes, and move, too. I've seen a bush masquerade as a lurking man and brazen it out until I was all but near enough to touch it. "Taking cover," I panted.

Well into the field I cut my pace, dropped, as Conan passed me, rolled over swiftly into a group of several stacks, and simply crouched beside one. Our pursuers passed by ones and twos but halted a little beyond, where the tangent the riders had taken led to a meeting. I didn't want to risk showing the white of my face for a look, but I gathered that they were in a satisfactory state of puzzlement.

"I don't know where they went," I heard a man admitting. "I saw 'em one minute, and then they were gone."

"Gone, Hell!" Gregory said angrily. "They couldn't run that much faster than you. They're hiding here somewhere. Now you men on foot hightail back to the fort and try to see that that damned fire doesn't burn anything else." He next harangued the horsemen. "On the off chance they're still legging it, spread out and ride hard till I give the word. If we don't locate 'em by then we'll turn and walk back slowly. It'll be easier to spot 'em going toward the fire. Look behind and under anything big enough to hide a runt flea. Now get going, all but Henri, Louis, and Charles. This is where we lost 'em, so I want you men to stay here and ride 'em down if they try to break cover."

Keeping my hand out of sight, I used my sleeve to brush my hair over my eyes and twisted my head to glimpse the men walking back to the fort. As tired men will, they straggled along separately, most of them silent while waiting to get their wind back. The last one, however, was humming a certain song between reaches for breath. That man was Conan, and I rose to fall in behind him.

"Hey! Who's that?" one of the watching riders called.

The entire band of us halted, men without faces in the dark. I didn't dare speak because of my accent, but my friend gasped out an oath. "My name's Conan," he said sarcastically. Several laughed, the mounted man cursed the night, and we all plodded on again. Luckily there was too much general tiredness as we progressed uphill into more and more light for anyone to pay attention to anyone else. Moreover, the excitement over the manhunt was nicely balanced by the excitement over the fire. Men approaching it, inevitably looked at it and little besides.

Nevertheless, we had to continue straight toward the fort or draw suspicion. Fatigue seconding my anxiety to escape attention, I walked with my head bowed, reckoning the odds. With the riders decoyed to the north side we might be able to make a successful break for it. Or there were even grounds for hoping, what with everyone concentrating on the fire, that we could slip past unnoticed.

Suddenly I groaned as well as I could with what breath I had. A rider was coming down hill. That he would discover our identity seemed sure, although on the long chance he wouldn't I continued to eye the earth. In another second he was right on us, and I hardened my muscles for action.

"I never thought I'd see a good horse thief like you out for a stroll," the fellow said conversationally.

As my head snapped up I saw Conan's doing the same. Father Clovis was grinning down at us. "I was just going to see how the hunt was prospering and maybe offer my ecclesiastical services to Finnian here when they hanged him—if they waited. But it looks as if the Devil's at his old tricks, mothering his own." His face sobered. "I wish I could give you this horse, but Gregory would hang me instead, and I wouldn't like that. Anything else I can do?"

"You might ride around to the southwest woods fringe and whoop for Fulke to come running," Conan said. "Thanks Father."

"Welcome as wine." He grinned again. "Nice fire you started, Finnian. Hated to leave it."

He changed his course, riding briskly now, and we dawdled upward. Opposing the urge to hurry was the necessity of regaining a little wind before we should be called upon for more violence. That would probably come when we reached the gates.

No doubt we were observed by men on the wall, but we weren't recognized purely because our presence was so improbable. Those ahead of us, who had stretched the distance between us while we were talking to Clovis, had already entered the fort by the time we were in the shadow of its walls.

Our luck had been good, and we couldn't expect it to hold.

A man glancing down was impressed by our bloody and battered condition. "Looks like you boys made the mistake of catching up with Conan," he gibed.

"Aw, go to hell!" Conan growled.

Only then apparently did it strike the fellow that he couldn't identify us as colleagues. "Say, who are you?" he demanded. We quickened our pace, but before we could goad our tired legs into running again he had discovered the truth. "It's them!" he yelled. "It's Conan and the bard! Hey! You in the court, out and get 'em! It's Conan and the bard! Right here, I tell you!"

I couldn't be sure how much of a spurt was left in me, but I didn't try to hoard my strength. The one man who succeeded in clearing the gate before we reached it had seen too much of us to want to tackle us unsupported. Taking one look at us bearing down on him, he sprang back so hastily he fell. As we sped past I saw at least three on whom we wouldn't have much of a lead, and others were swarming after them. Still I knew some of them had also taken more exercise then they wanted, and as followup for a hard day in the fields, to boot; and there was no longer the imminent threat of horse pursuit.

They were trying to arrange for that, however, for men and women were ballooning the news to Gregory. He and his dragnet might be out of hearing, but the men he'd stationed by the grain stacks were assuredly not. And they would be all that was needed.

We were plunging down the south slope, and that fact alone allowed me to maintain any speed. Suddenly I knew that I would be finished when I reached the bottom. "Fulke!" I cried desperately, but my voice had no strength.

Glancing back, Conan saw my plight, for the leading pursuers were almost on me. "Fulke!" he boomed. "Here!"

My ears were ringing, and I couldn't be sure whether there was an answer or not. But even if he was on his way the minstrel would have to come fast to do us any good.

A second later, indeed, I stumbled for weariness and fell. "Fulke!" Conan bellowed again as he turned to pull me to my feet. Then we stood back to back while they swept around us, trying to beat us down by their weight of numbers so that Conan could be taken alive. In the heat of action none of us heard the running horses.

My legs played me false as I swung at a man, and I was on

the ground again when Fulke larruped into them with the two lead mounts. Those of them who were not knocked down scattered to get their bearings. Conan himself had been tripped in the course of their rush for safety, but he rose promptly, hauling me to my feet once more as he did so. "Fulke!" he cried for the last time.

Locating us, Fulke wheeled to gallop back through them. Conan heaved me into a saddle and scrambled up on a horse himself just as they closed in on us again. We rode down one or two of them, and I realized with what little perception remained to me that we were free.

Chapter
Sixteen

ALL my mental and physical faculties were being used to keep me in the saddle, but Fulke, who was leading the way, was riding with his head over his shoulder. "Three horsemen by the gates," he announced, "but they're just sitting there."

"I guess you were something of a surprise to them, Fulke." Conan, beside me, was apparently also watching. "So-ho. There goes one back to break the news to Gregory. Well, we've got a handy lead."

"We'll need every inch of it," the youngster commented. "Their horses haven't been all over France today, the way ours have."

Nevertheless, we weren't crowded, though our horses would never have guessed it from the way he hustled them. A modicum of strength had returned to me, and I was breathing normally by the time we reached the trail. Fulke had left some branches across the road to mark the turning. He scooped them up, and, single file and on foot, we entered the forest.

Our mounts had no breath to lavish on whinnying, but we took them quite a ways in lest their stamping around betray our whereabouts. Naturally they knew about the trail, but without a marker it would take a lucky man to find it without careful search; and we could use all the time procurable for rest.

They overshot, possibly working on the theory that they might overtake us while *we* were searching for the path. At any rate we heard the whole gang clattering by at a good clip just as we were tethering our steeds. That done, we felt our way back toward the road so as to be in a position to keep track of developments.

Worn though Conan and I were, the sickness of exhaustion was over, and we could now begin to savor our triumph. It had been a whirlpool of a night, and the fact that we had won through to more life was heady knowing. It was as if we were both a little drunk, and we giggled like schoolboys on a nocturnal pilfering raid while we whispered questions and discussed lively moments.

"That was smart work, using ogham," Conan complimented me. "Lord! I hadn't thought of that for years."

"What gets me," I said, "is how the devil you managed to be one of the parade when Gregory ordered all the runners back to the fort."

He chuckled. "Oh, that was easy. I took a dive just after you did, but I jumped up to run right behind them. They'd just met the horsemen, so they didn't notice. I figured they hadn't bothered to count themselves when they slithered down the wall, and naturally nobody could see to identify anybody else. They were looking for someone who was hiding, not a man in plain sight."

"Good old Clovis certainly played his hand well," I observed. "I hope he gets to be pope."

"He'd make a good one," Conan agreed. "That grace of his was a masterpiece."

"He told me where to look for you," Fulke put in, "so I was half way to you when I heard you call."

"He's all right," Conan reaffirmed the general opinion. Then he thought of something. "By the way, Finnian, where the devil did you come from? Not that I wasn't glad to see you." He reached out to grip my arm, and I felt good.

"Well, that's something of a story, too," I said, proceeding to give the gist of my recent experiences. We had shifted to reminiscence of our first meeting when we heard the enemy returning. They were moving slowly, looking for the trail, and we rose in case flight should be necessary.

"Here it is!" one of them exclaimed excitedly.

"What do you expect me to do about it?" Gregory asked sourly, "cut it up and eat it? Now look. If they've found it already we're licked, but they may not have. We may have chased them past it, or they may have ducked into the woods to keep from being chased past it. But this is the way they've got to come if they're going to do any more traveling tonight. Ten of you will stay here in ambush with me, and the rest will go back to the fort. If there's anything left of it to go back to, that is."

Gregory had had a bad evening. His prize had escaped and bid fair to get away entirely, a good deal of his property had been destroyed, and several of his people had been killed, not to mention all that were wounded or badly knocked about. Chilbert, moreover, might not be at all nice about Conan's loss. My shoulders shook. The more bile traitors had to drink the better I liked it.

The only thing that detracted from an otherwise thorough triumph was the knowledge that Chilbert, in spite of all we had done, was preordained to profit. He would be disappointed at finding that Conan had given him the slip for yet a second time, but Gregory had attempted his last political horse trading as an independent agent. He, his troops, and his strategically situated land would be ruled by the count from now on. The alternative was facing Conan's wrath unaided.

Our pursuers crashed into the woods on the other side of the road, murmuring sullenly. Then at Gregory's word they were silent. We, too, refrained from further speech and movement. It got cold there as the night wore on, but we who had been so near the colder realm of death, had no complaints. Nor was the day far off, as Gregory had pointed out. In an hour or so we felt the breeze that often ushers in the dawn, and the rustling of the leaves it stirred blotted the slight noises of our retreat.

It was while we were still only part way to our mounts that we heard horses from southwards on the road. "Chilbert!" Conan whispered. "It's too bad we can't wait to see them meet and hear what they have to say."

But instead we stole along the path more rapidly still and reached our animals just as the fading of night was perceptible in tiny patches through the trees above us. Behind we could hear Gregory's men talking again as they got ready to greet the newcomers. Under cover of that we got under way, afoot until the trail could be followed with the eye. Then we mounted and increased our pace in proportion to the visibility until we were riding as fast as conditions would permit.

The horses were in somewhat the same condition as ourselves, sufficiently recuperated to go on albeit stiff and sore. Conan and I had bruises and cuts to boot, which were painfully lashed now and again by branches, but we were too delighted with ourselves to let such things worry us much. We talked, joked and sang until the midday warmth worked on our sleeplessness. Mine soon became the source of a dull agony, and the rest of the day was a succession of wakings barely in time to save myself from falling out of the saddle.

As a matter of fact, I was all for resting during the afternoon, but Conan, aside from his natural longing to get home, took the sensible position that an hour's respite would only serve as a teaser. So on we went somehow, the others in not much better shape than I myself and caught sight of the fortress just after sundown.

People rushed out to meet us as soon as we were near enough to be identified, but I don't know much what was said except that everybody was glad. I just grinned at them vaguely. "Don't ask them any questions now," Ann squelched the insistently curious. "We've got the answer to the only important one, and now they're going to rest."

Jean was there to steady me as I slid from my horse, finally at home, and right behind him I saw Marie. Maybe I'd spoken to her before, but I thought she looked as if she expected me to say something. I blinked at her. "Hello, Marie! I'm thirsty."

It was a simple statement of fact, but they suddenly howled with laughter. "Glory be to God! He's ready for a drink again!" Jean shouted. "Get the man wine before he kills somebody!"

But I wasn't ready for a drunk—what I had really had in mind was water—and I couldn't have killed a butterfly.

A half cup of the wine they brought vanquished me. I hardly recollect being helped to bed.

It was late the next morning when, after looking out at a wet, chilly day, I washed and slouched stiffly into the hall. There seemed to be quite a few things the matter with me, but the one of which I was most conscious was lack of nourishment.

The rain had stopped the harvest, and the household was assembled around the fireplace. Conan and Fulke were already breakfasting, and the rest were impatiently waiting for them to finish and give out the details of our exploit. My advent elicited boisterous greetings. "Here comes another man to eat us out of house and home," Rainault issued a general warning.

"I suspect it's been done already, judging from the way those two gobblers are going at it." I looked at Ann anxiously. "Is there anything left?"

Conan grinned as she kissed me good morning. "Nice but not sustaining," he remarked. "But you don't have to worry, brother. She's so afraid there won't be enough for you that she's practically starving me to death."

"I cooked one goose for only three men," Ann said, "but Conan's idea of sharing it is to give you and Fulke the feet and the feathers."

I smiled at Marie as I sat down and abruptly recalled that I hadn't expected to return when I set out. Well, it had happened that I had, and I was glad that it had so happened. I was even gladder when I saw the portion of goose I was receiving. Ann had certainly seen to it that I wasn't scanted.

I ate hugely and drank plenty of wine, a thing I seldom do in the morning. But they were in the mood to indulge me, and I was in no mood to stop them. My veins glowed pleasantly soon, and I was drowsily happy, liking myself and everybody else.

"Now let's hear about it, and don't leave out anything," Ann commanded when we were through.

Personally I had no intention of exerting myself to construct a coherent narrative. I stretched out on the floor before the fire. The bear rug was otherwise satisfactory, but I kept shifting my head to find just the proper spot. Then suddenly to my intense surprise Marie matter-of-factly seated herself on the floor and took my head on her lap. It was very comfortable, and I sighed contentedly as I looked up at her.

"You're extremely beautiful, but I'll probably go to sleep," I murmured. "Do you mind?"

Her hand felt fine upon my brow. "No, sleep will do you good."

Somehow I had never thought of her as being kind. I half closed my eyes, putting in comments as they occurred to me, while Conan and Fulke carried the burden of the story. Well fed, well wined, well liked, happy with achievement, and cherished by a pretty girl, I have never experienced such complete, though passive, satisfaction. The tale and its attendant ejaculations of excitement and approval grew farther away. As I had prophesied, I slept again.

When I waked everybody but us two had gone. The fire had died out, and, though a glance told me it was now sunny outside, it was damply cool indoors. I sat up and looked at Marie. "How long did I sleep?" I asked guiltily.

"Only a couple of hours." She smiled and held out her hands. "Help me up."

I grew more contrite, seeing how stiffly she rose. "Hell, I'm sorry! You should have roused me." I was touched by her consideration and kept hold of her hands.

"Oh, I remember a time when you did something for me," she replied. "And you've earned a little coddling today." Her smile changed to a grin. "You took to it like a kitten." She was feeling very friendly and wondering if I was going to kiss her.

"I enjoyed it," I assured her; and then I resolved her doubts. She had a warm, generous mouth.

One good kiss deserved another as far as I was concerned, but she shook her head. "It's only recently that as something to kiss you've ranked above spiders. I've got to get used to the idea."

"Well, if we can't make love let's at least be comfortable," I accepted her attitude. "Let's go out in the sun and bake the chill out of us."

People hailed me as we walked across the court in amiable silence, but all were too busy to do more than proffer a word of congratulation. As a matter of course, we sought the low place in the wall where we had sat a couple of nights before. It was warm but not hot, and the slight breeze was fresh from a washed world.

"I thought you weren't coming back," she said after a moment or so.

"So did I," I chuckled, "but with a couple of dozen sword swingers herding me I forgot to be choosy about places. As a matter of fact, I forgot I had intended to go anywhere else until this morning."

"I suppose we should be grateful for your absent-mindedness."

"Why not?" I asked. "I am myself. I like being with everybody here." I looked at her. "How about you? Are you going to get along all right?"

"All right," she echoed the words flatly. "I like the people, too, and Ann's been most kind. She says she's glad of my company." Marie set her lips. "She'd better be. I don't see how she's ever going to get rid of me."

An orphaned and landless girl has a tough row to hoe; and I was particularly concerned to think anybody was depressed on this day when I was feeling so triumphantly pleased with life. Noticing my look of commiseration, she instantly smiled and took my arm.

"I'm sorry, Finnian. You're worrying about me, and I shouldn't have said anything to make you do so today. You've earned carefreedom and rest; and the rest, at least, you'll certainly need. There's going to be high feasting tonight, and everybody will want you to drink with them."

"I'll try to accommodate them," I said mildly.

"I bet you will. And once you have been so obliging what will you do?"

"I don't know any more." I laughed ruefully. "Sometimes I think I'll never get out of this country. Certainly no plans I make to that end come to any account." I was more serious than I seemed, for I was thinking once more of the Pictish priest and wondering if I was doomed to remain there while my life lasted. And suppose I was?

I mulled that over, and my mind, always apt to go rabbit chasing when not disciplined to bear on a specific problem, hunted out the possibilities of such a situation. There could be far worse dooms than living where I was, providing Chilbert didn't win the anticipated war. I would be among friends, with a record of service to ensure my welcome. More than that, I'd be the chosen peer of the man in power, and as such a recognized leader. Therefore, if Conan won I could have holdings and followers of my own.

The vision grew, awing me. Since schooldays I had had no companion for long, and I had accepted that as inevitable. I had never owned more than I could carry with me, though often considerably less. Now the odds were one in two that chieftainship would be all but thrust upon me. And one of the responsibilities of a chief as well as the ordained procedure for a man with a hall of his own was to get married.

I thought that out and shook my head dazedly. If the logic of events was as implacable as it seemed, I would marry the girl beside me. As a woman she was looking for a place of her own with a man she could like. With my newly won land I would need or ask no dowry, and Conan and Ann would give their approval. So much for her side of the bargain. As for me, I admired and trusted her, having seen her bearing in hard circumstances. She was a girl, too, that a man could make love to with conviction.

My glance, which had been wandering, returned to give her a veiled scrutiny. "Still drowsy?" she asked.

I came out of it. "No, just mooning," I confessed. Aware that all the foregoing had been built on the shadowy base of hypothesis, I felt silly. But the train of thought had left its mark. I closed one eye slowly. Suppose the hypothesis became reality. And after the logic of events had married a man off, did it stay around to help him out in the pinches?

Conan had been inspecting the walls with Ann, and now they were drawing near the part where we were sitting. "How do things look?" I called, knowing almost as well as he did but eager to start a conversation that might free me from further disturbing speculation.

They picked their way across the unevenness of the uncompleted stretch to join us. "Apparently nobody was loafing while I was Gregory's guest. If it wasn't for the harvest it'd be finished now." He patted a stone as he and his wife seated themselves. "In a few weeks I'm going to have a place Ann can hold without looking up from her sewing. Then if certain polecates stay alive it won't be because nobody tried to kill them."

"Gregory wouldn't happen to be the first by any chance?"

He sighed. "Gregory would happen to be a polecat, but not one that I'll kill. I led three men into that trap of his, and to pay their way out I'll guarantee not to follow the matter up." He chuckled. "After all we fined him pretty heavily what with one thing and another. I think he wished God had made him a good boy before the night was over."

"How are you going to negotiate with him?" Ann asked. "Sending a man or a few men would just give him additional hostages."

"Right as usual, girl," he nodded. "No, I'm going to visit the Abbot in a couple of days to offer a personal thanks for the help he gave. I'll ask him then to act as go-between, and I have no doubt he'll be willing to send a man on this simpler, less dangerous mission."

"There's excitement by the gate," Marie remarked. "Maybe Gregory decided to make his offer beforehand."

We looked up with interest to see a horseman enter and dismount, to be hidden from us in a swiftly growing group. At about the point where impatience was driving us to call out to them we saw Fulke hurrying toward us. "It's a stranger, Conan," he announced. "He claims he's just come from the other side of the Loire, he isn't sure whether or not he knows anybody here, and he wasn't sent by anybody."

"Well, feed him and keep an eye on him," my friend directed.

"Yes, but he says he must speak to you personally, and that doesn't jibe with the rest of his talk. I think he's a spy."

"A lot of men are these days," Conan said. "Make sure he hasn't got any knives hidden on him and bring him over."

The young man Fulke and Rainault escorted between them looked tired and not too well. His features were handsome for all their drawn appearance, and he carried his compact, slender figure as if he knew he was a man. He halted to look up at us, gazing inquiringly first at Conan and then at me. As our eyes met his face lit up with genuine pleasure. "Hello, Finnian!" he said enthusiastically. "I told you I'd remember."

Everybody was staring at me expectantly, but nothing registered in that first astonished searching of my past. "Maybe you remember, but it's obvious that Finnian doesn't," Conan remarked. "Where did you meet him?"

"You're Conan, I take it?"

"Yes. I was told you wanted to speak to me. But let's get this point straightened out first."

"Surely." The newcomer turned his eyes to me again. "You fished me out of the river and made the monks look after me."

I knew who he was then, of course. Still, considering that I had never seen him erect and in full control of his faculties before, it wasn't strange that I hadn't recognized him. "That's right. Glad to see you up and about. The Danes put an arrow in him," I explained to the others.

"You certainly get around and meet the people, brother. Can you vouch for him, now that you place him?"

"Yes, I think so," I said. "He comes from too far west to know Chilbert."

"The name is Raymond, in case anyone's interested," the fellow said.

"There remains to be explained," I pointed out, "how it happens that you elected to come here."

"Well, I had to go somewhere. The monks had their hands full of trouble without an unwanted guest, and I was able to walk by the time the Dane scare was over. The scum turned back when they saw what strength Chilbert had against them."

Having warned Thorgrim that such would probably be the case, I nodded. "Well?"

He gestured with both hands. "My chief and my people were killed and the hall burnt. I had no wish to go back and see the charred carrion, so I decided to look for a place in the vicinity. From what I could gather there was no leader worth tying to on the south side of the Loire, but I learned that across the river there were men who were doing things. I didn't like what I heard about Chilbert, and I'm not a priest."

He had looked at Conan while making the last remark, but now he turned to me again. "The Danes had left some horses without owners. I wasn't up to it, but Gaimar caught one and got it across the river for me. He told me to tell you he was sorry for being a louse."

"He's one no longer." Though puzzled, I was pleased, for I hate to think sourly of a man with whom I'd shared pleasant times. "But see here. What the devil made Gaimar think you'd meet me in these parts?"

His eyes gleamed. "It seems that Gaimar had a lot of non-monastic acquaintances."

"He did," I chuckled.

"It seems, too, that although you never said where you came from he'd heard a story of a bard who'd stood by Conan in a walloping good fight. He couldn't figure out what you were doing at the abbey, but he always thought you were the one."

"I owe him something for keeping his mouth shut," I said.

"Well," he concluded, "that decided me that the trip up here would be worth it. I knew if you were for Conan he must be all right."

My helpless glance brought a grin from Conan who, I could see, had already made his judgement. "I'll take him on if you say so, brother. How do you want him counted?''

It was not only because I was partly responsible for his presence or because of a man's obscure urge to continue being helpful to anyone he has once assisted that I was moved to say what I did. I had been favorably impressed by his directness and his general air of competence as he told his story. "Until he's well, as my guest. Thanks, Conan.''

Raymond's face lighted, then composed itself as he voiced his appreciation. My words had granted him the most favorable position he could have wished for. Under other circumstances he might have had a long pull proving his right to membership in the inner circle of the household. And once accepted there he could not well be relegated to the outer reaches.

"Glad to have you," Conan said and turned to Marie. "Would you see to it that Finnian's friend has the meal I think he could do with?''

She jumped to the ground and smiled up at me. "As one of your waifs and strays I'll be glad to help another.''

We looked after them briefly as they walked from us. "Nice-looking pair of youngsters," Conan commented, yawning.

Chapter
Seventeen

"SPEAKING of Marie," my friend went on after a moment, "Ann informs me of another piece of business you've done for us. Who was the chief you snatched her from?"

He didn't know Thorgrim, but having done viking work himself, he could see exactly what I had been up against. He whistled as I started to sketch the scene, but I didn't have to take the matter seriously now. I proceeded to fabricate a grotesque picture of my own fright, the manner in which Thorgrim had been carried away by his sense of drama, as well as his later realization of having been sold, and Marie's valiant struggles to keep from being rescued. Conan roared at the comedy of it, but Ann laughed only a little.

"It seems that everyone here is in your debt, Finnian. I wish there was something we could do for you."

"We could give him a drink," her husband said hopefully.

Ann gave up. This was our day, with our big celebration imminent, and from now on nobody could make either of us serious about anything. "And I suppose," she smiled, "that at least one of us could give himself a drink, too. I'm going in now to see about the final preparations for the banquet. I'll have the wine sent out."

When we saw the decanter we sauntered over to the table and seated ourselves with the deliberation of men who approach a great task with full respect for what has to be accomplished. We sat slowly, backs leaned against the hall, legs stretched out to the exact and carefully found point of comfort, and brooded, solemn-eyed, on the cups my friend was gently filling. Then we eyed one another, seeking inspiration for the toast.

"Wine and whisky for our friends," he intoned.

"Amen," I said. "Whey and water for our enemies!"

"Mixed!" he said.

We held it on the palate, swallowed and sighed. It was from the bottom of the cellar. I closed my eyes, then opened one. "There are only two people I can think of right now who deserve a wine like that."

He nodded. "This is one of the times when I'm profoundly impressed by the exquisite rightness of things."

The feast began early, for Conan wanted the men to get their celebrating over with in time to rest up for a full day's labor the next day, a necessity in view of the pressing tasks on hand. Nevertheless, when we were called to eat we had a craftsmanlike foundation, neither so large that food might make us feel sodden nor so small that food might make us feel sober.

By design we entered last and paused with genial self-consciousness to hear the shouts of greetings. Hell, it was our party. "Shall we give it to 'em now?" Conan asked.

"I was never one to keep a good song from anybody," I assented, and we promptly boomed out some lines hatched between us by the aid of the uncritical heat of wine.

> "Who looks like a toad that a snake's half swallowed?
> Who stinks like a corpse that a wolf's half hollowed?
> Whose plans were a traitor's? Whose plans weren't
>   followed?
> Gregory's! Drink his soul to Hell!
>
> "Who harried this kite and mangled his pinions?
> Who burned up his crops and slaughtered his minions?
> Who and with what swords? Conan's and Finnian's!
> Wine for the brands, and drink it well!
>
> "Who bellowed for kegs of wine by the wagon?
> Who poured it in cups the size of a flagon?

Who then walked off with no trace of a jag on?
We know—wahoo!—
> *but*
>> *we*
>>> *won't*
>>>> *tell."*

Everybody was already in a good humor, and our own very ripe good humor but served to heighten the general tendency. They whooped, and we saluted them while taking stock of the seating arrangements. Our two empty seats were in the middle of one side of the family table, of course; and Ann had thoughtfully arranged for Fulke to sit next to us in his earned place as one of the honored. Beyond him were Jean and his wife, while Rainault and his were next to where I would sit. Ann and Marie were beyond them again at one end of the board. Raymond was not there, having evidently elected to sleep.

It was customary to keep the side toward the generality in the hall open, but there were unusual and unbalanced features of the placing. "You are not sitting next to me, my little dove," Conan called out deeply.

"I am not, my hero," Ann called back with serene firmness. "I have no intention of having my ears deafened and my ribs bruised when you start showing how you and Finnian massacred armies."

Conan laughed. "My wise woman!" he praised her as we finally advanced to seat ourselves. "You know, I think we've come to the right place, brother. They have wine here."

"Providential," I pronounced. "Shall we have a toast?"

"Naturally. I suppose you have sense enough to know whom we're going to toast first?"

I caught Marie's amused eye on us and winked. "Fill the cups," I challenged, "and I'll prove that I know."

Conan handed mine to me, and we rose. "We'll drink now," he began loudly, and as he spoke everyone in the hall started to lift his wine. Fulke was imitating the others, but I reached over and spilled his to the floor. "To the man who brought the horses to the men who needed them!" my friend went on. "Were it not for him we'd be feeding crows instead of drinking with you all tonight. To Fulke!" And we two, at least, drained our cups to him. Others might not give him justice, but we appreciated to the full the special courage and coolness required for waiting, inactive, for the right moment. When every sort of devilment is breaking loose within sight and hearing, it's harder to stay still than to act.

Fulke was stunned and embarrassed, which was as it should have been. A cocky youngster is as unpleasantly hard to overlook as a neighboring goat on a damp night. Conan picked up the lad's cup, filled it and thrust it before him. "You can drink this next one," he smiled.

Still red, Fulke looked up. "Father Clovis?"

"None other," I assured him, "and we'll throw the Abbot into the cup for good measure."

After Jean, his good-natured face laughing with wine, had toasted the chief and Rainault had called for a drink to me, we sat down to eat. I understand it was a particularly good meal and that I ate like a starving bear, but I have no recollection of that. All I can remember is that Conan or I would stop every now and then and loudly propose to the other some new thing to drink to. The only one I can bring back was dedicated to the life-long sacrifice the capon had made for us.

While we were getting our second wind after the feast, Fulke sang for us. He had a pleasant voice and played well, though the viol has but flimsy tones if a man is used to the power and sweep of the harp. As I listened dreamily, I looked around, liking what I saw and counting it my own. No idea could have startled me just then, but actually a startling thing had taken place in my life. I was thinking of this place as my home and of these people as my clansmen.

And why not? It was a fine thing to see them, young people and old, hearty and happy at the feast, snug in their fortress. And each of them would always have a smile or a good word for me. They already looked on me as a leader; only my acceptance of the status was needed to make it official. As for those at the table with me, it was not likely that I would ever again find so many I liked as well.

I looked them over, finishing with Marie. The insidious thing about conceiving the idea of marrying a particularly pretty girl is that the more a man thinks about it the more reasonable it seems. A little pulse of passion stirred in me as she caught my glance, smiled, and resumed talking to Ann. No, there didn't seem to be any sense in going anywhere else, now that I rationally considered. The Lord could attest that I'd done all the traveling, and more, that I'd ever benefit by.

A bard didn't have to keep moving except in pursuit of new audiences, and as a landed man I wouldn't have to scratch for such a catch-as-catch-can living. That would be a fine thing, too, for instead of using good effort to turn out a lot of popular nonsense I could give my time to writing something I could be proud of, maybe. And the matter of a livelihood aside, I could get more done if I didn't have to be always on the go. Take Virgil and Horace: they stayed on the premises and got things accomplished. I nodded a head full of vague plans for master works.

Fulke had finished another piece and was being called on for more. I looked at his instrument enviously, wondering where and how I was going to obtain another harp. I could make the frame and string one myself, but where I'd get the proper stringing was something else again. Possibly, I thought hopefully, Fulke himself had the craft of preparing the gut.

When he begged off to rest awhile, the women cleared away the dishes and left us with the wine. In token that we were resuming our obligations I filled Conan's cup and my own. "You know," I said, my face aglow with the sudden inspiration, "there's someone to whom we owe attention that we haven't fixed up this evening."

He eyed me with interest. "Who could that be?"

"The lad we both love—Chilbert!"

"Right, by God!" Conan brought his big fist down on the table with a bang. I caught up my cup in time, but he slopped the others and flipped Rainault's neatly into his lap. Everybody but the latter was delighted, and he was appeased as soon as his cup was filled again. "Now about Chilbert," Conan said in a businesslike voice.

After a weighty discussion of forms and styles we decided on something approximating the Irish satire. With this to go on we set to work, gravely weighing the abusive values of words and metaphors until we'd hit upon our theme. Then with Conan supplying hints and occasional epithets, I set to the making. By dipping a finger in wine I was able to keep track of the rhymes and key words.

Loud talking and louder laughter were incessant in the room. But we had attained that hushed clarity which attends the later stages of a careful wine drunk. Other beverages do not grant this Indian summer of the brain, and our fellows might not have been sharing its charm; but we were fully endowed. We worked with unperturbed concentration, pausing only to pour and drink. Finally, after mumbling it over together a couple of times, we shouted for attention and gave it to the world at the top of our voices.

> *"Had I been a bunion or a fiend's hang nail,*
> *A louse on a viper, or an eel gone stale,*
> *I'd have hated to be slated*
> *To doff my breeches,*
> *Fated to be mated*
> *To the bitch of bitches,*
> *The whore*
> *Who bore*
> *In her festering belly*
> *The crawling corruption, murderously smelly*
> *As the oldest member of an ancient eggery,*
> *Ranker than Judas, Ganelon, or Gregory—*
> *That thing called Chilbert, fish-scaled and verminous,*
> *His face the spit and image of his terminus;*
> *His sum a belch fathered by thin, sour wine,*
> *A participle dangling on a vile bard's line,*
> *A tick and a leech and the sweat of a craven*
> *Fused to a cheese in the crop of a raven,*
> *A walking hare lip, a dung heap slug,*
> *A pustule on the rump of an idiot bug!*
> *Here's to you, Chilbert, may the Devil's tail spike you!*
> *May you marry a ferret and have children just like you!*

It was an immense success. The men were riotous with laughter and demanded repetitions we were nothing loth to give. After each every man present would toast Chilbert with solemn ceremony. He should have been there.

But by the time we got tired of that we were merely started with song. It didn't matter whether or not anybody else joined in or even listened. We sang in French first, then switched to chanting Latin poems, Irish ballads and Danish lays.

Then the good talk began. And here, too, one language was not enough for the largeness of our minds. We exchanged viking experiences in Danish, talked of school life in Gaelic, and mooted points of scholarship in Latin. We told jokes, both those of the flesh and those of the spirit; we reconstructed philosophies and smashed them with a quip; we drank to heroes, retold the lives of saints in a way that seemed unbelievably funny at the time, though the bawdy details now elude me, wrangled over poets, and wondered at the terrific intellect of the man who'd invented wine.

We were having a marvelous time, but the others must have got tired of us. Most of them, mindful of the day of drudgery to follow, had left in a body fairly early. At what time we were deserted by Jean and Rainault I can't say. I remember that we were intimately alone, and that the fact wasn't of sufficient interest to make us comment.

Yet at a certain point, a few cupfuls left in the last flagon notwithstanding, we looked at each other thoughtfully. "We have had about enough," Conan spoke for both of us. "There's no use in overindulging ourselves."

I was shocked at the idea. "Certainly not!"

He rose with immense dignity and nearly tripped over something. Looking down to see what his foot had caught on, we saw Fulke, prone and sleeping with quiet soundness. The lad must have felt it was his duty to try to keep up with us.

Conan stroked his chin broodingly. "What do you think can be the matter with him?"

"I don't know," I answered worriedly. "He must be sick or something."

"You'd better take a look at him."

I rolled Fulke over, which was a mistake, for he immediately began to snore. Rolling him quickly back on to his stomach, I stood up, shaking my head. "Why, he's been drinking, Conan!"

"No!"

"You don't think I'd say a thing like that about anybody unless it was so, do you?"

"That's true. What do you think the world's coming to, anyhow?"

"No good, I'll bet," I said darkly.

"That's my own suspicion. And to think such things can happen in my house—*my* house!"

"He's only a youngster, too."

"Hardly more than a boy." Conan's face was now stern. "Well, let's put him away now. We can lecture him in the morning."

That was the end of that great night. Grinning at him affectionately, we picked Fulke up and went happily to bed.

We were a little subdued the next morning but had no regrets, realizing that a man cannot always walk the world as a giant. Conan spent the morning surveying the progress of the harvest, while I looked around for a suitable piece of seasoned timber to use for a harp frame. Finding one that would serve, although not of the best wood, I set to work. Albeit not an expert, I could fashion one that would do until I could secure one made by a master.

Later Raymond, still wan but looking much better for the good rest he'd had, found me and conversed awhile. He proved to be an intelligent, likable youth, and I made up my mind that I had done Conan a good turn by taking him into the household. He on his side was well pleased with everything.

"This is a fine place," he stated, and I could see that he was already considering it possessively.

I was rough-hewing my timber down to workable dimensions and didn't look up. "You won't find a better one," I said with conviction.

"I know that," he said confidently, "because you brought me here."

My head jerked up at that and I stared at him, speechless.

"You're my luck," he informed me with cool assurance. "I had bad luck before I met you. I had a chief I couldn't like much and who ran things ill. Matters kept on getting worse, and the Dane raid just killed the place before it died. I nearly died myself, but I didn't because of you. Then I didn't have any particular place to go until I heard that Conan was a friend of yours. He turns out to be a real chief and a friend to follow—I've found out how his men feel—and his place is strong and living, with good people in it. And because of you I have a chance to show I deserve a place with the leaders. I'll keep that place because I'll work and fight well, and good service in a friend of yours will be rewarded."

I was a little nonplused, and he noticed that. He smiled a little. "You see, I'm really your man; maybe the first you've ever had."

This was true but none of anybody's business in view of my new aspirations. "What makes you say that?" I growled.

"Marie told me about you. She says you don't want either to follow or lead.

Only a woman would know that about a man on the basis of no evidence at all. Still it was pleasant to know I was one of her topics of conversation. "H-m-m," I said noncommittally, mentally promising myself that she would see that I could run a house and rule those in it as well as the next man. I returned to my hacking, making a good resolution with every chip.

"Conan's chief over everybody but you," he pursued, "but I'll follow him only if you have no present need of me yourself."

He was not without humor, but he had a dominant and direct purposefulness that, seeing myself one of its stepping stones, I found embarrassing. I straightened up again and looked him in the eye.

"I may want you later," I said, dimly envisioning a fort and hall of my own where this young fellow might have an honored post, "but you came here looking for a niche for yourself, and the place isn't mine. If Conan accepted you as my guest, that only holds good while you are convalescent. Once you are well enough to hold up your end there's only one man you can work for here. That's Conan. If ever I have an establishment of my own and positions to offer, it will be because I ask, and he grants, a favor."

He nodded cheerfully when I'd finished. "It doesn't matter from which of you I take orders. For once I know that I'm in a place where I have a chance to get somewhere. You're my luck, and whatever you advise will be good for me."

With some moodiness I looked after him. Every canon I had for judging character told me he was the sort of man you'd want around when the going got rough. But though I had an instinctive admiration for him I could not feel the warmth I'd experienced toward many another man. There was nothing wrong with his avowed lust for getting on in the world, yet I couldn't see why he had to talk about it. If it happened, well and good, but if it didn't, why, there are plenty of men, no less grand for being landless, to split a bottle with.

Conan would be a power because his natural efficiency set him to coping with conditions that angered him. He, however, took his abilities for granted and never palavered about them or the success they achieved. But I wasn't being fair to the youngster in holding him up against Conan. Not many had the latter's faculty for living in most good corners of life.

There was a clattering on the bridge, and I looked across the court to see the man himself enter the gates. He had dismounted and was walking toward me when a guard on the wall halted him. "There's a rider coming," the fellow called down. "He's in a hurry, too."

Chapter
Eighteen

CONAN stood undecided a moment, then went up on the wall to see for himself. These were days when a rider might well be bringing a message that would radically change the state of things. I went on with my work until I heard somebody yell: "No, there are two of them!" Then curiosity sent me up on the wall also, where I shouldered my way to stand beside Conan.

He nodded to me, and we silently watched them draw near, pushing tired horses hard. After a little my friend whistled and slapped his thigh. "It's the Abbot, by Jesus! Take a good look, Finnian."

I shaded my eyes. The rain the day before had laid the dust, so the still distant figures could be seen clearly enough in general outline. They were churchmen, all right, and one of them didn't look like an ordinary monk. "It might be the Abbot," I said cautiously.

He snapped his fingers, more excited than I had ever seen him. "Man! I hope it is!" he said with a fervor I understood. He'd been trying to win the Abbot as ally for a year now. If the prelate was coming to visit him it might mean that he had at last decided to seal the entente.

The Abbot was big news, and the possibility that he was arriving took everybody from work. Jabbering speculations, they swarmed up to point and stare. One child, with a boy's genius for such things, fell off the wall into the moat. Even the

Abbot couldn't compete with that, and the laughter while the brat was being fished out served to lighten the waiting.

Conan's attention had not been diverted, however. "It's he, all right," he said, quiet and contained now that he was sure. "Everybody off the wall except the guards," he ordered. "And when he comes don't crowd around him as if he were a dog fight." He touched my sleeve, and we descended to the court. "Send him to us in the hall," he told the gate warden.

It was nearly lunch time, but as the meal was to be served outdoors the hall was an empty place. Conan ordered wine which we sipped disinterestedly, in strange contrast to the night before. Most of the time he paced up and down while I tapped out tunes on the table with my fingers. Then we heard the horses coming over the bridge. Conan seated himself with a great show of nonchalance and turned his head with easy naturalness when the door opened. But it wasn't for the Abbot. One of our own men entered.

"The Abbot says he'd like for you to come outside first," the man told Conan. "He says he has something he'd like to show us all."

That was a puzzler. Conan stuck out his lip, shrugged, and rose. Something strange, we saw at a glance, was undoubtedly in the air, and we approached the churchman watchfully, though with outward cordiality. The Abbot on his part was neither friendly nor inimical. He greeted us, but he was terse and hard-eyed.

Seeing his mood, Conan waived ceremony. "My man said you had something you wanted to show us."

"I have." The prelate beckoned to his follower, who stepped forward with a sack of soft leather. "Yesterday," the Abbot announced, "a peasant of the abbey's brought me this. He said a horseman gave it to him with the message that it was from Chilbert and that I should pass it on to you after taking what was mine." He had spoken in a loud, resonant voice; and, looking around, I noticed that every man and woman in the place was watching and listening from some point or other.

Conan never took his eyes from the churchman's face. "From Chilbert," he murmured. "So!"

"So!" the other repeated after him. "I looked in the bag, and this is one of the things I found." Grimmer than ever, he opened the sack with great deliberation, looked to see what he wanted, then thrust in his arm. When his hand came out it was holding the head of a man by the hair.

The bloodless thing had belonged to no one I had ever seen; but Conan's oath was terrible with wrath and sorrow, the women shrieked, and the men groaned. This was one of the men who had gone into Gregory's fort with Conan. We had been so sure that Gregory would dare do nothing to them, and apparently *he* hadn't. It was Chilbert who had sent the message.

The Abbot nodded bleakly, handed the head to the monk with him, and reached in again. Even though those assembled were anticipating the other two they could not forbear to curse and moan when the sightless heads emerged without their bodies.

"Now I'll show you my gift," the Abbot said, looking from Conan to me; and before we had time to wonder he drew out a fourth and held it high. It was my turn to cry out in helpless rage. Sardonic even in death, Father Clovis was smiling horribly. I felt nauseated with grief and shame. He had been murdered, alone with them all against him in Gregory's fort, and it had been at my request that he had entered the trap.

Conan and I looked at each other wretchedly, then turned back to the waiting priest. "What happened?" he asked, his voice suddenly harsh with emotion. "This is all I know."

"Come on inside," Conan said, and we led him between us, snarling at anybody who wasn't quick to jump out of our way. "Fulke!" Conan barked. "Post men at the doors with orders to let nobody enter; nobody at all!"

Without speaking to each other we marched to the table, and I poured wine for the Abbot. Pointedly he pushed it aside. "Not until I hear," he said. We made no comment, for we were on trial, and we knew it. A man of his had gone in to help us, we had got off comparatively unscathed, and the man had been left behind to die.

"You know the first of it, brother," Conan muttered, so I gulped some wine and delivered a detailed account of what had taken place after we'd left the abbey. Later Conan took up the tale with careful circumstantial accuracy. The narrative took some while, but in all that time the Abbot said not a word. He just sat there, shifting his eyes from one to the other of us constantly. If we'd been telling anything short of the strict truth I don't think we could have finished.

"And the last thing we know," Conan concluded, "is that he told Fulke where we wanted the horses. He was in no danger then, certainly, or if he was he didn't know it. There was nobody to stop him from heading straight on back to the abbey."

To our infinite relief the Abbot reached out and thoughtfully began to sip his wine. "Clovis went back," he said, looking as if he was actually seeing what had occurred, "because he didn't want anybody to connect him, and therefore the abbey, with your escape. Those were my orders. But he disregarded his orders at one point, and that's what tripped him. Somebody must have seen him talking to you when he met you coming up the hill."

I groaned inwardly, knowing that it was on my account that Clovis had taken unnecessary chances. "Even if they did see him," Conan objected, "why shouldn't he talk to us? They couldn't have caught him at anything else or they would have stopped him. The abbey has no quarrel with me, and the mere fact that he didn't betray me on sight couldn't be taken as proof that he helped me."

"No," the prelate agreed. "But don't forget the heads were sent not by Gregory but by Chilbert. He'd be an angry man at finding, and Gregory a humble one while admitting, that his prize was gone."

Chilbert must, indeed, have slavered with fury, and at another time we might have enjoyed the thought hugely. We could laugh at nothing then, however. "All right," Conan picked up and followed out the suggested line of speculation, "Chilbert had Gregory on the run, maybe he even accused him of selling me back to myself. In any case he wasn't cutting much of a figure, and Chilbert treated him like a vassal, taking charge of his fort while he investigated the circumstances of the escape. He found that I had three men there, which would serve to clear Gregory perhaps, but he killed them out of spite. As for Clovis—"

"He might have shown he was amused at your escape," the Abbot said sadly. "He would laugh, you know."

"That," I said, "or the coincidence of Clovis' arrival a few hours before mine may have been more than he could overlook."

"That's likely to be it if he was convinced that you were the bard in question." Conan refilled the cups and put his elbows on the table. "It would eat his brain, if he knew that the man who had hoodwinked him this time was the one who had previously clubbed him, stolen his pet horse, and snaked me out of a hot hole once before. It might well make him crazy enough to kill any possible accomplice."

The Abbot nodded. "Be that as it may, my man is dead, and Chilbert is the avowed murderer. You have used the word 'crazy,' and the count never did a madder thing. No doubt he imagines in his growing power that he can intimidate the abbey by such a gesture." He put both clenched fists on the board before him. "All he has done is to declare war. Had Gregory protested, or even killed Clovis, I would have been willing to concede some justice; but Chilbert was only a party to the business through duplicity and arrogance. He has murdered for spite, as you have said, and he will be paid for it."

The Abbot next leaned forward a little. "Conan," he said challengingly.

My friend's voice was quiet. "Yes?"

"You have offered alliance in the past, and I refused to commit myself. Probably I was wrong."

Conan waved the suggestion of guilt aside. "There was nothing, as you saw it, to be gained by fighting before you had to, and you argued reasonably that I was too much of an unknown quantity."

"Exactly. But now I see that though the abbey will still gain nothing concrete by fighting, Chilbert means to swallow us if we don't. And the fact that Gregory is now his man puts him in a good position for it. I always knew that the count wanted us to pay tithes to him, of course, but the killing of our envoy and the flaunting of that killing before us shows that he now thinks he has the force to crush us into helpless submission. I'd hoped that I could remain a balance of power that would leave us all free to guide our respective peoples as we see fit, but Chilbert won't accept so rational a situation."

"No," Conan agreed. "I'm no fool to want empire. I only want my people to be let alone to live as men. Chilbert does want empire, and he wants nobody to live as a man except himself."

The prelate slammed the table with the flat of his hand. "He wants to rule everything, so I say he shall rule nothing." His strong face was seamed with lines of determination. "If you'll ride with me now—for I think that now before he is ready to take the aggressive is the moment for the first blow—I pledge that the abbey will stand or fall with you."

So the pact was made at last, and we would take pleasure and confidence from the idea later. Just then, however, we could only remember that it had been formed because of a man we'd rather have alive. Subduedly we drank to the entente, then Conan ordered lunch to be brought inside to us. We ate sparingly, each one mulling over plans and contingencies in silence, then Conan sent for Jean and Rainault. After a few words of explanation to them the council of war began.

"Chilbert will no doubt be south again on his own proper holdings," the Abbot said. "He'll be getting ready to move against us right after his harvesting."

"We're all waiting for that to be over," Jean remarked. "Naturally there's a temptation to gang and hammer them right away, but that means starving through the winter. There's not much point in winning a victory if you're going to be a skeleton after it."

The Abbot signified agreement. "All right. But they are probably reasoning that we are so reasoning." He looked at Conan, his eyes far back in his head. "We've both had men murdered by a dog who did it just to defy us. I think the best cure for the arrogance of that dog is to prove that we can carry the war to him."

"That's true." Conan was thinking it out carefully. What with the harvest and the building of his new fort he had two vitally important projects that were occupying the full time of all his men. On the other hand the moral effect of an unexpected raid would put Chilbert and his allies healthily, if temporarily, on the defensive. And proof that Conan and the Abbot were acting in concert would give them much more to consider.

Meanwhile I also had been giving the proposition attention. If my knowledge of the situation and terrain had blank spots it was none the less generally sound. "Look, Conan," I said. "That day I first met you; whose lands were you on?"

"Both the Old Farms are mine, but I was being chased off Chilbert's land—Oliver's holding." His eyes lighted, then he squinted. "You're right, brother."

"What's he right about?" Rainault demanded.

Conan drained his cup and thrust it aside. "We can't afford

a real invasion now any more than Chilbert can, but a quick harrying would be worthwhile provided there is a definite objective to pay the price of the risk. Chilbert's own fort is too far away and too strong to consider now, but Oliver would be easier pickings. We might get near enough by night to be on him before he could crawl in his hole and pull it after him.

"He'd do for an object lesson if we bagged him." The Abbot drew his lips back from his teeth. "He's one of the canniest chiefs, not counting Gregory, that Chilbert has under him."

"He is also," Jean put in, "the next best louse, even counting Gregory. I rode up one time after he'd tied three peasants in a shack before he fired it." He grimaced savagely. "They weren't quite dead when I got there."

"You may get a chance to remind him of that," Conan said.

Rainault, who was captain of the garrison and who therefore went on expeditions only in cases of extreme emergency, looked at the rest of us with disgusted envy while we concluded our plans. "If this undertaking is satisfactory to you," Conan said to the prelate, "I'll contribute a third of the men I've got working on the fort. I can spare no more of them. The harvesting, you will understand, can't be interfered with at all."

"Most of us are busy at it, too," the Abbot said, "Yes, the plan is acceptable, and I'll match you man for man." He considered a moment. "The Old Farms would be the best place to meet, and the southeast corner of the far clearing would be the nearest point to Oliver's hall."

"Right," Conan said. "At sundown tomorrow?"

"A good time," the Abbot stated as he rose to leave.

There was mutual confidence, but it was all too solemn and businesslike for any show of cordiality or enthusiasm. We four saw the churchman to the gates and bid him a quiet farewell. Then Conan swore feelingly. "I've got to tell Ann I'm riding again," he said morosely.

"You won't have to wait long," Rainault remarked. "Here she comes now."

I watched my friend put an arm around his wife and enter the hall with her, then I snapped my fingers. For once there was someone for me to talk things over with, too, and I went eagerly to find her.

I may have swaggered a little as I did so, for I was exhilarated by the knowledge of my new position. This time I was not just something caught between the anvil and the hammer but a man striving to achieve definite goals whose winning would have a permanent bearing on my way of life. Why hell! and I shook my head at the amazing rightness of it, I was going out to fight for my chosen clan, my own land and living, my own woman. The more I thought about it and all it implied the more it went to my head. For the first time in my life I was contemplating battle with something like pleasure.

On the other side of the hall I found Raymond and Marie, still seated at one of the otherwise empty lunch tables. She looked up to search my face as I stood smiling at her. "What happened?" she asked.

"Oh, Conan and the Abbot made a treaty," I said easily. "Mutual aid, stand or fall."

"And?" she prodded.

"And they're going to start activities right away. Or tomorrow, rather."

Her quick concern was gratifying. It was childish to take such delight in it, but I couldn't remember when I'd had anybody concerned about me before. "And does 'they' include you?"

"Surely," I said, a little surprised. I thought she would have taken that for granted.

She stood then, her eyes very large and serious. Raymond rose, too. "I wish I could go with you," he said wistfully.

With an expansive smile I clapped him on the back. "Don't worry about it. This is just a small raid. The main party won't come off for some while. By that time you'll have enough meat on your bones to stand the gaff."

"Yes, but I wish I could show you and Conan what I can do," he mumbled miserably.

"You'll have plenty of time." I took one of Marie's hands. "Will you get the hell out of here?" I asked him pleasantly.

He started, then smiled slowly. "I'll be up to see you leave tomorrow," he promised as he sauntered off.

The girl's mouth twitched to a smile an instant before she resumed her sober appraisal of me. "You came to tell me right away," she remarked strangely.

"Of course." I was so obsessed with my new point of view that I couldn't fully appreciate why she might be struck by its suddenness.

"That's nice," she decided. "Is it going to be dangerous, Finnian? No, that's nothing to ask you after what you did for Conan. You don't think in such terms."

I stared at her. God Jesus! If she only knew how scared I had been. I thought women knew everything about men, and sometimes I was convinced men were as strange as goblins to them. "This may not amount to anything at all," I told her frankly. "Unless we're lucky it's only a gesture to give Chilbert and his hangers-on pause by letting them see that we're acting in unison and are so far from being intimidated that we dare invasion. Of course, if we happen to stumble on something we may achieve practical gain as well."

"You're speaking of yourself as part of this." Her free hand motioned to include the court, then she put it on my arm. "Are you really, or are you thinking of that man?" She shuddered. "That fourth head that the Abbot showed us, I mean. I heard you cry out, Finnian."

She was all sweet comprehension then—everything that I could ask of a woman. "That man was dear to you, wasn't he? What was he like?"

I tried to tell her about it. I wanted to be able to talk to her naturally as Conan talked to Ann, but I began at the wrong end. "Oh, I only saw him two or three times."

Her face grew blank, and I knew that she had been anticipating some tale of life-long friendship. "You see," I said earnestly, "he was killed not only because the Abbot sent him on a ticklish mission but because I was a man he'd do something for."

"And you felt that way about him. But why, if you hardly knew each other?"

"Well, there are plenty of people you like just because they're pleasant fellows who happen to infest the premises. Every now and then, though, you meet a man who actually knows what you're saying and doing. Clovis was such."

"You're funny and always will be," she said, but she reached up to pat my cheek. "You don't do anything for rational motives the way anybody else might. All the others have axes to grind; but you're going along because Chilbert murdered a man who laughed at the right time, or something." She looked at me with affectionate amusement. "And you'll never change."

I almost told her that I already had changed, that I was fighting now in hopes of earning my own land and hall. I almost told her that I knew the woman I wanted in my house, but two things deterred me. One was that the instinctive feeling that it would be better to wait until I had something specific to offer. The other and more forceful was the knowledge that this moment when she was lovely with warmth intimacy was no time to waste on words.

With her pliant strength she was a fine woman to hold, and the way she answered my kiss showed she had good, hearty passion to meet a man's need. But here in the court by daylight prolonged embraces were not in order. Reluctantly I dropped my arms and perched on the table beside her. Our talk was desultory, but its very casualness betokened the new strength of feeling between us.

Chapter
Nineteen

WE started before dawn, for we intended to rest both horses and men halfway there so that neither would be too tired for night travel. Early as it was everybody was up to see us leave. Marie looked pale and fragile under the single torch that lit a corner of the hall. I said farewell to her last and made no bones about the fact that I was not giving her a mere kiss of friendship.

As I was turning from her I caught Ann's eye upon us, a fleeting look of speculation lighting her anxiety at Conan's going. Few women are ever too busy for matchmaking, I reflected as I followed Conan out. In this instance, I reasoned, it would be a good thing. Ann would probably brace Marie about it, with the lack of reticence concerning mating peculiar to the female. Yes, a little talking it up ought to help me along, and I had a pleasant vision of the two women discussing Conan and myself with respective possessiveness.

True to his word, Raymond was there to give me a leg up. It was a nice gesture from a man not yet any too well, and I shook his hand cordially. "Don't let anybody walk off with the fort," I told him.

"It'll be here," he promised. "Then Conan gave the word, and we left.

We slept through the hottest hours of the day, as per schedule, and, after eating, rode the few remaining miles to keep tryst. It was still a little short of sundown when we arrived, but the monks were already there. While our men and the fathers fraternized, the Abbot and a priest called Father Jacques sat apart under a tree with Jean, Conan and myself.

"I've got a man who can lead us there in the dark," the Abbot began briskly. "It'll be slow going, for the horses will have to be led, of course. But as it's only about twelve miles we can make it before first light. So if none of Oliver's villeins get wind of us and manage to warn him, we might accomplish something worthwhile."

"Let's decide what we're trying for," Conan said. "Naturally what we see when we get there may change our plans entirely; but it's my conclusion that we'll have the best chance of drawing more blood than we lose by laying off in the woods and waiting for them to come out. That's a pretty strong fort of Oliver's and liberally garrisoned, to boot. We can't storm it with the force we have."

"Just what have you in mind then?" Father Jacques inquired.

"Well, it's harvest time, so if it's fair weather a good part of the garrison will come out to work in the fields. Maybe they'll even be moving far enough away from the fort for us to be able to cut them off."

"You're right," the Abbot declared. "Then with half the defenders driven off we might be able to break in and take Oliver. Or he might make it easy for us to snap him up by coming out to take a look at his crops."

"There's a pretty good chance of that," Jean opined. "It wouldn't be reasonable for a man to stay in his hall all day during the harvest."

"Let's get there," I said as Conan looked to see whether I dissented.

That was a brutal night of endless slow motion. It's bad enough to go for hours through a benighted forest without having the faintest concept of time or distance. But when one also has to lead a horse which takes the sensible view that it's all a lot of foolishness, exasperating hard work is added to weariness and boredom. In the earlier stages I tried to relieve the tedium by singing, but I had to interrupt myself so often to swear at my mount that it was hardly effective entertainment. By midnight even the cursing had become routine and dispirited. We kept moving only because we knew we were going to.

There was still no sign of darkness lifting when the word was quietly passed back from our guide that we were on the edge of Oliver's cleared land. We all fumbled around until we found a place to tie our mounts. Then we sat dully in the pre-morning chill and watched for the sky to change. It did after a while, and we roused ourselves to steal up behind trees and bushes on the forest fringe and peer out at the fort.

The earthworks looked quite high, and it was a place of some size. About half a mile away it was, and the intervening fields were only partly harvested. A road ran out from the gate, at right angles to our course but soon switching away east. By the time it was light enough for us to make out all that I could descry the watchers on the walls, and I studied the fort more closely. As Conan had stated it was not a place likely to be taken suddenly or with ease.

I looked at my friend where he lurked by a large oak, and he signaled that he'd like a word with me. We had to be careful about speech, because a voice can carry surprising distances over open fields; and we therefore retired a certain distance before holding a whispered council with the Abbot concerning the orders for the day. These were in chief an embargo on speech, a ukase against approaching the clearing unless so commanded, and an admonition to keep weapons from exposure to any trifling gleam of sunlight. If they detected us before we were ready to act our painful trip would be fruitless.

We set men to keep track of developments, then ate a cold breakfast washed down with wine. That fought off the cool dampness, and we felt more cheerful. "I bet Oliver wouldn't enjoy his own breakfast if he knew who'd come to visit him," Conan chuckled.

"You don't think he likes us?" I asked, wide-eyed with hurt.

"Why, I suppose he figures we were pretty hard on him last time," he said judiciously. "But you know how it is. You get carried away by the spirit of the thing."

"Certainly I know how it is," I assured him, "and I'm a trifle surprised that he isn't big enough to look at it from that angle. I wonder if it could have been your bouncing that stone block off him that he objects to. Come to think of it, he wouldn't speak to us after that."

"It could be; it could be," Conan's lips were pursed in thought. "I wonder if he keeps any cats now?" he asked reflectively.

I snickered, then smiled inwardly as I happened to notice the others present. Jean was red-faced from effort. He wasn't used to controlling laughter. Father Jacques was looking nonplussed, while the Abbot was regarding us with patient benevolence. He was a man I much admired, but folly was beyond him.

About an hour later the sentinel we'd posted returned to say that the men were leaving the fort for the fields. We sneaked forward with what haste was commensurate with quiet, but to our intense disappointment they turned off to work on the other side of the fortress. We debated attempting to skirt the clearing but decided against it. Not only would the odds favor the betraying of our presence if we moved by daylight, but we would lay ourselves open to the danger of being cut off and trapped.

After sending our guide to watch the harvester, with instructions to set fire to the crops if we should succeed in distracting them by an attack of some sort, we sat like ravens waiting for a battle to leave them corpses. It was doubtless exceedingly boring to some. I made myself comfortable, adream with my new prospects. I didn't even bother to look very often, being certain my attention would be called to any important development. It was almost noon when that happened.

"Finnian!" Conan whispered excitedly. "What do you make of that?"

Peering forth, I was brought sharply back to actuality. A troop of horsemen was on the road, not departing from the fort but going towards it. This was something that called for a prompt decision. If they didn't prove too numerous they might be the victims we were awaiting.

Gambling on the probability that Oliver's watchers would be preoccupied with the men on the road, Conan risked sending a man up a tree to count the newcomers. Meanwhile every man stood to his horse.

Conan and I caught the man to silence his fall as he dropped to the ground. "Over twenty, maybe thirty," was his report.

We numbered, thirty-five ourselves, which made attack feasible if we made sure of getting out from under before the garrison could help their friends. We looked at the fort once more to make certain. There was no excitement there, which meant that the newcomers were recognized allies, and therefore our foes.

"Our horses have had a good rest," the Abbot said. "We should be able to charge through and drive back before they can be reinforced. If we regain the woods before they catch up with us they'll have a hard time cornering us."

"They might not enjoy it if they do," Conan observed. "We'll hit them as they round the bend, I suppose?"

It was the obvious place, and the prelate nodded. "Give the signal," he whispered as he turned toward his horse.

Our foe was still a good distance off, but the horses were moving at high speed. They were so patently making the old meal-time spurt that we grinned. "Those nags have their hearts set on hay," Conan said with satisfaction. "They're going to be hard to turn for anything so nonessential as a fight."

I left him and returned with both our mounts. All the others were already astride, edging cautiously nearer to the clearing. We waited a moment longer, by which time the leaders were almost to the bend. Conan gave me a knee up and vaulted astraddle his own horse. "All right," he said quietly.

Our crashing through the brush out into the open was their warning, but by the time they comprehended the extent of their danger we were well on our way. There was a stretch of barley to surge through first, then there was new stubble, and the horses could run. Meanwhile there were shouts from the wall and startled yells from the men on the road. The startled yells insured the riders startled horses and ones that had no liking for veering to face us. Their solution of the situation, as Conan had predicted, was to keep on bolting for the oats.

The drawback to that idea as far as the enemy was concerned was that we could undoubtedly reach them before they reached the fort; so unless they lined up for a countercharge we'd wash them away as a freshet does sand. They tried to meet us as soon as they decided they couldn't avoid us, but, fighting their nervous and indignant horses, they couldn't attain much momentum.

As I shrugged my shield into place and drew my sword, I was looking them over, mount and man. "There's Oliver himself!" Jean cried with fierce triumph, but it wasn't a rider that held my attention first. My eye was taken by a splendid bay, the finest horse I had ever seen. I didn't need to strain to see who was on it. "Chilbert!" I called to Conan.

He looked, then headed directly for the count. "He's mine, brother!" he cried, and I accepted that. Oliver was the one I would try for.

They did their best to meet us, as I've stated. For a moment I could see their wrathful or frantic expressions, those of men striving but knowing their hopeless disadvantage, and then we were on them. I don't know whether I killed anyone on that charge or not. As Oliver had shifted his position by the time we encountered them I contented myself with indiscriminate hacking.

But the massed force of our run was terrific. We blasted them apart, knocking some from their mounts and riding them down, wounding some with our swords, killing others. "They got between us, God damn them! I had him, and they got between us!" I heard Conan lament as we turned to bite them again.

They had attempted to reorganize, but they were too hard hit. I heard Oliver shrieking excitedly and Chilbert crying orders in the peculiarly cold voice I remembered him using just before he murdered the Saxon youth. As I turned my mount I saw men issuing from the fort. No doubt the harvesters were on their way also, and well armed, too for no sane men would work in the open without weapons handy.

But we had time for one more good charge. However, they saw at the last moment that they couldn't succeed in crystallizing effectively. Or rather Chilbert saw, and they scattered before us at his command. He was right, for though it proved utterly fatal to the fragment we caught, more escaped our compact onslaught than would have survived if they'd stood against us.

Chilbert himself killed a monk who sought to block his retreat, coolly avoided Conan's attack and hazed the bay away at a terrific speed. My friend started to follow, but I had had that horse under me and knew what it could do. "No use!" I called. "He can be back from Rome before you're halfway there."

Conan was some strides ahead of me, but, remembering my knowledge, he turned to aid in making as much havoc as possible before we had to break away. But there was no one, we discovered, whom we could now catch with safety. The un-maimed and still mounted survivors were too near their swiftly approaching comrades to make following them worthwhile. Our men reined in to jeer loudly, and a few engaged in pilfer-ing the dead and wounded.

But there was one major episode of the fight left. The Ab-bot had headed Oliver off and was remorselessly intercepting each dash to rejoin his friends which the redheaded man made. Finally the latter charged in desperation, and that was his undoing. The churchman warded a sword blow, then a sec-ond. A moment later he found the opening he wanted and swept his own blade through Oliver's neck. The head actually lofted a little before it struck the ground, bounced and rolled.

Leaning from the saddle the prelate speared the head with his brand and held it high. "That's for Clovis!" he shouted after Chilbert. He was no ritualist then.

We took one final survey of the possibilities and instantly decided they were and would remain unfavorable. Chilbert knew what he was doing and had stopped his mounted men until his foot troops from the fields, now nearly flush with them, could arrive to form a line which could fold and trap us if we were fools enough to ride into it.

Had I been in Chilbert's place I would have done exactly what he did. The odds were that we would have been carried by the heat of success to essay further damage. But Oliver's death had cooled most of us. Thirty thousand Olivers would not compensate for Father Clovis as a man, but in their value to their respective factions one could be crossed off against the other. Likewise two or three men lay dead for each of the fellows assassinated in Gregory's fort, and others, if they sur-vived, would not feel well for a long time. We had done as well as we could have hoped for and a little bit over. The more we lingered the more we would jeopardize our gains.

"Come on away!" Conan ordered. "And make it fast!"

A few, made wild by triumph to the point where they con-sidered themselves invincible, hesitated in wonder at this order for retreat. The Abbot glowered at them. "Anybody who wants to stay and fertilize Chilbert's fields can do so," he said. "The others will come along now!"

When we fled Chilbert was after, but that was more for the morale of his people than anything else. As mass tactics would be rendered impossible by the trees, his advantage in numbers would be largely nullified. Attacking us would resolve into a haphazard business with only such unpredictable gains or losses as would develop from a series of single combats. Or such would be the manner of it until the foot soldiers arrived. The latter could come in among us with knives and pikes to bring down our horses.

They would take a little time to arrive, however, and within the border of the woods we halted and faced our immediate pursuers for a stalemate. They were hoping still that fool-hardiness would put us into their hands, and I could see Chilbert glaring fiercely willing us to stay where we were.

Conan winked at me. "Give them a sword song, brother," he urged. We were gay with triumph as we had something of a right to be, seeing that the swift blow, which we had pushed ourselves hard to make possible, then waited cannily to deliver, had succeeded with a cost to us of but one man. The loss of Oliver would tell heavily on Chilbert not only because he had been a valuable lieutenant but because word of it would rapidly go everywhere, diminishing the count's prestige. Scoring the first gains is always and naturally taken for a powerfully fair omen.

Feeling as I did, I welcomed Conan's suggestion, and I saw that the monks were looking at me with as keen anticipations as our own men showed. At the moment there wasn't a one of them from the Abbot on down who was thinking in any terms but those of a warrior. I looked at the enemy, who were also, though sullenly, giving me their attention, and I laughed. I would need no harp to help hold this audience. As for the song, it was easy to decide upon, for there was only one of the sort I'd ever made in French.

> *"Women save things; men are spillers,*
> *Renders, breakers, cleavers, killers.*
> *The sword knew that.*
>
> *I was glad; my hand was ready,*
> *For the call was stirring, heady*
> *When the sword spoke.*
>
> *'Have done now with loving, laughing,*
> *Hunting, sleeping, singing, quaffing,'*
> *The sword said. 'Seek!'*

'What?' I asked, 'should I be finding—
Land or cattle for my minding?'
    The sword said: 'No!'

'Would you have a man my questing,
Met in pride but left unjesting?'
    The sword said: 'Yes!'

'Would you have him broken, battered,
Carved, left bloodless, headless, shattered?'
    The sword said: 'Right!'

'Any man could suit your needing
For a life let out by bleeding?'
    The sword said: 'Wrong!'

'There's a man for whom my hating
Might be ending him know sating,'
    The sword said: 'Good!'

He was tall, a strong one, daring,
Facing us unawed, uncaring.
    The sword said: 'Strike!'

Smiling first, he soon was shrinking;
And as it bit deeply, drinking,
    The sword said: 'Ah!'

We were savage at his worsting,
And, though slaking, still athirsting,
    The sword said: 'More!'

Finding man, we left him cuttings
Fit for kites at twilight gluttings.
    The sword said: 'Done!' ''

"Done!" all our men echoed at the top of their voices and
cheered, while our foemen scowled at us, muttering. But Chilbert looked to see that his harvesters had almost caught up.
His face lighted with the assurance that he had us, but Conan
chuckled. "Good-by, Chilbert."

"Home!" the Abbot ordered tersely, and we wheeled. Our

scout, who had rejoined us to report the crops not dry enough for burning, led off briskly, and we swept after him. Chilbert followed us for a ways, but once again he was forced to concede that there was little gain in attacking, even if he could catch us, once his footmen were outdistanced. So he gave up, and we strung out in single file, tired men but talkatively delighted with ourselves.

The Abbot, whose stronghold was by far the nearest urged us to rest there before continuing on to the fort. Keenly as we were looking forward to reporting our success to those anxiously waiting at home, the good sense of the churchman's suggestion was obvious. So we headed for the monastery, excitement seeping from us to leave us worn, drowsy riders.

Chapter
Twenty

WE were halfway home from the abbey the following day when we noticed considerable smoke a couple of hundred yards south of our path. Any sign of fire in a forest country must be investigated, so we promptly tethered our horses and went to take a look. It was a brush fire, fortunately already dying down for lack of wind, and we made short work of beating out what was left of it.

Jean looked around to make sure of his bearings. "Bertram lives around here," he told Conan.

We were starting to leave as he made this remark, but Conan halted abruptly. "That's the charcoal burner?"

"Yes," Jean's gesture indicated general rather than specific knowledge. "But it's not far from here," he said positively. "It might be the source."

"We'll find out," Conan stated, and we advanced gingerly, coughing because of the smoke but not too much bothered by the heat. The forest was moist enough to save the big trees from firing. Only the brush and some saplings had caught.

"There's what's left!" one of the men exclaimed, pointing to a small, smoke-misted clearing. There were undoubtedly the ashes of a shack there. As we approached I noticed that a couple of the base logs still glowed dully. With our smarting and weeping eyes we were slow to make out details or to tell wood from other charred matter, but suddenly Jean swore with hysterical horror. Any man would have under the circumstances. He had just stumbled over the badly crisped body of a woman.

In another minute we discovered the corpse of a child. "You can't tell whether fire killed them or not," Conan said, coughing. "Make a good search for Bertram."

"Maybe he went to the fort to tell you about it," someone suggested. But he hadn't.

We found him after awhile, half in and half out of the spring. He had a sword wound a man could put his foot in, and he was burned away in the legs. He had probably been left for dead and had somehow reached the spring in an effort to save himself from the flames. His misfortune was that he had succeeded. Terribly enough, he was still alive.

We didn't know it at first, and Conan rolled him over to certify his identity. "It's Bertram, all right," he said; and the combination of the fact that he had been stirred and all the noise we made coughing brought the fellow to.

I think the stunning intensity of his pain was its own anaesthetic, for he didn't groan. He just opened his eyes and spoke like a man just waked from a drunken stupor. "Conan." The word had no emotional content. It was just a dull statement of realization.

I, who had never seen the man before, was hard put to look at him. It was doubly bad for Conan. As this man's chief he owed him protection. But, too, once that had failed he owed him vengeance. He bent very close, unable to touch him again for fear of adding to his misery, but trying to reach him by force of mind. "You're right; it's Conan, Bertram. Who did it? Tell us, man! Who did it?"

We were afraid he wouldn't answer, but he did finally. He was completely detached, so much so that he didn't seem to be answering a question. Rather he gave the impression of having changed the subject after a suitable pause. "Outlaws."

Only one local band of outlaws was known to me personally, so I naturally thought of it and of the leader who had used me as his zany. "Ask him if it was Piers," I said.

But, whether he knew or not, he was too far gone to tell us that. Our queries, however, had apparently started a disjointed but not unrelated train of thought. And what he said hit each man of us. "They didn't have to rape and kill the little girl."

Conan gave me one look, and I know at that moment we

were all glad of the smoke which granted us pardon for coughing, clearing our throats, and having tears in our eyes. "No," Conan said very gently. "No, Bertram, they didn't have to rape and kill the little girl."

With an inhuman, writhing motion the charcoal burner twisted over on to his stomach again, and Conan rose, motioning to Jean. There was only one thing left that a friend could do for that tortured wisp of a man. Jean crossed himself, asked Christ for understanding, drew his sword, and killed him.

After giving all three members of the family shallow burial we went seeking signs of the outlaws' path of advance. We found their tracks shortly, and after following them a little ways to make sure of where they were heading, we ran for the horses. None of us said anything lest he be guilty of crying a false alarm, but all of us had the same fear curdling our stomachs. The tracks of those murderous woods scurriers seemed to be leading toward Conan's fort.

Suspicion became conviction down the path a way, for they had cut into it. We growled and gave our horses all they could take without breaking down short of the miles they had yet to go. Our feelings of triumph and self-satisfaction had been obliterated by Bertram's fate, and we were soured, silent men. We had our minds on the uncompleted portion of the fort; and there was more to worry about in that we couldn't judge just how large a force was preceding us. The tracks told only that it totaled a considerable number.

I myself could not shake the notion that Piers and his crew were the raiders in question. I didn't reckon them a powerful force alone, but I recalled his boast that he could muster other outlaw bands at will. That was a boast I had once laughed at, but it summoned no mirth now. Besides, who could predict what one lucky charge might accomplish against a makeshift wall? For a moment before I suppressed it, shuddering, I had a picture of that rabble pouring into the court, mad for theft and desecration.

"It's probably Piers," I said. Not that the remark meant anything in particular. I was merely speaking out of nervousness.

"Very likely," Conan said. "He's got the largest of the outlaw bands. But, of course, there's no constancy in the size of those gangs. He may have more than we figure."

"I've been enjoying thinking about that, too," I said. "One of his scouts might have seen us riding to Oliver's and figured it was a good time to attack."

"Very likely," he agreed soberly. "Well, we'll know soon."

It was anticlimax when we did. The outlaws had made across fields to the fort, but there was now no sign either of battle or of burning. Moreover, men were stirring about outside the walls with every appearance of casualness. Faintly we heard the watchman's cry telling a bunch of raiders was sighted, and those without started to run for shelter. But that was standard practice. We were reasonably sure that the men were ours, and we slowed down, though still puzzled as to what had become of the rievers.

We got part of the answer when we were near enough to see that some of the men we had thought harvesting had been digging holes. They were partly filled up again, but it was easy to see what they were for. "A raid beat off," Jean said, and once more we hurried our mounts.

Our people were all on the wall when we rode up. My eyes found Marie where she stood and waved, a breeze pressing her dress closely against her body. It was a grand, lovely sight, and I was moved by pride and desire.

"You needn't have gone off," Rainault called down. "We just had us a fight by staying right at home."

Now that we were relieved of anxiety about the fort we remembered Bertram. "Was it Piers?" Conan demanded.

The question surprised Rainault a little. "Yes. Why?" Conan's tone had made it obvious that he wasn't just asking to ascertain facts about the raid.

"We'll tell you in a minute."

When we were inside and gathered to talk I had my arm around Marie as if it had been a lifetime habit. "What happened here first?" Conan wanted to know.

Rainault, as garrison commander, made the report. "About two hours ago Piers and his buzzards showed up. The immediate problem was to keep them from destroying the crops."

"Right. Well?"

"I sent out horsemen under Fulke for that. But Piers didn't try to do anything but attack the fort. He had us split up, he saw the weak spot in the wall, and he may even have known that you were away."

"I think he did. So?"

"So he rushed the wall at the weak point, and we were there waiting for him. If he'd won right away he would have been all right. As it was we held them off long enough for Fulke to come up and take them in the rear. They left after that. We hazed them into the forest, but with you absent and things being as they are I couldn't spare enough men to make following worthwhile."

"Sound, and damned good work!" Conan praised him. The elbow of the arm that wasn't holding Ann jabbed Fulke in the ribs, and the younster gasped for breath. "What did you drive 'em off with," the chief asked, "that viol of yours?"

"Let us have no mock of minstrels," I said in my deepest voice. "Minstrels are the preservers of fame."

"And the prime destroyers of all known drinks," Conan rejoined. Then we were serious again.

"Did we lose any men?"

"Nah," Rainault said. "I've been making the business out for more than it really was. Those outlaw bands never plan anything; they just do it, and if it doesn't work they quit. We'd roughed 'em up so by the time they'd got across the moat that there wasn't much left of their ambition to take the wall. Some of the lads were cut up, of course, but only one got a bad dose." He looked at me. "Raymond wasn't fit to go on the wall, but he did it against my orders. He'll be all right, Finnian, but he got another nasty wound simply because he wasn't strong enough to ward blows."

That was foolish of Raymond, albeit a nice kind of foolishness. Yet seeing that he had been accepted on my word I felt pretty good about it. "That's a good whelp of yours," was Conan's recognition.

Ann looked at me with an unwonted trace of archness. "Marie's looking after him for you," she stated.

Her words combined with Conan's made me know a chief's pride for the first time in my life. My grip tightened on the girl's waist. "I'll see him," I said. "Where is he?"

"I had him put in your bed, Finnian. He needed comfort."

"Naturally," I conceded cheerfully, "and I won't be needing a bed tonight, anyhow." I glanced at Conan. "I'll be ready to ride by the time a fresh horse is saddled."

"We'll leave in five minutes," he said, as I led Marie off by the hand. Raymond was awake and smiled at me in weak apology. "I always seem to be no good for anything when you come around," he complained.

His courage in the face of actual incapacitation had really moved me, and I told him Conan's remark to cheer him up. He didn't have much, if any, fever this time, nor a very bad wound. Loss of blood on top of weakness due to the same cause was his only real trouble.

"I've got to leave again," I told him after briefly sketching our success and the wherefores of the new business in hand. I was holding Marie to me, strong with the happiness that comes to a man from knowing that the full use of himself is drawing him toward the attainment of known and worthy goals. "You'll look after him for me?" Unwittingly I was making a question with the identical words of Ann's statement, but the ostensible meaning was unimportant. In reality I was hinting to her of a life to be, during which we two as leaders should be holding ourselves responsible for the lives and well being of our followers.

"I'll take care of him," she promised me. "Will you take care of yourself?"

"I've always made that my earnest concern," I declared, "but now I see more sense in so doing than ever before." It isn't hard to get a woman to take any remark personally, and the look I gave her left her in no doubt that she was pointedly referred to in that one.

She flushed, half smiling and half serious. "I can count on you for that?"

"You can," I assured her, wishing that poor Raymond could take up his bed and walk. Then I heard Conan's shout and made hasty farewells.

It was not only the thought of what had been done to Bertram and his family that impelled this new expedition. The real point was that when Piers grew bold enough not only to run wild on our territory but to attack the stronghold itself something had to be done about him. The next time, should he strike, for instance, while the garrison was drained of men for the fight with Chilbert, he might do some real damage.

"They won't go very far," I spoke from my knowledge of this feckless band. "As long as Rainault didn't follow them into the woods they'll settle down before sunset. And as long as they have no reason to expect us they won't have watchers —ones that will stay awake, that is. The only thing they'll keep on the alert for is loot."

Within the trees their trail was plain as a road, but we halted after about a mile, and Conan sent my old host, Thomas the hunter, ahead to scout. The afternoon was well gone, and if our calculations were correct they would be camped somewhere comparatively near. As for our horses, though they'd enable us to catch up with the outlaws, they would be no good to us when it came to an actual attack in the forest. We had agreed upon the obvious course of jumping the enemy on foot and by night.

A couple of hours passed during most of which we lay on our backs talking drowsily. We hadn't had a great deal of sleep recently, and once or twice I, at least, was on the verge of dozing off. Finally, however, speculations as to what was delaying Thomas roused us, then made us restless. We were sitting up, watching with disturbed impatience, when he eventually reappeared.

We jumped to our feet and met him. "They're about three miles ahead," he told Conan. "Less, if anything."

"You're sure they're going to stay the night there?"

"Sure. They were alrady making fires and rowing over soft places to bed down."

"Anybody see you?"

"*Them see me* if I didn't want 'em to?" Thomas snorted with a craftsman's offended pride. "Hell, I went all around 'em and scouted 'em good, and they ain't even worried enough to have guards around."

It was still light, but dusk had already arrived there under the trees, and the birds cheeped with that aloofness they manifest at day's end only. "That's fine," Conan pronounced. "We'll move up a couple of miles or so, then eat. By that time it'll be dark, and we'll see what can be done to educate them."

Thomas took us as near to our quarry as he thought feasible. Then while the meal was being prepared he went over the remaining ground once more to make certain that he could guide us through the imminent night. "They're making more racket than a herd of hogs," he chuckled when he returned.

I grunted, remembering. One of the hardest things that I had had to bear during my sojourn with those people was that there was never a moment of silence among them. Once they were settled around their fire or fires it would be no trick to steal upon them. Nevertheless, we waited the little while till full dark before we got under way.

Thomas went first, with Conan, then myself and the others in single file behind. We could see well enough to keep from stumbling or bumping into each other, and the hunter, spotting his landmarks and signs with amazing precision and swiftness, considering, led us at a fair rate of speed. After a little, though, he was relieved of the necessity of exercising his skill. Faintly at first but soon drowning out all other noises of the forest, we could hear the voices of the outlaws. Bred to yelling each other down, they invariably spoke several times more loudly than need be, and in harsh, far-carrying tones.

This notwithstanding, we did not grow careless. On the contrary we slowed our rate of advance, and if one of us happaned to cause any extra-sharp snapping of branches we all halted, trusting that thus the sound would seem to blend with the inevitable cracklings and rustlings of any forest. Then at last we caught sight of their fires, two huge ones.

"See which one Piers has settled down by," Conan whispered, and once more the woodsman was off, marvelous in his silence. We waited, listening to the mouthings of the unsuspecting folk ahead. They were making an ugly, patternless racket, and from where we stood it sounded all but inhuman.

"Now I know why a hawk dives down on a bunch of magpies," I muttered to Conan. "It's just to shut 'em up for a minute."

"Some of these magpies will shut up for a long time," he prophesied.

A minute later Thomas stole out of a shadow. "He's by the fire to the right," he reported.

In relation to our position it was the furthest away, and we set patiently about the task of quietly reaching an attacking point. From then on our orders were to keep together and work as near to the outlaws as possible.

For a while I had hopes that we would be on them before they knew it, but one of the men tripped and fell headlong when we were still about fifty yards short. They hushed instantly, and my skin prickled with a hunter's excitement as Piers himself called: "Hey! Who's there?"

Conan was not the man to give him a chance to find out by easy degrees. "At 'em!" he yelled, slamming through the underbrush. We obeyed as well as circumstances would permit, and after a few strides they weren't so adverse. The firelight picked out obstacles for us, and I can recall stumbling only once.

Of course, what with dodging trees, we couldn't go at top speed, but we were still able to reach them before they were sure what they were going to do. Or rather before Piers was sure what he was going to do. Most of them followed the animal instinct of their kind to duck for cover first and ascertain the exact extent of the danger later. There was much squawking and shrieking as women chivied their young into the dark, cursing betimes as men shoved past them.

Piers and a few fellows had tried to organize resistance, but when they found nobody was listening to them they also turned to escape. It was too late to avoid us then, though. We were already in their camp and in full career, while they were just getting in motion. Conan cut down one man from behind; and as the others whirled on us desperately, I leaped past him to get at Piers. I had promised myself that I would do that as soon as I knew we were on his trail.

His eyes told me that he recognized me, but for once he had no time for words. There was great strength in that frame of his, but he was not a skilled swordsman. The rest of the skirmish was over, but Conan knew that I wanted to handle this fellow myself. "But don't kill him, brother," he begged. "I have something for him."

Acquiescing, I turned Piers and worked him toward the soaring fire. He still hacked manfully until the intense heat began to singe and blister him. Then he suddenly dropped his blade with a groan. "Get him!" Conan barked and four men sprang to drag him to a cooler spot.

Whistling to himself, my friend sauntered around the fire, his face turned up to the illuminated branches. "Bring him here," he ordered; and Piers, wondering and sullen, was hustled before him.

"I've learned to tell you from a pig," Conan said, smiling in a way that the outlaw couldn't have enjoyed. "Isn't that nice?"

He stretched out his hand, and Jean gave him a coiled leather rope. Piers howled and almost broke loose by his frantic squirming, but additional hands made sure of him and tied his arms behind his back. Conan meanwhile paid no attention but, still smiling, carefully fashioned a noose. "Up Thomas," he said quietly, handing the coil to the woodsman. "Boost him, two of you."

In a moment Piers interrupted his own ravings with a squeal as the noose dropped down from the branch to hang level with his eyes. Conan swept it roughly over the outlaw's head. "Hoist!" he commanded.

If there were any there who felt compassion for him I wasn't one of them. "He kicks a lot," I said critically.

"He isn't used to it yet," Conan explained. "He'll get over it pretty soon."

He did, and we left him aloft for his fellows to see and think about.

Chapter
Twenty-one

THE next two weeks were fine ones for me. I was in almost continuous, purposeful action, and the physical weariness I knew by nightfall but added to my sense of accomplishment. Through it all, indeed, I experienced a sensation that nothing but the writing of poetry had previously given me. I was achieving something at once spiritual and concrete, and had knowledge of what I was doing while I was doing it.

It was a new existence that I was isolating and fortifying for myself. In the little nation which Conan was consolidating I was recognized as his alter ego, second only to him in authority, and I drove myself mercilessly to make sure I earned my rating. What we had to do in the short time before hostilities would be forced was to visit friends and waverers, giving them final notice of the conflict and its significance. With the friends all we tried to do was to show how confident we felt. As for those as yet undecided we made capital of our new alliance with the abbey, how we had just killed Oliver before Chilbert's eyes, and one more thing. In essence it was that when we were victorious we would remember who had helped us—and who hadn't.

Sometimes Conan and I traveled together. More often I acted independently, leading my little troop of followers to outlying strongholds to palaver and take careful note. Word of the business at the Old Farms and the work at Gregory's had got around attached to my name, and I was well received even by the hesitating. Never a diffident man, I yet entered all places with a new and surer confidence. All knew that I had power in the land and might well have a great deal more.

That was pleasant, and the fact that my followers liked me was better. But what really made the world gay with promise was the thought of Marie. She was never on my lip but always in my mind. And at night when my mission had been disposed of I had little to say over my wine in the brief interval before fatigue sent me to bed. When not addressed I would hold her in my thoughts, marveling that there could be a future which might house us together.

Once when Conan and I made a trip together night caught us in the forest. We were all tired men there by the fire, but I was happy with the friendship I bore them, especially one. And I was happy with the thought of having a home in a land where men looked to me, a home with a woman in it who'd bear me a son. Conan, son of Finnian, men would call that boy. But that was further away. The girl's warm beauty was with me there. She was a darling to whom I would be good because no other course was conceivable. It was a great and strange thing to come to after my years of wandering as a lone hand.

Thinking of her so, I sang as I had not for years, if I had ever thus sung before. It was a song I had made for a chief's wedding once, and the passion I had tried to put into the words was a moving actuality in my voice. The song was in Irish, but the men did not need to be told what it was about. They listened soberly, each staring at the fire and thinking of his own woman.

Midir's finding of Etain after she had been lost to him for several mortal lifetimes was the subject.

> *"She was lost, she was gone,*
> *His darling, his sweeting,*
> *And time maundered on,*
> *Yielding no other meeting.*
> *No meeting of lips, no smiles, no embraces,*
> *No charming his eyes with that face of all faces.*
>
> *She was stolen by art,*
> *Tricked from him by magic,*
> *His winsome sweetheart;*

And his godhead was tragic.
Yes, tragic to know that no kindly morrow
Could cut short his life to free him of sorrow.

'I will find her again!'
His heart cried, but: 'Never!'
His brain muttered then,
'Once she's lost, gone forever!'
Forever long gone, the voice that would bless him;
Gone the slim arms that would hold and caress him.

Night and day all alone
He wandered then, broken,
Each minute a stone
Crushing hope by its token.
A token of love's final no—she had perished;
Dead, the small, lovely one whom his heart cherished.

But he looked for her still
For the cheat hope-giving
To lessen the chill
Of the need to keep living.
The living though lifeless while she was missing,
The sweet, the kind one no more for his kissing.

But it happened one day!
Fate softened; he found her,
Though still the spell lay
On her spirit and bound her.
It bound her, kept her from knowing her nearest,
Her lover, her friend, her heart's ease, her dearest.

By his sleights, with his skill
He won her back, breaking
The charms a dire will
Had spun, banning her waking.
Awaking to old joy, heart and lips mated,
Giving the healing he'd hopelessly waited."

When I had finished and Conan roused from his thoughts
of Ann, I could tell by his face that he knew that I had not
sung merely because I'd felt like singing. Whether or not

he had guessed before, he knew then that something had happened to me, and he asked me a question that, I am sure, had long been on his mind. "You will stay with us, brother? There will be plenty of land if we win, and chiefs will be needed."

I looked at the fire instead of at him. "I might throw up a hall of my own if I could find a woman to put in it. Not much use of one without the other." Of course, he knew the woman I had in mind as well as I; but I wouldn't name her, so he couldn't.

He put his hand on my shoulder an instant in that warming way he had. "You might find one that wouldn't know any better."

"One took you," I retorted, "so no man should give up hope." We turned in shortly after that, but the dreams of good days to come followed me into sleep.

As for Marie herself, however, I scarely saw her in all that time. I was only at the fort briefly, and then only to make a report or get a few hours of needed rest. Everybody was working furiously, the women as well as the men, to get ready for the expedition or siege, whichever it was to be. On the two occasions when I managed a few words alone with her she was unwontedly shy and hesitant, and I was sure that Ann and she had been talking things over. But I said nothing particular to her, for it was no time for courtship. There was too much to be done; and also there was little use in talking now until and if I should find myself a survivor of the onrushing war.

As it turned out I couldn't even say farewell to her when hostilities were renewed. The news was sudden and desperate when we got it. Conan and I had met at a rendezvous to discuss our success with each other when a rider approached on a horse which had worked to get him there.

"A man came from the abbey this morning, Conan," the fellow's news ran. "Chilbert's attacking him with all the men he can round up! His riders were over the border when the messenger left."

We calculated. "Some of them could be at the abbey now," Conan said, "but not the main body of his horsemen; and his foot troops will be another day and a half behind."

"At that they'll be there before ours," I said.

"By some few hours," he agreed thoughtfully, "and naturally they won't want to wait around for us. The Abbot may need every man we can rush." He chewed his lip a moment then rose, having made his decision. "We'll send them to him anyhow. Finnian, you'd better take the men with us, pick up what mounted men you can without going too much out of the way, and ride to the abbey. The Abbot won't waver, but the moral effect on the others will be bad if Chilbert arrives and there is no tangible evidence of our support."

"Right," I said, preparing to mount.

He was moving toward his own horse. "Rainault and Jean will have dispatched the muster call everywhere by now, so we ought to be under way by noon tomorrow. Send if you see there's real need for hurry when we get there. Otherwise I'll coddle the men and let them save their energy for fighting."

"All right. Give my love to Ann and so on."

"I will," he smiled; "especially to so on. See you at the abbey, and don't kill Chilbert before I get there."

"Not if he behaves himself," I promised as we saluted and turned to go separate ways.

So for the third time I approached St. Charles Abbey, thinking sadly and bitterly that this time no Father Clovis would stand above the gates to bandy words with me. One other thing that distinguished this visit was that I was not, indeed, halted and questioned at all. One of the monks who had been with us on the raid against Oliver was on guard. He hailed me excitedly from quite a distance, and the gates were wide and welcoming when we arrived.

It was just after sunup, but the court was noisily abustle, swarming with monks, the troops of chiefs who held their land from the abbey, and refugee villeins. Under other circumstances the presence of so many women and squalling brats in a monastery would have been a scandal of dimensions.

The Abbot and I greeted each other like the old friends we were coming to consider ourselves. "Good," he said when I told him that Conan would follow with his full strength. "Come on up on the wall, and I'll show you the smoke from their fires. They're not cooking fires either," he added grimly when we'd climbed aloft, "unless they've left men inside their homes for the fun of it. They do that sometimes."

"So I've heard," I grimaced. There was no doubt but that Chilbert would use every cruel trick in his reputedly extensive repertoire to frighten people either into flight or into volunteering abject submission to him.

"We had a brush with their vanguard yesterday evening,"

he continued, "but they didn't essay a serious attack. They were trying to lure us back toward their main army, whereas our strategy is to keep out of a major engagement until Conan joins us. But Chilbert, I take it for granted, has had us well scouted and will make at least one big effort before Conan arrives."

From my observation of Chilbert at Oliver's fort I judged him a man who knew his way all around the battlefield. "He'll try," I agreed, "although if his footmen don't get here by dark they may wake up to find all our men here, too. Shall I chase a man back to tell Conan to rush his horseman?"

"I'll send someone," he said. "Let your lads and their mounts rest up now."

After seeing that my men had food and a place to bunk I napped a few hours myself, but I was up before noon. A troop that had been out scouting was just entering the gate, and I went over to listen while they made their report to the Abbot. They hadn't caught sight of any foot soldiers yet, but they had seen two or three times more horsemen than had been around the day before.

"And there are doubtless a good few you didn't see," the Abbot said. "Are they mostly encamped or are they on the move to any particular point?"

"Most of them are to east of us, though I'm not positive they're massing for attack from that point." The fellow shook his head. "The woods is sure full of them!"

"The woods is a good place for them; let them stay there," said the prelate. But they didn't take advantage of his permission very long.

A small group of monks had been stationed a half mile off by the next of little houses which belonged to the villeins. Seemingly the leader of the enemy vanguard had looked the situation over and decided he could sweep away the defenders and fire the huts before we could mount and intercept. For the scouts were just taking their horses to the stables when a guard on the walls cried: "Raid! They're raiding the cabins!"

"Many?" the Abbot snapped.

"Lots more than our outpost there."

The churchman ran to look for himself while I sped to collect my men. They and a lot more were tumbling down out of the loft where they'd been taking their ease, and everybody started to scrambling and jostling to get his horse out into the court. "More of them!" the watcher informed us hysterically. "As many again!"

This was evidently going to be a real battle, but the Abbot was notably deliberate as he ordered men to their positions on the wall before he dispatched any to support the fathers by the shacks. I had fished my followers from the crowd expeditiously and had them marshaled, waiting. But the reserves had already gone before he turned to me. "Will you stay close at hand outside, Finnian? We won't need any more men yonder."

Some of my fellows, keyed up for fighting, began to grumble, but I silenced them. This was the Abbot's hold, and he was in command. Still I didn't want to miss what was going on, and I led the way swiftly to a point whence our view of the proceedings was complete.

The two large bodies of enemy horsemen were separated from each other by about a furlong. Estimating their numbers, I clicked my tongue. They'd outnumber those we had defending the position by a tremendous margin. In fact without depleting our garrison we simply couldn't match them in numbers.

I looked at the Abbot, but he was following developments with stolid interest. And yet instead of withdrawing what was at most only a skirmishing force from the path of the enemy's mounted army, he had ordered out patently inadequate support. It made me nervous; but he was a man who didn't do things without knowing a reason, so I watched further.

For a while it looked a race as to which side would reach the cabins first, then it seemed to me that the invaders were slowing, deliberately letting our men beat them out. Only at that moment, so large and sudden had been the excitement, did I get around to realizing that the destruction of the shacks was not worth such a great effort on Chilbert's part. And a careful look at the rear body showed me that it was swinging toward the abbey itself.

My trust in the prelate had so far not been misplaced. He had foreseen the enemy's maneuver, and, due to the fact that he'd carefully played up to it, I assumed he had some countermove in mind. It would have to be a good one, for Chilbert's thrust could be terribly disastrous to us. Naturally anybody could now see what they were up to, and they couldn't actually get to the gates ahead of our retreating men. Not ahead of the first men, that is. But only two or three could ride in abreast, and while the rest waited their turn the fore could reap them by a charge.

Certainly they thought our fellows would run for it, for all at once even the leading raiders gave up pretense of driving toward the cabins and raced for the gates. That many of them we could beat back, saving our fleeing men by a sortie, but in the time required to do so their reserves could have a crack at storming the weakly defended walls.

I glanced at the Abbot again to find he was looking my way. "Feign flight," he called down, "but stand off on the other side of the fort where they can't see you. Then when they arrive do whatever seems reasonable."

Just after we'd taken our station I heard the hoofs pounding, then blown horses snuffling before the gates. Sweeping all the way from the woods east they'd had a long sprint, and undoubtedly they'd been pushed hard all day. "The fools stayed where they were! We've cut 'em off!" a voice I knew cried. The speaker was Chilbert himself.

"And now what are you going to do?" the Abbot asked him calmly.

The count laughed exultantly. "Chop 'em into bits while you watch!"

"How are you going to catch them on those tired nags of yours?" the churchman asked contemptuously. "By the time you race back to where they won't be waiting for you, you couldn't run down a badger."

The second section of raiders was galloping up, the sounds told us. "Hey! Chilbert," one of them called "those fellows never even tried to make it here. They must have some reason for staying outside, eh?"

I had finally figured out the answer to that one, and Chilbert, with his general's eye, would grasp it on the instant now that he'd paused to take stock. Taking a fort like the abbey was nothing that a man could do with one hand. If he dismounted enough men to make the effort a good one, the riders hovering around could charge in to raise the devil with him and drive off his horses. Still, having swooped on the fort with such dramatic speed, he couldn't leave without making some sort of gesture.

"Come on," he said angrily after naming the several men he wanted to accompany him, "we'll look this box over."

When I heard that man riding toward the side of the abbey where I saw skulking I knew just how I'd fill in the Abbot's blank orders. Passing the word, I plunged for the corner and got there just in time to hit the little knot of reconnoiterers. I made a vicious cut at the count himself, but the great bay saved him, rearing and whirling out of the ruck with amazing agility. Chilbert saw me, and the sudden recognition in his eyes was pure hate if I have ever looked on it. He tried to swing his mount back toward me, but it had been badly startled; and he could do nothing for a second against its frightened strength.

It and two more horses, one riderless, caromed into the rest, and that was all we really accomplished before we ran on with premeditated discretion. But the effect, if far from overwhelming, was good. By making the count flounder helplessly within a thumbed nose of his own men we had augmented their uneasy bafflement, the offshoot of having been generally outsmarted.

Some of them broke ranks to follow us but resisted at Chilbert's savagely voiced command. He had more important projects in mind, and, looking back, I could see him grimly resume his tour of the fort. That completed, he merely ordered his men to stay where they were and remain alert.

He was not so ill off at that. He had been permitted to bring his army up in good order and to mass it before the gates, effectively sealing the abbey. If his footmen arrived before our reserves they need not fear a sortie. As for my men and the monks without the walls, we'd then be wrong no matter what we did. If we left to harry the foot troops his horsemen would have a free hand to storm the stronghold.

As defense for the Abbot's strategy, beyond the immediate check it had served to bring about, there was the clear point that he was achieving the delay he wanted. And in the minor matter of the villeins' cabins he had scored, having so far secured them from damage.

So balanced, each side hoping for the help that would mean decisive power, we passed an agonizingly long afternoon. I spent the first part of it with my head over my shoulder, looking for allies, and the second with an eye on Chilbert lest he try to snap me up in a surprise move. With several hours in which to recuperate, his horses might be ready for another swift charge. He wouldn't abandon his strategic position, but a

picked troop might bag my worst mounted men if I allowed it
to get the jump on us.

Whether Chilbert actually contemplated such an attack I
don't know, for a shout from the wall did away with that in-
terlude's curious mixture of boredom and suspense. "Men
from the west!" a monk cried joyfully. "Riders!"

With a yelp of pleasure and a sigh of relief, I turned to see.
That would be our own vanguard sifting out of the woods in
satisfying numbers. I looked excitedly toward the foe again,
but, of course, Chilbert, his advantage nullified, was preparing to leave.

The newcomers were led by Conan himself, and when I saw
that I hastened to meet him. "I thought I'd better come along
with the van to make sure you weren't bungling the business,"
he greeted me.

"Why you might as well have stayed home," I told him.
"Why, we had Chilbert trapped right between us, and—"

He appraised the size of Chilbert's departing force.
"Trapped?" he asked politely.

"Safe as a bear with its tail in the ice."

"Anything really happen?" he wanted to know.

"Mostly scouting and maneuvering so far, but if he finds
his foot troops in amongst those trees there he'll maybe be
back again."

"Jean should have ours here sometime in the morning," he
said, "and the rest of our horses should be along by dark
tonight."

"The Abbot would like to hear about that," I suggested,
and we cantered toward the gates.

Chapter
Twenty-two

THOSE Chilbert was awaiting did arrive, our scouts reported, but by then night was crowding dusk. So while not relaxing vigilance, we set our minds forward to plan for the morning. Night is only an aid to an attacker if he be unexpected.

At once conferring and observing, a group of us could see the long line of the enemy camp fires flare up one by one against the black rim of the forest. To westward a similar but much smaller series of blazes showed where our own troops were bivouacked.

Conan turned to the Abbot. "I'll harry them and squeeze them against your wall as best I may; but I don't want to get tied up in a real melee till my walking boys come along."

"Understood," the Abbot nodded. "They've got to have adequate horse support when they come into the open."

As we were trying to join our followers a little later Conan broke a thoughtful silence. "They've got more men than I figured they could muster. Chilbert must be reaching way out east."

"They have a lot more than I'd like them to," I said. "We'll have plenty to do trying to check them until the rest of our army arrives—and maybe after that. Still they'll be well occupied trying to take the abbey."

"Perhaps. The walls are strong enough, but that place was built as a house of God first and only fortified as an afterthought when times got nasty. There's neither hill, water, nor rock to abet the defenses. It just sits there like an egg laid on a flat stone. We're lucky there's a tough chick inside.''

"There could be better locations," I admitted. "That level sweep on the north side is an invitation for attackers to gather around and put up scaling ladders."

"That's where they'll operate from in the main," he agreed. "Though if it's a clear day they may try the east wall first while the sun's low enough to be in the monks' eyes."

We were up when night started to fade. There was no rain, but it was going to be a gray day. "That means we take our stand to the north," Conan said as we wolfed our breakfast. "And I don't think they'll keep us waiting long."

The only moving things in a dim forest, we were drifting toward our post when a scout's report vindicated my friend's prophecy. The foe was preparing to move, and we speeded up in order to be ready for them. Because of the murk we couldn't yet see them when we reached the clearing, and even the abbey looked to be no more than a curiously edifice-like arrangement of clouds.

We remained in the deeper obscurity under the trees and held our gazes eastward with the patience of sure expectation. The visibility improved rapidly, but our ears first gave notice of their proximity. Soon then we saw a great wave of them coming over a little rise, mounted men on each side of files of footmen, and another following as the first spilled down into a hollow. It was while they were emerging from this to the level on which the abbey stood that we met them. They heard us running, but though they were forcing their horses we were in the position of riding down hill at them.

We didn't try to strike their entire front with our inferior numbers but instead attempted to fold up the nearest flank with the force of a phalanx hammering the wings of successive separated lines. It worked well, but all I can clearly remember is feeling my shield jarred by blows and seeing some of the enemy tumble to the ground. Then we were through them, completing a semicircle in our race back to the woods. If they wanted to follow us and put off the storming, well and good.

Some probably were for doing it, but Chilbert bawled orders to close ranks and keep on toward the monastery. Seeing that this was the case, we gathered again, cut an arc through the forest so as to be opposite the vulnerable wall, and approached to see what precautions had been taken against us.

Chilbert's mounted troops had been augmented, too, since the previous day, and he could afford a considerable force to keep us from climbing on his back while he assailed the abbey. Having spotted us, they were prancing forward to be ready for us if we should choose to strike into the open again, when we suddenly recognized their leader.

The sight of him was too much for Conan's usually cool head. "Gregory!" he shouted, surging forward with all of us pell mell at his heels. "Do you remember me, kinsman?"

No vituperation could have added anything to what was implied in the tone with which he uttered that one word, and Gregory felt the full, savage impact of it. Perhaps the disastrous results from his original betrayal had made him superstitious. At any rate he was an awed and miserable man who did not want to meet Conan. In place of giving the word to countercharge, as his men were expecting, he just sat there, vaguely fingering a sword he wasn't going to draw.

Then suddenly Conan's imminence was too much for him. He whirled and bolted right through his own men, ruining the morale he had already impaired and spreading panic as he went. It was a rout almost before we hit them. Those we couldn't catch to slay fled toward their main body, with Gregory leading them by two lengths. And so it happened that an army which had every right to think it was comfortably protected turned, startled, to find its rear guard thundering toward it, unchecking.

Chilbert, who had been directing preparations for the attack from behind the main lines, swung around, wild-eyed, and roared for them to halt. As I knocked a man from his horse and looked forward for another victim I witnessed an irony whose dimensions I could not then spare the leisure to appreciate. Quickly appraising the extent of the danger, and as swiftly discerning its source, the count dashed to intercept his fleeing lieutenant. As the latter perforce drew rein and hastily started to fabricate explanations, Chilbert heaved up the great axe he was carrying. Without opening his mouth to reprimand, curse, or otherwise give notice of his displeasure he delivered a blow which cleft Gregory's steel cap and only bogged down somewhere in his chest.

But no measures were stern enough to stop that flight immediately, and Chilbert himself had to side-step or be run down. He tried to make the rest of his followers divide and let the rear guard through, then close in on us as we followed. But it was too late, and the stampeded men we were driving ran on to smash in among the ranks of their fellows and ride down comrades afoot.

Because of the confusion they scattered we were an organized body impinged on individuals who had to shift for themselves. And where they wanted to shift was out of our way. We on our part could no longer retreat. We had to have the wall at our backs before we halted and reversed our direction.

We gained the wall without difficulty, but in so doing we sacrificed the momentum that had been our most potent weapon. Nor could we hope to pick it up again on the charge back. By the time we'd turned to face them they were beginning to form ranks against us once more. Still, though they were in numbers to eat us alive once they had fully gelled, they would be no great danger to us for a few minutes. And if the Abbot was the man I thought he was this period of their disorganization would not be passed by.

Everything had happened so rapidly, with results as amazing to us as to them, that until the moment of our turning I hadn't entirely comprehended what a blow luck had let us strike them. Having their rear guard routed almost before it took the field must have given them the idea that irresistible power was against them. There must have been something peculiarly unnerving, too, in the experience of being ridden down by their own comrades.

With the wall to keep us from being bothered from the rear, we were able to form an effective wedge and had no trouble in beating off such ill co-operating groups as tried to crush us. Elsewhere, however, Chilbert was doing a masterful job of re-establishing morale. A magnificent, huge figure on a magnificent, huge horse, he was savagely dominant. He didn't shame so much as cow them into renewed aggressiveness. I think most of them were more afraid of that one man than they were of all of us, their avowed enemies.

Conan had his ear cocked, his face the picture of action waiting to happen. "He'll come," I said confidently. Then we heard it.

"*Domino gloria!*" rang the cry from off to our left, and we knew the monks were boiling out to hammer the enemy into greater uncertainty.

"Come on!" Conan yelled, and we started boring into the mass, hewing furiously.

We were taking a line that would, we believed, unite us with the priests. If our two forces succeeded in meeting, the prefatory havoc would be a great blow in itself. And once combined we would be in position to tear even wider, less repairable holes in their divided array.

Chilbert appreciated the situation, of course, and rushed group after group into the shrinking space between us. The very fellows who were nipping at our heels were called off to take their places in the wedge he was driving. With each yard or so, therefore, the opposition was growing more stubborn. The value of our boldly followed-up opportunism was being abrogated by sheer numbers, cumbering the swift, decisive action which alone can render a markedly outnumbered force effective.

With that impatience with fact familiar to desperate need I wondered why things that were going to happen couldn't happen when they would be of some use. Now was the moment for Jean to appear. The foe could spare no horsemen to rip into his men, and those men would supply just the added weight we wanted.

But Jean didn't come, and Chilbert put yet more pressure on us. Satisfied with his marshaling efforts, he was at length ready to take personal part in the battle; and he waved his heavy axe, shouting for men to follow. After a while, a tiring, winded man, I was no longer sanguine as to the outcome. We were practically stopped, and unless the monks were more successful the enemy might pin us back against the fort and whittle us down. I listened as best I could, but the Abbot's deep, certain voice seemed no nearer.

Nevertheless, we were holding our own, if no longer accomplishing any more than that, and as long as we could keep from being crushed and scattered there was hope that we could wear them down. And then if our foot troops arrived—

Meanwhile the count was working his way along the battle front. He was striking an occasional blow, but mostly he was searching for something. From the vicious delight of his expression I knew what that something was when Conan abruptly plunged toward him with a challenging cry. Each of them, for this one time, had the same idea, arrived at the same reason: to kill the other would be at least half as good as winning the battle.

But encountering a picked man in a melee is difficult to achieve. It so happened that when Chilbert was finally able to sweep toward us in a surge of men and horses it was I that first encountered him. I slashed at him, missed him for the second time in two days, and cut short the resultant oath to duck under his axe. No doubt my impression was heightened by excitement, but it sounded like a high wind as it passed my ear. By the time I was ready to strike again he wasn't the man I struck. We had been parted in the turmoil.

Some yards to my left Conan and Chilbert had at last succeeded in meeting and were struggling at once with their horses and each other. I began to fight my way toward them, but too many others were essaying to do the same thing for me to make swift headway. At such instants as I could spare from defending myself I watched a duel in which both men were hampered by the crush. They would be forced apart, then come together again, roaring for their respective followers to make room.

Skill at horsemanship was naturally discounted by the circumstances, but at that the bay nearly ended the fight. To my horror I saw him rear up and overbear Conan's mount which staggered and fell back on its haunches. This was Chilbert's moment, and he took a full, two-handed swing with all his tremendous might.

I felt as I had once felt when a wave had picked me off a viking ship and before I knew it was going to put me back. But Conan, instead of trying to keep his seat, had used his hands to vault backward and slide toward the rump. The blow that would have sliced him as a similar effort had split Gregory landed instead on the half-stunned, struggling horse.

The moment that it took Chilbert to pull his weapon from the now totally collapsing animal was his bad luck. Conan stretched out a hand to grip the axe's handle, and so used Chilbert's own strength to keep from being rolled on by his dead mount.

With a mighty wrench the count pulled his weapon out of the animal and away from Conan's grasp, but by then my friend was braced, one foot on the ground and one foot on his fallen horse. Now it was he who was in a position for an overhead, two-handed sweep. He had the start of Chilbert by just that trifling edge that matters. He hewed the count's left arm where it showed beyond the shield, and slashed again to lay open the thigh. His foeman tried to swing his axe with one hand, but it was easily warded. Conan's answering cut took him in the face, and the combat was over.

Whether Chilbert was dead when he fell to the ground, or whether some horse's hoof ground out what life was left in him nobody knew, and we were all too busy to find out. Chilbert's men who were there to see were at first even too maddened to feel dismay at his loss. They surged at us in a furious effort to ride Conan under, we flung ourselves in front of him, and there were a bloody few moments before he was safely remounted on a masterless horse.

Once in the saddle he started to shout: "Chilbert's dead!" And we all took up the cry. "Chilbert's dead!"

This was not merely a boast of triumph; its purpose was to tell the count's men they were leaderless, make them think what that meant, begin to wonder what they were going to do. It turned out that they weren't going to do very much. When we drove at them again they commenced retreating; and I could hear the Abbot absolving the souls of the men he slew as he moved steadily nearer.

We chased them, but, once they had broken, our object was not to kill. Conan and I stopped soon, watching the flight and trying to realize that it was all over. After a few minutes we were joined by the prelate. He, too, was dazed by the suddenness of victory.

"Well, it's done," he said. "With Chilbert slain they won't have another try at us."

"No," Conan agreed.

We lapsed into the inertia that follows completed violence. "I still don't see how it happened," the churchman said then.

"It was one of those things." Conan tried to spit, but his mouth was too dry. "If there'd been any other man leading the rear guard it would have been different."

"Who was he? I saw Chilbert kill him, but I didn't get a good look at him."

"Gregory," I said.

The Abbot's eyes grew round. I had never seen him laugh before, but he did then. "How Clovis would have enjoyed that," he remarked wistfully, and all three of us gave a thought to that man before he spoke again. "So Gregory didn't want to meet you?"

"No, but as I couldn't foresee that, I didn't really have any business charging him before the rest of his army was occupied with you at the abbey. Then when he turned, one thing lead to another. At that I wouldn't have followed in so deeply if I hadn't been sure of you."

The Abbot accepted the tribute with a gesture. "Chilbert, though I don't say he deserved better fortune, surely had a right to count on it. I thought for a while we'd be lucky to get off with a draw."

"He was a capable bastard," I said, and we let that stand for his epitaph.

We looked around. All of the enemy who could manage it were out of sight, together with most of our men, although some of the latter had hung back from the pursuit to round up riderless mounts. The people who'd been left in the monastery were out finding what of the men left on the field had enough life to make salvaging possible. The Abbot sighed.

"Before we have to find out how much in the way of friends and man power this victory has cost us—"

"And how many women we'll have to tell that they'd better start looking for another man," Conan took him up soberly.

"Yes, before that, too, and so while our only positive knowledge is of good, let us go over to that tree," he pointed to an isolated oak, "and sit quietly to think of this new power we have."

With those words he was no longer a comrade in arms but an older man and a priest. "A good idea, Father," I said, using the term of respect for the first time since he had shown us Clovis' head.

We dismounted to let our horses graze where they would. It wasn't a far walk to the abbey, and they had earned their leisure. We stretched out in the shade, only then appraised of how worn we were. All of us had sundry nicks, scratches, and cuts of varying length and depth; but in view of what we had come through they didn't seem worth a great deal of thought.

In a moment or so, however, the Abbot sat up, unbuckled his sword, and threw it from him. "It's a futile hope in times like ours, but I trust I'll never have to use that again. In any case I won't have to use it as much from now on. There will be respites, and I can build as I have never had time to do before. The abbey will start to house scholars instead of soldiers as soon as I can find the men to teach."

I raised up on one elbow. "I know the man for you!" I said excitedly, and launched into an enthusiastic description of Father Michael. "He's the one to teach your teachers," I concluded. "I've met scholars in my time but never one to touch him. And he's wasted there, breaking his heart among louts who don't know a poem from a papal bull.

He eyed me with paternal indulgence. "There are more things to scholarship than poetry."

I shrugged. He was a churchman, and in any event he had a right to his own opinion. I even had the caution to refrain from telling him that Father Michael did not think so. "But he's your man," I said earnestly. "You'll never find a better."

"I'll send to see if he will come," he promised. "What will you take from our success, Conan? Will you seize Chilbert's land? The abbey wants none of it."

"Nor do I, Father," my friend said. He rolled over on his stomach, selected a piece of grass, and started chewing it. "I'll offer alliance and what protection I can give to any man who wants to hold from me, but I'm not a conqueror. I have land, and there's room enough for my friends to live uncrowded now that the master landgrabber has been done away with.

"Like yourself I know I'll have to fight again, but I'm stronger now. It'll take a great army to take that fort of mine, and nobody can stay long in my country who cannot take it. I'll have my friends build of stone, too, and in the shadow of those stone forts our people will be safe, assured that when they marry the roof will stay above the heads of their wives and children." His clenched hand hit the ground. "I'm only a chief because I can give them that thing as other men cannot or will not."

"Excellent, my son," the Abbot nodded, turning his attention to me. "And what will you do now, Finnian?" His eyes twinkled. "I recall that on the occasion of our first meeting you would have none of us. Will you find a place here to suit your requirements?"

Having no such claims in the direction of constructive benevolence as they, I was a little embarrassed, but Conan saved me. "Of course, Father. We'll find him a place off in the woods where everybody will be safe from hearing his harp and songs."

The prelate smiled in recognition of the intent rather than in appreciation of the jest. "And now," he said, shifting to a kneeling position, "as men who have been granted good fortune by God today, let us offer a prayer."

We followed the Latin with him until he became largely silent with more personal communication, only a mumbled word or so conveying the general tenor. From similar murmurings I knew that Conan was also praying. I thought of Marie instead, which perhaps came to the same thing, involving as it did contemplation of the *summum bonum*.

We had finished, and the Abbot was retrieving his sword in sign that he was ready to leave when I noticed Conan's foot soldiers, already emerged from the forest and marching sturdily toward the abbey. A knot of horsemen led them, and I could make out Jean at their head. I nudged Conan, and we stretched out again, chuckling.

"Jean!" Conan bawled.

He located us after peering, halted his men, and trotted across fields. The Abbot, seeing that we were not for immediate going, saluted us and strode off. We watched him approvingly, then grinned lazily up at Jean, who reined in to stare, nonplused. "Hello, Jean; what are you doing in these parts?" I wondered.

He scratched his head, knowing that something was going on but not sure what. "Where's the war?" he asked finally.

Conan and I looked at each other. "Did you hear of any wars around here, Finnian?" my friend asked curiously.

"No," I yawned. "Somebody must have given him the wrong directions."

"Sure," Jean said, pointing to a corpse about a hundred yards away, "and I suppose he's just a landmark.

"Oh," Conan drawled, "you mean *that* war. Hell, that war's all over!"

Jean gulped and goggled at us, unable to assimilate this. "It is?"

"It is."

"You mean to say I had to yahoo those poor devils afoot all through a moonless night," Jean, a harried man who had had no sleep, was angry now, "and you couldn't even wait till we got here before you finished up the war?"

Conan choked at the bathos delivered thus seriously. "I'm sorry Jean," I apologized. "We just didn't know our own strength."

That and the look on his face finished us. We turned over on our stomachs and writhed in a great joy of laughter. Then after another indignant second his own usually ready guffaw resounded to swell the chorus. It was well, for we needed that laugh. Soon we rose to attend to the bitter business of seeing who was lost, crippled for life, or maimed in some lesser degree.

Chapter
Twenty-three

IT WAS over another week before we turned home again. The military rout was complete, but to insure against combines of chiefs who might try later reprisals we visited the more important ones. To the amenable we promised protection and alliance, to the sullen we pointed out that they had got off easily but wouldn't next time.

True to his word, Conan seized no occupied land, but all empty and doubtful country contiguous to his borders he preempted. His purpose was to settle it, establishing a fortified buffer to give pause to later aggressors. He did not even confiscate any of Chilbert's mobile property as indemnity, though we did raze his fortress as an object lesson. Then we made sure that his land was partitioned among five men, so guaranteeing that none would fall heir to dangerously heady wealth.

The endless conferences were a bore, but a necessary bore. By showing men the dirt we could rub their noses in while never doing it, or even mentioning the dirt except in allegorical terms, we made, if not friends, resigned enemies who congratulated themselves that things were no worse. Some might be friends later, others not; but all were impressed. Our power was a byword, and it would take some outsider to rally local men against us.

Such an antagonist might and would eventually materialize, but in the interim our might would be increased. There's nothing like proof that one can gut a man to inspire him with consideration for one. Only the few like courtesy for its own sake.

Notwithstanding the swank, heavy politics, and monotony, I wasn't unhappy. Indeed, though I did my part reasonably well, I believe, I was in a trance of anticipation the whole time. I functioned by rote, and my life was elsewhere. Conan noticed and gibed me about it, though he, too, was chafing with impatience to get home.

Then the great moment came when we actually started for the fort. And brutes we were about it, pushing tired men to the limit of their endurance and almost beyond, nagging and cursing everyone's slowness. We were as weary as anyone, but we didn't care.

The end of our patience came during a rest on the march not ten miles from the fort. The men were supine, exhausted. I followed their example for a moment, then sat up restlessly. "Let's ride," I said to Conan. "We can't wait for these turtles till Christ comes again!"

His eyes were red from lack of sleep, as no doubt were my own. Yet he scrambled to his feet on the instant. "Right!" he said. "They can find their way home!"

Knowing how much I prized it, he had given me the great bay; and he himself had confiscated an excellent horse to replace the one Chilbert had killed. Worn too, they still had enough more vitality than most of the other mounts to save us a good hour or so.

We were happy men as we rode, proud of achievement, glad of life, liking the future. We sang in spite of our dusty mouths, and each laughed at everything the other said, whether he had listened to it or not. Conscious as we were of our pleasure in each other's company, our minds were ahead of us. We'd done a good job, and we wanted to tell our women about it.

Naturally messengers had brought the general good news to the fort, but that wouldn't spoil the personal conferences we were anticipating. When at last I saw the walls of the stronghold I drew in my breath like a child at sight of a honeycomb. I had dreamed of it, and here it was. Before an hour had passed, I swore, I'd ask my girl to share my well-earned winnings.

The watchers had marked us, and everybody in the place crowded around us, asking questions. Conan kissed Ann and then bellowed at them, grinning. "Can't a tired man get any privacy with his own wife? We'll talk it over in the morning, but let me alone now."

In spite of his good humor he made his point sharp enough, and they left us. I looked around, feeling cheated and terrifically disappointed. "Where's Marie?" I asked.

Ann looked at Conan and received no more help than a fatuous smile. Her eyes seemed very serious. "Why, she's in the hall, Finnian."

"Anything the matter with her?" I inquired anxiously.

"No. She wants to see you, but not with other people around. She has something to say to you."

Private talk with her was what I myself earnestly desired. "That's fine!" I said, brightening. "I've got some things to say to her." I winked at Conan, and he laughed gaily.

Ann suddenly broke from her husband's arms. "Go over there," she called over her shoulder, pointing to a deserted corner of the court. "I'll send her out to you."

Conan slapped me on the back. "Good luck, brother! Marie's a fine girl." It was the first time her name had been used between us.

So I limped stiffly across the court and leaned against the wall. I wouldn't look at her as she came up to greet me. I'd wait to see what her spontaneous words of salutation would be. In a minute I heard a step, but not a woman's. I turned my head, annoyed. Raymond was approaching.

I was feeling too pleased with the world to be angry, but if there was anything I didn't want around then it was another man. "Glad to see you up and about," I told him, "but I'll tell you more about that later. I'm waiting here for somebody now."

He drew a breath and braced his legs. "I've got to tell you myself," he said in a flat voice. "You want that girl, and so do I—but she wants me, not you." He spread his arms. "Hit me! Kill me, if you think you've got the right! But it won't change that."

I stared at him, feeling stunned and battered. My intense fatigue didn't let me react very fast, and the preconception I'd lived with so long was not easily displaced. But even though I didn't grasp the full import, I knew, thinking back. It was this of which Ann had tried to warn me.

I couldn't say anything, so he went on. It must have been hard work for him, but I only appreciated that later. "You wouldn't have done it to me, maybe. I didn't want to do it to you. It just happened." His mouth worked. "I knew you wanted her, and you've been my friend and more than that. You're my chief! But she and I—after the first week or so we knew." He drew himself up, quivering. "What are you going to say? What are you going to do?"

I looked at him dully, feeling all my weariness then with a vengeance. Well, if it was so, it was so; but I didn't want to talk about it any more. "It's all right," I said.

He broke the skin on his knuckles hitting the wall. "It isn't all right, but—"

I smiled, though not much. "But you'll do what you're going to do, as everybody else does. And why shouldn't you? God knows I don't want a woman who doesn't want me." I touched his arm lightly. "You're friend still, but let's drop the subject."

With one last hang-dog look he left me, and I gazed out through the open gate and across the dropped drawbridge, symbols of the new peace in the land. The burn of the pain would come after a while; now I was merely getting used to the knowledge that preceded it. The vision I had been living with and on for the past few weeks had been all imagination. No, not entirely that, either. She had had it in her mind also, but only, humiliatingly enough, because there had been nobody else around. Then along had come this one lad, and he had really proved sib.

I wanted to sit down, but there was no place unless I walked for it, so I just stood there. There would be no woman, no son, no hall. Somebody else was drawing near, and I looked around with sodden irritability. It was Marie herself, the last person I wanted to see.

"Raymond told me." Then I said to her what I had said to him. "It's all right."

But she wouldn't go away. "I'm sorry, Finnian," she informed me.

My nerves were jumping, but I tried not to raise my voice. "It's over," I said. "Words are good for nothing now."

Her face was drawn with effort, but she continued to face me. Women fight for what they want with as much courage as men, and with more specific knowledge of their needs; and she wanted something of me. "There's something we've *got* to talk about," she said desperately.

I felt like a sick man without strength enough to strike at a hovering gadfly. "What?" I asked.

"You'll be going away now, won't you?" she remarked rather than inquired.

Glancing through the gate again at the road beyond, I realized what had been on my mind since Raymond had spoken. Yes, I would be going away. There would be no use remaining, seeing that I had nothing more to do there. I would be welcome to stay with Conan, but even in my lost state of mind I shied at the picture of myself as the favored and indulged hanger-on, growing more purposeless by the month.

No, the whole bright concept of existence there had depended on Marie, and it had shattered because of her. And she knew that, as well as what I would do about it. Abstractedly I wondered how she could know that much about me and still feel alien. But she did. Remembering, I saw that she had always liked me, yet been repelled.

"You'll be going away?" she repeated to force an answer.

"Sure," I said. "Now won't you go away yourself? I don't feel like conversation."

Her next words, however, intrigued my distraught attention. "But if you stayed you could have all the land you wanted. Conan would give you anything."

I looked at her curiously before I nodded. "Yes, he'd give me anything except Ann and his half of the bottle."

She moistened her lips. "We need that land, Raymond and I. Conan would never give us any, because he'll hold us responsible for driving you away. But if you're not using your land, there's no reason why we can't."

"I haven't got any land," I said brusquely. "It's all Conan's."

"Yes, but Conan owes you something, owes you a lot!" She reached out her hand. "Ask him for land! Raymond's your man, and you can tell Conan that he'll hold it in your name. Look, Finnian! Conan needs chiefs. I've heard him say so myself. And Raymond would make a good one."

She wasn't just praising her lover. She was telling the truth. I would be doing no disservice to my friend by sponsoring this lad's promotion. He would, I was convinced, do a good job. Marie was leaning toward me, peering to read my mind. "Finnian!" she cried urgently. "You must!"

I glowered at her. A bargain that would favor all parties and wouldn't harm me waited but my word. If I failed to give it I'd feel small and mean about it the rest of my life; and of that she was keenly aware. I tried frantically to find some excuse, but there was none. She had me cornered.

"I'll speak to Conan," I told her, still somehow keeping my voice quiet.

"Oh, Finnian!" The wealth of emotion in her tone soured me yet further, because I knew it was really meant for another man. Nevertheless, she persisted in remaining.

"I—we have been good friends, Finnian," she said "and—"

"Well what do you want now?"

"You've meant much in my life, and right now may be the last time we'll really talk together." She drew a step nearer, so that our bodies were almost touching. "I'd like to kiss you good-by, Finnian."

A vein started throbbing in my temple, then at last my anger broke. "Kiss you, you conniving brat!" I roared at her. "I'd rather break your damned neck! Now get the hell out of my sight and stay there."

For once she had no answer for me. She turned away, sobbing a little, but I had no remorse. She had just kicked the only good idea for a life I'd ever had into pieces. Moreover, she had made me pay her dowry so that she could marry somebody else. Well and good, but kiss her on top of that! A man can be noble to just such an extent without turning his stomach.

Once more I looked out over the bridge, knowing with unshakeable positiveness that a clear way lay before me. No further incidents would occur to keep me in this country which had held so much for me. The power of the Pict, or whatever it was, was through with me.

Oh well! I began limping toward where Conan was waiting. Ann had sense enough to walk away when she saw me coming; but she would have told him, and he would know better than try to dissuade me from leaving.

He looked as done in and dispirited as I felt while I drew

near where he stood with sagging shoulders, gazing at me haggardly through sweat-lank hair that he didn't bother to brush
from his eyes. "Let's get drunk," he said when we had looked
at each other a minute.

"Thank God for the wine," I said.